In loving memory of my mother, Franke,
who believed in this story from the very first page—
and who believed in me, always.

CIP data for this book is available from the Library of Congress.

Published by Creston Books, LLC
www.crestonbooks.co

Type set in Garamond and Plantagenet Cherokee

ISBN 978-1-939547-48-4
Source of Production: 1010 Printing
Printed and bound in China
5 4 3 2 1

MIX
Paper from
responsible sources
FSC
www.fsc.org   FSC® C016973

ALL OUT OF PRETTY

INGRID PALMER

Creston Books

PART I

Chapter One
Now

The great poet John Keats once wrote, "A thing of beauty is a joy forever." Keats never knew my mother.

I glance down at my watch again. Three hours. That's how long it's been since Ayla left me in the car with a distracted wave and a promise to "be right back with some munchies." Right. I'll bet she bummed dinner off some guy at the bar and didn't bother to get anything for me. Now she's probably passed out somewhere. Or hooking up. Or maybe she can't remember where the hell she parked.

I never should have let Ayla go off on her own. I should know better than to trust a woman who can't even remember to pay the rent.

For about a millisecond, I consider hunting her down and dragging her drunk ass back here. Forcing her to deal with the cold, and the lack of food, and *me.* But when we first rolled into this tiny town, Ayla insisted on doing a drive-by of the local bars

1

and I saw the bouncers standing outside. There's no way I can pass for twenty-one. Most people don't even believe I'm sixteen until I produce my driver's license.

I drag my fingers through my long, dark hair. It feels greasy. So does my face, which I haven't washed properly in days. But when I lean forward and peer into the car's rearview mirror, the girl staring back at me somehow still looks pretty. I scowl at her. Then I grab a pen and start scribbling in my notebook, the ink making deep indents on the page to match the ones on my forehead.

The truth is, I used to like being pretty. I used to feel proud when girls at school wished out loud for my pale blue eyes, when boys stared as I walked past. It felt good, in the same way that spring grass tickles your toes or pearls feel fanciful looped around your neck. Even Gram would sometimes stand behind me, looking at our reflection in the hallway mirror, and say, "You're stunning, Andrea—inside and out." Then she'd beam at me like a proud mama bear, crinkling her nose until we both collapsed into giggles.

I can't remember the last time I giggled. I don't even smile anymore. If I feel my lips twitching, I push the smile down, kick it into the dirt. I hide—not just my smile, but everything.

The problem with being pretty is people tend to notice you. And these days, being noticed is the last thing I want.

My fingers ache from gripping the pen so tight. I stare down at my messy handwriting in the soft circle of light emanating from the roof of Gram's car, knowing I won't ever share the words I've written. They're just a rant. I've already finished the essay I *will* turn in to my English teacher when spring break is over. It's written in neat, vertical letters and it's full of the fun things I did on vacation, like going to the waterpark and exploring the science museum. I call it my Rough Draft of Lies. I hate lying. But I can't write honestly about the places I've been this week—or this year. It's remarkable, really, how many secrets I've accumulated in such a short stretch of time.

A dull thudding starts in my temples and I begin to feel lightheaded from not having eaten in thirty-seven hours, from the worry that's plagued me ever since we got evicted. Gathering our few blankets, I coil up in the backseat and rest my cheek against my dark green backpack. I lift my head slightly and punch the bag, trying to make the bumpy spots flat. If I can't have food, then I'd like a good night's sleep. In a real bed. Not in the back of Gram's Buick, with its stiff leather seats that remind me too much of her hands the day I found her.

Inhale. Exhale.

It's so quiet that the smallest sounds are amplified. Like my breathing. And the lone moth repeatedly throwing itself against the windshield, attracted to the red glow of the dashboard security light. The *thwp-thwp* of its wings beating against the glass makes my own limbs ache in sympathy. Maybe I should shoo it away—or put it out of its misery. The frost will claim it tonight anyway. But that would mean unknotting myself from my own fragile cocoon, and I'm not that selfless.

As time ticks by, the only thing keeping me remotely warm is my increasing anger. The bars must be closing, so where the hell is Ayla? My stomach rumbles and I press my fingers against its

3

hollowness. I stare out the window at the ink-blotted sky, where the moon hangs like a sentry between heaven and earth. Even if Ayla keeps pretending, I know we're in trouble. Just like I know the sixteen cents in my pocket will buy me exactly nothing at the 24-hour gas station across the road. I also know there's a dumpster on the other side of this lot. My eyes flick toward it.

Before the thought has a chance to warp into an actual plan, bright lights blind me, a sharp wind whips into the car, and pointy-nailed fingers poke my shoulder. I shield my eyes, hoping it's not a cop. Instead, I see Ayla's gorgeous, flushed face blocking out the moon.

"Wake up, wake up!" Her voice is giddy and high-pitched. She definitely scored dinner or she'd be growling and swearing at me. "Come on, Bones, we got a place to stay." Bones. This is what she calls me instead of Andrea—the name Gram chose when I was born. I wish I could say Ayla's nickname for me is a term of endearment, but I know better.

Tugging off the blankets, I sit up and squint into the cold darkness. My lungs protest the frigid air, making me cough. A rainbow halo is smeared around the one lit parking lamp near the street. There's a man under it, smoking a cigarette. He's tall and strong-looking, not the cleanest sort. He doesn't look at me. Just at Ayla in her tight black skirt and shimmery top.

"That's Judd." Ayla smirks, like he's some knight in shining armor. "We're going to crash at his place."

She leans in to gather her belongings, which are strewn across the front seat of the car. I steal another glance at Judd, and he smiles. It's uneven and awkward, an expression I can tell he avoids. *Huh,* I think. *We have something in common.*

In the hazy lamplight I see that Judd's hair is dirt brown where it's not receding from his forehead. His face is long and fierce, like the skin has been stretched too tight. He might have been decent-looking at some point, but he's at least ten years older than Ayla and he seems…haggard. I don't bother pointing this out. I know Ayla's giddiness is a ruse. She's playing Judd, using him for what we need. She's a parasite. And so am I, by default.

Yes, I used to like being pretty. But if it means ending up like Ayla, I think I'll pass.

Chapter 2
Then

I was worried about a *boy*, of all things. Not my upcoming exams or the math algorithms I hadn't nailed down. Nope, nosiree. It was nine o'clock on a Wednesday night and I was curled up in our living room chair, stewing about the fact that while plenty of guys at school flirted with me, Ben Stankowski looked away every time I glanced at him. Every time! Even Delaney was stumped. At lunch she'd pointed out that Ben was in all my AP classes, on the yearbook committee, *and* in student council with me. Clearly, we were perfect for each other. He just didn't seem to know it. Delaney thought I should take charge and ask him out, but how could I make the first move when I couldn't even make eye contact?

So that's what I was thinking (okay, obsessing) about when Gram walked slowly into the living room and proceeded to stare at our just-bought Christmas tree. She had this nostalgic look on her face as she touched two fingers to her lips and inhaled the tree's sharp, piney smell. Like she was inhaling a memory.

"Who was on the phone?" I asked, doodling Ben's name in the margin of my composition pad.

Gram opened her mouth and then closed it, like she was searching for the right words and couldn't find them. Which is why I knew what was coming. I scribbled harder in my notebook, sorry I'd asked.

"It was Ayla," Gram finally said, sinking onto the couch across from me. "She might be coming home soon."

"You mean she might be coming for a visit? She doesn't live here," I corrected.

"No matter what, she's still part of our—" Gram began, then fell into a ragged coughing jag. I frowned. She'd kicked the habit a few months ago, but thirty years of smoking had taken its toll. "Can we please discuss Ayla politely for once?" she said after catching her breath.

My frown deepened. Though I hated disappointing Gram, I was *so* not in the mood to hear one more horror story about my mother.

"Actually, I can't discuss anything," I said. "I have a history paper due tomorrow." This statement was one hundred percent true. I just omitted the fact that the paper was already written and tucked neatly in the "completed" side of my homework folder.

But Gram knew I'd never wait until the night before a paper was due to finish it, and her skeptical gaze warmed my face. I felt myself getting angry. Why was she pushing me to talk about Ayla now, when she knew how heavy my workload was, when she knew I had exams coming up...when she knew how much it bothered me?

She also knew I usually gave in.

But not this time. *At some point,* I wrote to myself in the notebook, *you have to take a stand.* Refusing to discuss my mother, while kind of pitiful, was my stand that night.

Still. It was rare that Gram and I were at odds, and the whole thing turned me sour. *Leave it to Ayla to cause problems without even being around,* I thought bitterly. It hadn't always been this way. When I was little and Gram talked about Ayla, I listened so hard, I swear my ears ached afterwards. I hung onto Gram's words, sifting through them for any detail that would link me to my mother. Back then, the stories were sweet fairytales—about a teenage girl with soulful eyes and the poise of a ballerina, flying off to have adventures.

It wasn't until I got older that I saw the truth: those soulful eyes were usually bloodshot, the ballerina pose was actually Ayla retching in the bushes, and the adventures…well, they weren't appropriate bedtime stories. I'd heard enough.

As if reading my mind, Gram pressed her lips together. "People change, Andrea. She wasn't always like this. It's important that you remember that."

"My grades are important, too. Way more important than *Ayla,*" I snapped, then felt bad when Gram flinched. After all, it wasn't her fault her daughter was a mess. Gram had raised her the same as me. But Ayla was an addict and I was headed for the Ivy League…hopefully. Ayla's shenanigans had shadowed my life long enough. "I'm sorry, Gram, but I can't just drop everything. Not for her," I added in a softer tone.

After a short silence, Gram reconsidered. "Then we'll talk tomorrow after school. No excuses, okay?"

"Okay," I agreed reluctantly, gathering my books. "I'm going to finish this in my room. G'night." I mustered a small smile.

"Goodnight, sweetheart."

As I skirted past, I couldn't help noticing how tired Gram looked. She was only in her late fifties, but her slender shoulders had carried too much heartache over the years. On nights like this, her whole body sagged with it.

In the back of the house, I paused outside my bedroom door, feeling guilty for ducking away. Gram was always available whenever *I* wanted to talk. I peeked back around the corner and saw a worn blue photo album lying open on Gram's lap. I watched her gaze at the childhood pictures of my mother, her hand gliding down the page like she was stroking the fragile wings of a tiny bird.

My heart hitched, then hardened. Gram would never stop hoping to save Ayla, but as guilty as it made me feel, I had no time for wounded birds.

The next day at school, I barely had time to eat lunch. Christmas break was a week away and I had a million tests and projects to do. My own fault, I knew. At the beginning of the semester, both Gram and my guidance counselor had urged me to take a lighter course load so as not to burn out, but this was how I liked it. Mach 10. Warp speed. Basically, no time to dwell on things like mothers snorting cocaine off your Hello Kitty plate and grandmothers calling addiction centers for advice on how to help said mothers.

"Earth to Andrea…" Delaney plopped her lunch tray onto the table next to my books and papers.

"Hey!" I watched my math notes go flying. "I need those."

Delaney scooped them off the cafeteria floor but refused to hand them over. "Stop studying for two seconds and listen. I have news." She blew out an exasperated breath that made her thick bangs flutter and fall crooked against her forehead.

I felt exasperated too, but I knew from experience that the fastest way out of this was through it. "Fine, I'm listening. What's up?"

Settling into her seat, Delaney smiled. She loved the limelight—even if she had to demand it. "Okay, my news first. Last night at rehearsal, the dance teacher chose *me* to do the solo at our competition in Chicago this weekend!"

"Congrats, Dee, that's awesome," I gushed. Irish dancing was to Delaney what academics were to me. She lived it, *breathed* it, and her passion showed in every step. I wasn't surprised Delaney was picked. She was hardcore. Which is probably why we were friends.

"Yeah, I'm kind of a big deal now," she joked, pounding her toes against the floor in an excited little jig.

Glancing at the clock, I asked, "What's the other news?"

Delaney peeled open her yogurt cup, grinning. "I infiltrated Ben Stankowski's inner circle."

"What? How?"

She laughed, delighted by my reaction. "I cornered his

sister—nerdy little freshman—and she spilled the goods on Benny boy."

I wasn't sure whether to be happy or horrified. "And?" I asked.

"Well, he doesn't have a girlfriend. Has *never* had a girlfriend. He wants to go to MIT, so he's always studying or building rockets in his backyard. Oh, and big surprise—he's painfully shy."

I nodded, confirming that his profile made sense. In fact, I probably could have guessed it all. But what Delaney didn't know about Ben was the way his lips pursed when he was thinking, the way his whole face came alive when he engaged in a classroom debate, the way his dark brown eyes watched things—saw things— so intently. Things that weren't *me,* anyway.

Delaney continued, "He sounds painfully *boring* if you ask me, Andrea. But he's perfect for you."

I wondered if I should be offended. "Are you calling me boring?"

"No. You're too adorable to be boring. I call you other things…Dedicated. Driven. Diva."

"Diva?" Now I *was* offended.

Delaney's freckles spread across her cheeks as her smile widened. "Oh wait, that's me."

"Yeah," I agreed with a laugh. "So why won't Ben talk to me, oh wise diva?"

"You've tried all your usual moves?"

I nodded, though I wouldn't call them *moves.* Typically, all it took to get a boy interested was a cute outfit and a flirty smile. From there, a conversation began. But not with Ben.

"I have a new theory," Delaney said. "Maybe he doesn't

want to get too close to the competition. For class valedictorian?"

I blinked. Hadn't thought of that. "Yeah, maybe," I said. There were a few other contenders, but I *was* Ben's biggest rival academically. Speaking of academics, my eyes skipped to my math papers laying on the table, and Delaney sighed. When she pulled out her phone I knew she was about to text her dance friends—her *best* friends—who didn't go to our school.

"Okay, okay. Back to your books, girlie."

I snatched the papers. She didn't have to tell me twice.

When I burst through my front door later that afternoon, the first thing I noticed was that Gram had strung the lights on our Christmas tree. They blinked a cozy hello between the branches.

I tossed my backpack on the couch and yelled, "Love the lights!"

The TV was droning in the kitchen, so I figured Gram was in there getting dinner started. Maybe she'd forgotten all about that "Ayla talk" we were supposed to have. If so, I wouldn't be the one to remind her.

"Guess what?" I called, slipping off my shoes. "Ben actually spoke to me at the student council meeting today. He asked if I was doing Quiz Bowl next semester. Which I might, if I can squeeze it in…"

Technically, Ben had asked a whole group of us about the Quiz Bowl thing, not just me. But I still considered it progress. When Gram didn't respond to my news, though, I figured she wasn't in the mood to hear about it. Boys were always a hit or miss topic.

I unpacked what I needed for homework and headed toward the kitchen, balancing a mountain of textbooks. Ugh. Maybe I *should* have taken a lighter course load.

Halfway down the short hall, I noticed a stream of clear liquid pooling between the kitchen floor tiles. I frowned, confused. After another step I spied a silver pot flipped upside down, and my heart flipped too.

"Gram?"

As I rounded the corner, my books spilled from my arms in a waterfall of flapping pages. Gram was in the kitchen, but she wasn't hovering over the stove or watching CNN on the small countertop television like usual. She wasn't sitting at the table with the photo album open, waiting to have our talk.

She was lying on the floor in a heap, silent and crooked and cold.

Chapter 3

Now

The blackness of the parking lot swallows Ayla as she gestures impatiently for me to get out of the Buick. "We're gonna go in Judd's car," she says.

I climb out of our makeshift home, clutching the two bags I keep close at all times—my school pack and a small duffel stuffed with every article of clothing I own in the world—four tops, two sweaters, a pair of jeans, and a long black skirt. The skirt I planned to wear to Gram's funeral. The funeral I didn't get to attend.

"We'll come back and get the Buick tomorrow."

I watch Ayla lock our car and stuff the keys inside her purse. I always watch the keys.

"It's too far to try and follow in the dark," she adds as we walk to where Judd is leaning against the lamppost. I'm so weary that my shoes keep catching on the crumbling asphalt. If I had the energy, I'd call Ayla's bluff. There is only one reason we can't drive the Buick—it's out of gas.

I shuffle along three steps behind where Ayla is swerving and clinging to Judd's arm. Either she's drunker than I thought or she's putting on a good act. *Men always want to feel needed,* she's told me many times.

Judd's car is black, with dark tinted windows, but still nicer than I expect from the looks of him. I sit in the backseat and stare outside, trying to memorize the turns and street names. It's too hard, too much. My brain is foggy, and I'm so hungry. As if on cue, my stomach lets out a loud rumble.

Judd's snaky eyes find me in the rearview mirror. "I've got plenty of food for you, girl. Don't you worry." He says it like he's some kind of hero, like I should jump into a song and dance of gratitude. I've only been living this way for a few months, but already I know not to trust any man who acts too eager to help us. I turn back to the window, silent.

My right hand slides over my left wrist, squeezing the silver beaded watch strapped there. The watch is the one thing of Gram's I took when we left Indianapolis. It's all I have left of her. That and the Buick, which I hate leaving behind. Already I feel stranded. Tears prick the corners of my eyes, but I wrestle them into submission.

Still, I know Judd sees.

His house is small, dirty, and remote. But at least it's warm. And as promised, there's food. I swallow over my parched throat as Judd shows us around. The kitchen is the only room I care about. I want to jump inside the bag of chips laying on the counter, but I wait until the grand tour is complete. Judd tries smiling again and points to a steep, narrow stairway off the hall. "There's a bedroom up there for you, girl. Real nice."

I don't return his smile. "My name is Andrea," I say tersely.

The awkward grin melts off his face. He turns away slowly and says, "Like I told you, there's plenty of food in the kitchen. Help yourself. Your mama and I are gonna...*dance.*" Judd laughs and slips his hands around Ayla's tiny waist, then slides them down her leather-clad butt as she shimmies into his bedroom. I hear her laugh with him, see the dented door close. And as I snatch the bag of chips and reach greedily for the fridge handle, I almost feel sorry for her.

After shoveling salami into my mouth, I load up my arms with two cans of soda, the chips, a brown banana, a jar of peanut butter, and half a loaf of bread. I want to eat away from the sounds of *them.* The stairs Judd pointed out are barely wide enough for me, but that's okay because my hands are full and there's no railing anyway. I lean against the wall and slide up slowly, into the dark.

The door at the top creaks when I push it gingerly with my toes. The first thing I see is the moon, bright and welcoming, wrapped like a present inside a hexagonal-shaped window. I instantly love that window.

The moonlight is bright enough for me to see a dusty twin bed. Dumping my spoils onto it, I search the sloping walls for a light switch. There's one near the door, but when I flip it, nothing happens. Then I find a single bulb with a string dangling from the low, unfinished ceiling, and pull it hard. The light flickers on, but the string breaks off and I'm left holding it, slack in my hand.

The room is really an attic, but it doesn't span the entire lower level. It's cramped and musty, and hasn't been lived in for a long time. Some little girl used this room once, though. I can tell by the faded flowers on the curtains in the other window—the high one that runs horizontal over the bed—and by the sheets, which are pale pink, and by the miniature porcelain horses lined up on the small shelf by the bed. I wonder where the little girl went, and why she didn't take those horses with her. I shudder away the possibilities that creep into my mind.

There's a hard-backed chair in the corner and a closet that's empty except for a handful of wire hangers laced with spider webs. This will do.

I drag the chair over to the door and tilt it back so that the top edge is lodged beneath the knob. Then I look back at the bed I'll sleep in tonight and the food spread on top of it. Taking a deep breath, I dive in.

My eyes blink open to warm sunlight streaming through the window. It is so nice not to wake up shivering. For a few lovely lazy minutes, I lay on the bed and savor it, but as soon as I hear footsteps downstairs, I bolt upright. The chair is still secured under the door handle. My bags are on the floor by the bed, packed and ready to go. Always.

I glance at Gram's watch. No way is my mother awake. It's only eight fifteen, and Ayla doesn't do mornings. Still, I'm ready to scramble in case Judd wants us out. You never know with Ayla's men. Some of them cuss and yell, like they don't even remember picking us up. Others treat us to breakfast at a Bob Evans restaurant.

I sit like a stone on the pink sheets and wait. Soon, knuckles rap against the stairway wall.

"You awake, girl? Get on down here." Judd's voice is all business. That fake syrup sound he tried on me last night is gone.

I slept in my clothes, even my shoes, so I walk to the stairway and start down, careful to keep my face blank. Judd is waiting in the hallway and today there is no crooked-toothed smile. There is, however, something different about him. Instead of flashy clubbing clothes, he's dressed in khakis and a sweater, hair combed to one side as if he's trying to look…normal. He gives *me* an unimpressed once-over, in my dirty jeans and wrinkled T-shirt, then grunts. "C'mon. There's work to do."

My eyes dart around. "Where is she?" I demand, but my voice betrays me by cracking.

"Sleepin'."

"What are we doing?" I find the courage to ask.

Judd looks at me as he picks something from between his teeth. "You didn't think you were gonna stay here for free, didja?" He laughs a little and it sounds so unnatural, like a lion trying to mew.

I gulp. We know nothing of this man, in his dingy house hidden deep in the woods. He could have Ayla tied up in that room, gagged, or even—

"Look, I got a business to run and your mama said you'd work for your keep. It's a fair trade, for food and shelter. Don'cha think?" Judd asks with arched brows, waiting for me to agree. I relax a little. If I'm working, then I won't owe him anything. Plus, the aroma of cooked bacon lingers in the air and that's as close to heaven as I've been in days.

Before I can ask what his work entails, there's a knock on the front door. No, not a knock exactly—a series of small, birdlike beats that seem endless and purposeful. Judd looks through the peephole, cusses under his breath, then opens the door all of two inches. He hisses, "I told you not to come here unless I called." And then I hear a young man's voice slurring his words, saying he can't wait, he has money...

Judd turns towards me, scowling. "Clean up the house, then eat breakfast. I'll be back."

After he slams the door closed, I peek through the window and catch a glimpse of the visitor's pimpled face, a jagged red scar etched above his right eyebrow. He looks a few years older than me—maybe nineteen or twenty. Judd grabs the collar of the guy's jacket and drags him to a path in the woods. The kid doesn't resist.

As soon as they disappear, I rush to Judd's bedroom door and turn the knob. Locked. I jiggle it and call Ayla's name, three times. She doesn't stir, but that's nothing new. I press my forehead against the closed door.

Damnit, Ayla. When are we gonna get the Buick?

After a minute, I head to the kitchen, resolved. I've survived in Ayla's world for months now, and even if Judd seems a little rougher than the hippie crowd she usually runs with, I can handle this. He's probably some low-level pusher—one of those guys who wants his next hit and a bit of business on the side to pay for it. Besides, this is only temporary.

It doesn't take me long to find, cook, and devour the bacon. I put the last two slices in a plastic bag and slide it inside my boot for later. Then I stuff cheese and pretzels into my mouth while I wipe down the kitchen counters, earning my keep.

Judd returns half an hour later. I'm scrubbing about fifty layers of soap scum off the bathroom sink when I feel his gaze on my back. I whirl around, but his gray eyes are not hungry like some of the men Ayla has brought into my life. They're just matter-of-fact, sizing me up as he leans against the doorjamb.

"Bones, huh. I can see why she calls you that. Not much to you. Pretty face, though." He sighs, like this worries him. "Hope you're stronger'n you look."

I'll give him strong, I think, hardening my face and lowering my eyelids. I clench my jaw tight and cross my arms loosely. This is the look I use on my classmates when I want them to leave me alone.

But Judd is no tenth grader and he doesn't shrink from a skinny little girl with attitude.

"Let's go," he barks, sliding on a backpack he pulls from the hall closet. "I'm behind schedule." Then his hand is pressed against my back, pushing me out the door toward that same path in the woods. It's a sunny day, but the crisp wind cuts through my T-shirt.

"Where are we going?" I demand, twisting around so I can keep my eyes on him.

"My office," he says without breaking stride.

Office? Out *here?* As soon as we're surrounded by the trees, panic sets in, and I try to veer sideways, out of his grasp. He responds with a yank on my elbow so powerful it rattles my teeth. "Stop squirmin'!" he hollers. Every muscle and ligament in his body is tight—his neck, arms, hands.

Judd must see the fear on my face because he sighs and tries on another smile like it's killing him. "Look, this is real simple. You do what I say and you can stay here with your mama, eat all the food you want, sleep in a nice, warm bed at night. But if you become more trouble than you're worth..." His sentence dangles and I wish he'd finish it.

Then again, maybe I don't.

Imagining the worst, my survival instinct kicks in again. "I won't be any trouble," I promise, letting him guide me deeper into the woods.

We reach a small clearing where three paths converge and Judd stops short. "My business requires a certain level of... discretion. Your mama says you know how to keep your mouth shut. That true?"

I nod.

"Good," he says. "But that don't mean I trust you." And with that, Judd's hand moves to the base of my neck, two of his bony fingers extended so he can control where I look. That's all it takes—two fingers.

My breath is shallow, and the feel of his hand so close to my face makes my stomach churn. Judd walks fast, and I walk faster to keep up. My long black hair blocks my peripheral vision.

On the ground I see sticks, rocks, leaves, and sunlight, all swirling in circles because of the way he keeps my head angled down. There are other paths that cross ours, turns we take that I know I won't remember. He doesn't want me to.

Finally, he grips tighter, halting me. His fingers slip off my neck. Looking up, I see nothing but trees, some with a coating of ice still clinging to their branches.

"Don't move." Judd slips on a pair of gloves, unlocks the door to a shed buried deep in the brush, and ducks inside.

For some reason, I follow his orders. I don't move. I am paralyzed in these woods, in this moment. Until I'm yanked into the blackness of the shed.

Chapter 4
Then

I don't remember calling 9-1-1. But I must have, because the ambulance arrived and someone led me away from Gram and into the living room. Everything was a messy blur of sirens and strangers, each moment spinning into the next like puzzle pieces that didn't quite fit. The newly strung lights on our Christmas tree, the tepid hands of a social worker, the promises recited over and again, as if repetition could summon a miracle: "We'll find your mother soon, Andrea. Everything will be all right."

I watched the paramedics take Gram's body to the morgue. Nothing would be all right.

The social worker drove me to a foster home. I heard her say how lucky I was that a family in my school district was willing to take me on such short notice. Standing on a dark doorstep, I stared at a holly wreath hanging from a crooked nail, then looked into the weary eyes of a middle-aged couple when the door swung open. I did not feel lucky.

I went to school the next morning because I had a geography quiz, a French project to turn in, and a yearbook meeting. Because school was the only thing that seemed normal. But when I got there, no one knew how to act, not even me. Not even Delaney.

"I feel so bad about your Gram," she said, tears pooling in her eyes. But she didn't suggest that I leave the foster house to come stay at hers. She didn't cancel her Chicago dance plans or insist I come along. She echoed the social worker, assuring me that my mother would come back soon. I felt something inside me latch down tight.

The foster people said to call them Charlie and Diane. Their house was eggshell blue. There was peanut butter smeared on the cabinet doors and a pile of plastic bowls set on the counter each morning. There was a guestroom full of futons and cots and kids. Charlie and Diane were used to this chaos. I was not. Between school and dinnertime, I wandered their neighborhood, just one subdivision away from my own. I could've walked home and let myself in with the spare key we kept in the planter, but the memory of Gram slumped on the kitchen floor kept me away.

My body repelled sleep, resisted the passage of time. It wanted to go *back,* not forward. Each night I slipped out of the room I shared with the four other foster kids and tiptoed across the hall cradling my backpack. I curled up in the bathtub and hugged my books, their familiar spines pressing into my chest, their words barricading my heart.

I had read countless stories about the fog of grief, but nothing prepared me for *this*. Gram was dead, Ayla was out getting high somewhere, and there was no chance of my father—whoever he was—coming to rescue me. It's not like I hadn't experienced loneliness before. As an only child, that's part of the deal. But I'd never felt this hollowness. I'd never felt so completely alone.

Lying there in the tub each night, I held my breath while pieces of the nightmare rained down on me like shards of broken glass. They cut deep like puncture wounds, barely visible on the surface. But damaging just the same.

Chapter 5
Now

The lock on the shed clicks behind me. Judd walks farther inside, but I stay by the door and let my eyes adjust to the dimness. There are several canisters lined against the far wall, a folding table, and drug paraphernalia similar to what I've seen Ayla use with her hipster friends. Also a box overflowing with teddy bears.

Judd half-sits on the table and lights a cigarette, sizing me up again. I'm breathing so hard but so quietly that my lungs ache from the effort. He stares like he's trying to decide something, and I suddenly realize how bad things could get if he thinks I'm too fragile, too naïve, too much of a risk.

So I cross my arms and pull out my toughest voice. "What are we selling?"

He steps forward and leans his face down close to mine, amused. "I'm a distributor of home goods." His breath puffs out, sending the rot scent of tobacco up my nostrils. It takes all my willpower not to gag.

I nod once. Then repeat his words. "Home goods. Got it."

He chuckles. "This might just work out."

Judd walks over and peels a lid off one of the black canisters. It appears to be filled with rock salt, the kind Gram and I sprinkled on our concrete path when it was icy. But the top part of the canister lifts out to reveal a second, hidden compartment underneath where I spy mountains of leafy green- and rust-colored cannabis.

Judd pulls out the buds and separates them into clear ziplock bags. He stuffs the baggies inside the teddy bears after cutting ragged slits into their undersides with a serrated knife. For the white bears, he pulls special baggies of snow white powder from his backpack and slides those inside as well.

My job is to sew up each bear with a needle and thread. Judd tells me to be quick about it because there are deliveries to make and that dipshit kid messed up his schedule. I'm no seamstress, and I keep poking myself with the needle and wiping the drops of blood onto my jeans. The shed is drafty and soon my fingers and toes are numb, but that makes the needle pricks easier to take.

"Be careful," Judd warns. "This shit's worth more than your life."

My life? Four months ago, I had a life. I was a typical high school sophomore, my biggest worry whether I got an A or B on a test. Four months ago I had friends, a home. A grandmother who loved me. Four freaking months. That's all it took to erase everything. To turn me into *this*. I know what I'm doing is wrong and dangerous to boot, but for all my supposed smarts, I can't think…

I can't think of a way out.

The shed is windowless so we work by the light of a few battery-operated lanterns. Despite the chill, Judd rolls up his shirtsleeves. On each arm I spy matching tattoos of a sword surrounded by flame. I consider asking about the tattoos, trying to play friendly, but then I remember how acting friendly worked out with Charlie, and I clamp my mouth shut.

Judd works fast and it's hard to keep up. When I quicken my pace, he encourages me with one word, "better." I don't need his praise, but I think about how good that bacon tasted and how soft the attic bed was, and I keep sewing. There are so many bears to fill, and it seems like we work forever in the cold, dim silence.

My mind is not silent, though. Now that I let him in, I can't get Charlie the foster dad out of my head. I keep picturing the day it happened, the way he sat so close with his hand on my shoulder, asking me about school, which subjects I liked best…the way he got me comfortable, got me talking, and then while I was explaining something about molecules, the way his hand slipped to my chest and his leg pressed down on mine, and his lips swallowed up all my words…

"*Get* your head outta your ass, girl. You're spilling it everywhere!"

Judd shoves me aside, snatching a small bear from my hands. It is leaking a fine stream of white dust—I must've punctured the baggie. He drops to his knees, trying to pinch up the lost white granules. It's hardly anything, and there's no way to salvage it, but he's frantic. Judd's fingertips scrape at the wood, collecting tiny bits of powder under his nails before he accepts the loss.

Cursing, he stands up and slams his elbow against the side of my face.

Letting out a sharp cry, I crumple to the floor.

There's not much pain, just the faint taste of blood where he loosened a tooth. That, and the wild animal feeling in my chest as I try to breathe. I stay hunched on the ground.

Judd finishes the sewing himself, muttering "worthless" under his breath every time he looks at me. I breathe raggedly and wonder what a person like Judd does with someone he thinks is worthless.

When the job is complete, he stuffs the bears into two backpacks—the one he brought along and a larger one that was stashed under the table.

"Get up," he growls, and I scramble. He straps the smaller backpack to me and hefts the larger one onto his own shoulders. Outside, his hand grips my neck once more, rougher and tighter, for the cold trek back to his house. The trees watch us go, their branches shuddering.

I don't open my mouth for the rest of the day, just do whatever Judd says as we drive from one shitty neighborhood to another. I carry the stuffed animals, though anyone with half a brain can see I'm too old for them. I hand the bears to the people inside the houses. Judd jokes with them—his dealers—but it's clear that they fear him.

I'm grateful for that fear when I notice some of their ravenous eyes on *me*. In one house, a man pushes up so close to me that I make a small whimpering sound. Judd's hand shoots out toward the guy's bearded face, squeezing the man's jaw until he cries out in pain. The message is clear—I am Judd's and I am off limits.

By nightfall Judd looks relaxed, maybe even happy. He smokes while he drives, listening to the radio and nodding to the beat of the music. Now that he's in a good mood, Judd looks at me with lighter eyes. "You screwed up earlier, but you'll learn. Gotta keep your focus, girl. Next time I'll take it outta your pay."

"Okay. Sorry," I croak and wonder which he would deny me—shelter or food.

Ayla is alive, content and lounging on the couch when we return. I don't know why I feel such relief at the sight of her, since the feeling is not reciprocated. Ignoring me, she smiles pretty for Judd. He groans with pleasure and falls on top of her, ready for more *dancing*. I rummage through the kitchen for food to take up to the attic. This time I take twice as much. I've earned it.

Before I leave the kitchen, Judd stops mauling Ayla long enough to raise his head and say sharply, "Bones. Be ready by eight tomorrow. S'gonna be a long day."

Upstairs, I gaze out the hexagonal window at the moon, a crescent tonight, and wonder if Gram, if anyone, can see me.

Chapter 6
Then

Four days before Christmas, I climbed off the school bus and trudged up the driveway to the foster home a few steps ahead of the other kids. It was officially winter break, and the frosty air slapped my cheeks as if to prove it. I yanked on the brass handle of the front door, ducked inside, and stopped.

There was a woman in the kitchen chatting up Charlie. Her voice was unmistakable—low and raspy. My backpack slipped off my shoulder.

"Forget how to walk?" grumbled one of the foster girls, shoving past. The others streamed around me, heading for the rec room in the basement.

My frozen cheeks suddenly flushed hot. I wasn't ready for this, for her, so I took the roundabout way to the bedroom. I sat on a futon and hugged my knees, took a breath in and blew it out slowly. Ayla was here. She'd come back for me. So many conflicting emotions rushed at me—anger, relief, fear—that I couldn't make sense of them. How would she be this time? Did I even *want* to go with her?

Then, through the wall, I heard Charlie say in his smooth-operator voice, "I can see where your daughter got her good looks," and Ayla flirt-laughed and I snapped back to my senses. I gathered my things.

"Here she is!" boomed Charlie, catching sight of me in the kitchen doorway, bags in hand. "We're sure gonna miss this one."

Slowly, I met Ayla's eyes. She wore a denim jacket and big hoop earrings, her dark, clean hair cresting her shoulders. She looked way better than the last time I'd seen her, so good that I wondered if she'd managed to turn things around. Like Gram always hoped she would.

"Hey there," Ayla said, half-friendly. Her voice sounded hoarse, but her pupils were clear. She spoke as if we'd seen each other hours ago, instead of months. "Ready to go home?" she asked, stubbing out her cigarette in a tin can with a picture of a purple beet on its label.

I stared at the can. I hated beets. They'd been served for dinner every night since I'd arrived here, along with some overcooked chicken in a thin mustard sauce. I remember how Diane had said matter-of-factly on my first night, *You kids eat what you're given, or you don't eat. Makes no difference to me.*

"Ready," I said, blinking.

"Thanks for keepin' her fed," Ayla told Charlie and stood up. My mother is tall compared to me, all leggy and lithe, and she was wearing four-inch patterned heels that day. I wondered how she could even walk in those things, but I was thankful she was *walking*, period, instead of falling down drunk or stoned.

Charlie followed us to the foyer. At the door he initiated a side-hug goodbye, but I slipped away before his arm could capture me. "Come visit anytime, Andrea," he called, all friendly.

I slammed the car door.

As Ayla drove us home in Gram's Buick, the pressure that had been squeezing my chest for days dissipated a tiny bit. Outside, the gray December sky gave the world a dusty look. The car's blinker clicked rhythmically, like a heartbeat.

"So they told you...what happened?" I ventured, staring at my hands.

Ayla's gaze rested on me for a moment. "Yeah. We'll be okay, though." She said it soft, husky. Tender, almost. Like the Ayla from Gram's stories.

I glanced up, surprised, but the woman who shared half my DNA was busy lighting another cigarette. She didn't look at me again. She didn't talk again either.

Three days later she charged into my bedroom, ordering me to hurry up and pack because we were leaving town, *now.* Her dark hair was tangled, her movements twitchy, and her eyes wild. I knew this woman—she desperately needed a hit.

My heart hammered as I shoved handfuls of clothing into my duffel bag. I wasn't ready for this. I hadn't even told Delaney about the realtor putting our house on the market. I guess a part of me thought if I pretended things were normal, they *would* be. How stupid.

"Let's go." Ayla plucked my half-packed bag off the bed and headed down the hall. I snatched a few books off my nightstand, shoved them into my backpack, and followed her to the living room. Then I saw the stockings by our fireplace and the Christmas tree in the corner, lights unplugged. It was Christmas Eve, I realized. My feet stopped.

Ayla whirled around, impatient. "Come on."

"Where are we even going?" I demanded.

"I got us a place." Her dimple showed when she smiled, proud.

"But we have this place."

"Not for long." She nodded toward the window and the For Sale sign visible in our front yard. "I got an offer."

I chewed my lip, hating that *she* got to make these decisions. Ayla! Who only ever showed up when she needed money or a place to crash. I didn't have any special love for Indianapolis, but this was Gram's house, full of Gram's things.

"What about school?" I pressed.

Ayla snorted. "You don't think they have schools anywhere else?"

"Yeah, but I have friends here," I said, my voice rising. "I'm on the honors track. I have a *life*."

Ayla rolled her eyes, then smirked. "You want to stay? Fine by me. When the new owners kick you out, I'm sure Charlie will be thrilled to have you back." She dropped my bag with a definitive thump and walked out the door.

The house got abruptly quiet. Flat light poured through the window slats onto the couch where Gram liked to read. Glancing at the bookshelves, my eyes zoned in on the blue photo album, the one Gram was looking at the last time I saw her alive. I shuffled over and ran my fingers down its spine. I stood still for a moment, letting Ayla's words bleed into focus. My mind flashed to the foster home, to the rainy afternoon with Charlie. That was all it took.

Tucking the album under my arm, I grabbed my bag and ran out the door, the memories and photos and knickknacks of my childhood all disappearing in a white-hot blur.

Chapter 7
Now

Judd's elbow leaves a sad yellow bruise on my cheek that makes me look tougher than I feel. He got his point across. I don't make any more mistakes. Each day I spend hours working in his shed, hiding drugs in various household items that we pretend to sell. I help him pack everything up, switch out his license plates, make deliveries. The dealers call me Bones now. I fear I might become her.

We're sitting in stopped traffic on our third day of deliveries when Judd glances at me across the front seat. His voice scratches at my skull. "You don't look much like her. Your mama."

"No," I agree in a neutral voice, knowing it's because of our eyes. Ayla's are auburn and sultry-looking. Mine are arctic blue and, nowadays, cold to match.

"She and I go way back, didja know that?" Judd's cheeks disappear as he sucks hard on his cigarette.

I did not.

"I saw a picture once, when you were a baby," he continues. "Somethin' about you made her real sad."

Yeah, I think bitterly. My *birth*. But I'm shocked to hear that Ayla ever kept a photo of me. Maybe she cared, back then. Gram said she stayed sober during most of her pregnancy. I try to imagine Ayla as the kind of mother who smothers her baby with kisses, who sings soft lullabies, who breathes in that new-to-the-world scent and whispers *I love you, sweet girl.*

It takes a lot of imagining.

"Couldn't believe my eyes when she walked into the bar the other night," Judd says. He shakes his head like it's the darnedest thing. I glare at his profile, imagine raking my nails down his face. "Guess it was fate," he concludes.

And then we are on to the next delivery and it is too late to quip, "Or just bad luck."

When we pull up to a dilapidated-looking Cape Cod house in a rundown section of Columbus, Judd cuts the engine and hands me a boy's winter coat from the box in the backseat. I know the drugs are sewn into the hood because I poked myself twelve times trying to get the needle through that slippery material.

Judd wraps his fingers around my chin and turns my face toward his. "You know the signal, Bones?" His stare is so intense that even if I didn't know, I would lie. After I nod, he says, "They know what they owe me. Don't give 'em the product until the money's in your hand. You put the money in your pocket. Then you walk out here—*walk,* never run—and put the money in my hand. Got it?"

"You're not coming in?" I blurt. The stupidity of my question earns me a hot glare.

I look up at the house, at the massive door with its peeling white paint, and wonder who's waiting on the other side.

"I don't have all day," Judd mutters as he shoves a cigarette into his mouth and flips open a small black notebook. My mind reels. I should have seen this coming. After all, what use am I to Judd if he has to escort me everywhere?

Transforming my face into a mask of stone, I get out of the car and climb the porch steps. I glance down the street at the long row of sad, saggy houses just like this one. Shutters falling off, broken windows covered with sheets. The pulsing beat of music pounding a few doors down.

I squeeze Gram's watch for strength and think of what she said the first time I had to present a project in front of my classmates—"No one can see your nerves, love."

On the top step, I take a breath and knock the way I'm supposed to. I know the signal.

"The fuck is it?" a voice thunders from the other side of the door, followed by raucous laughter. The guy must have seen me walk up alone. No one would respond to *Judd's* knock that way.

"Bones," I answer, proud of how tough and flat my voice sounds.

The door opens. I go inside and the door closes. There are a few people sitting in the main room, all staring at me, and one guy in the entry with sweat glistening on his big brown muscles. I don't look at his face, but I can smell his acidic body odor, like he was working out. He says something, but the words don't process over the thumping of my heart. I give up the coat before he produces the money, but he's good for it. Once I have the cash in my pocket, I'm outside and fast-walking down the steps to the shelter of Judd's sedan.

My hand trembles as I place the bills in his outstretched palm. Judd notices. He purses his lips and says gruffly, "They won't hurt you. They know you're mine."

As we drive away, I think about his words, how they make me feel safe in one way and completely screwed in another.

Chapter 8
Then

When Ayla and I arrived at The Lofts, a trendy hotel in downtown Columbus, I have to admit I felt a flutter of excitement. The lobby, decked out for the holidays, was nicer than any I'd ever seen. But when the lady at the front desk politely informed us that our reservation didn't start until December 30th and the hotel was booked until then, my mother, who is *never* in the right place at the right time, launched into a full-blown tantrum. As she ranted about *their* idiotic mistake, I tugged her outside into the cold.

"We'll stay at a different hotel for a few nights," I suggested.

But Ayla refused to spend her "fun money" on a week's worth of crappy hotel rooms. Instead, she drove to her friend Trey's apartment building, knocked on three doors before she found the right one, and sweetly asked the young man who answered if he remembered her from last year's Mardi Gras party and by the way, could she and her little sister crash there? The guy flipped a shock of shaggy blond hair out of his eyes and looked Ayla up and down, like he was trying to place her by her body instead of her face. "Why not?" he said, opening the door wide. I spent Christmas Eve sleeping on a stranger's couch under a stained blanket. Ayla stayed in the bedroom with her "friend," but I can tell you, they didn't sleep.

In the morning, we were kicked out early and unceremoniously. Ayla drove us to the bungalow of Scott and Sylvie—hippy-types who were generous with their food *and* their drugs. A small party was underway when we arrived, and there was a lot of giggling from the adults camped out on the porch. After gushing about how adorable I was, everyone pretty much ignored me. At least there was turkey for dinner.

The next day, Sylvie caught Ayla and Scott lip-locked on the porch and literally tossed our bags onto the lawn. Still floating high on Sylvie's cocaine, Ayla just laughed.

We continued couch surfing with random people. Most of them didn't remember Ayla, but they let her in because she was beautiful. By the time we returned to The Lofts and collected the keys to our suite, I was shell-shocked. That was how Ayla had lived for *years*.

But she had money now, and she paid for an entire month at the hotel up front, which made everything feel less transient than it was. The suite even looked like an apartment, with exposed brick walls and memory foam beds, a kitchenette and steam shower. After the previous six nights, it was a palace.

For a week I zoned out on TV and junk food—two things Gram had limited at home. Ayla and I operated like roommates—

eating take-out and talking only when necessary. She went clubbing every night and slept most days, so we were on opposite schedules, which worked out nicely. Often, I woke to find random men making coffee in our kitchenette. Some of them felt entitled to rake their eyes over my body, earning them my tough-girl look. Others seemed nice, but I kept my distance anyway.

The Lofts had a business center with four computers. I surfed the Internet, but didn't send emails. Or use the phone. Mostly I slept and cried and paged through the photo album looking at pictures of Gram when she was a young mother. Her hair was longer and darker then, her skin smoother. She looked beautiful. She looked *blissful.*

"What is that?" Ayla asked me once when she was bored. She hopped on my bed and leaned over to look, her chin pressing into my shoulder. I held my breath. She'd never sat so close. Then she took the album into her own hands, transfixed. It was all about her, really. Ayla in a tutu. Ayla in a swimming pool. Ayla blowing Gram a kiss. Poised and flirty and all smiles. *She* was the stunning one, even at age five.

As Ayla paged through the album, tears filled her eyes. When she was done, she took a ragged breath, handed the album back to me, and left the suite. She returned at five in the morning, shitfaced.

Whatever loss Ayla felt for Gram or *her* old life, I was certain I felt it deeper. I missed everything about home. Gram most of all. But also my books and my bedroom and—silly as it sounds—the filing cabinet with all my school papers sorted by subject and year. Everything orderly about my life had been blown away by the tornado that was my mother. For the first time in sixteen years, I had no plan, no motivation. I was simply caught, swirling, in her vortex.

"Here," Ayla said one night, switching on the overhead light and stirring me from sleep. I was nothing but a lump on the bed as she tossed a paper on top of the comforter and announced, "You start at that school tomorrow, Bones. I signed you up."

Under the bundle of covers, my eyebrows furrowed. Ayla taking initiative? Unlikely. I peeked out to see a thick, glossy brochure. I couldn't imagine my old high school spending one cent of their precious government funds on fancy marketing materials like that. Curious, my hand slithered out to retrieve it.

With a rigorous academic curriculum, I read, *Essex Academy is consistently ranked in the Top 100 public high schools in the country, number one in the state of Ohio for the past ten years...*

My mind woke up. My *heart* woke up. Excitement bubbled through my veins as I devoured the information...*Highest SAT scores. Ninety percent of graduates receive scholarships. Tier one colleges recruit the best and brightest.* I almost squealed. Graduating from a place like Essex, especially with honors, would increase my chances of attending an Ivy League university by so many margins I could barely sit still long enough to do the math. I took it as a sign. *This* is what I'd always wanted. This is what Gram would want for me.

Instead of sleeping that night, I paced and I planned. The next morning, I buried the photo album in the bottom of my duffel bag, drew on a thick band of Ayla's eyeliner, and embraced my new life.

Essex was everything the brochure had promised. I didn't try to make friends—I was there to accomplish a goal. I immersed myself in academics and didn't worry about anything else, including my mother. I was still naïve then. I felt more disgusted by her lifestyle than concerned about it infecting mine.

I didn't think about money, either, since Ayla always seemed to have enough. Gram's house had sold and I figured Ayla had inherited her savings. In February we moved into a small apartment that I found advertised on Craig's List. Life went on, clumsy but bearable, with Essex as the shining star in my universe. Until last week.

When the police showed up to "enforce our eviction," I was stunned. It was the first day of spring break and I'd been planning to spruce up the place with paint and pictures, to go grocery shopping and fill our bare cupboards since Ayla never found time. Eviction? It had to be a mistake. I tried arguing with the officers, then pleading. Ayla, who must've collected the notices, wasn't surprised. She had apparently forgotten to tell me that Gram's money was gone. All gone.

We packed our things and drove around Columbus trying to come up with a plan that *didn't* involve couch surfing. I was livid that Ayla had spent all our money, but yelling at her wouldn't bring it back. So I kept suggesting reasonable options for our future, many of which involved returning to Indianapolis, even though I already felt detached from my old life there. Ayla shot down my ideas, and soon we were forced to focus on our immediate needs. We rationed our last few candy bars and kept the Buick running to stay warm. In hindsight, that was a mistake.

On the third day, we loitered inside the bus station because it was warm—and populated. Ayla flirted with a few men, conned them with some sob story, and swaggered off with their handouts. Her efforts earned us each a soft pretzel and hot chocolate—our only meal that day. I remember Ayla watching me eat, smiling like she was proud of herself. I remember something inside me throbbing with pity for her—until the hunger pains snuffed it out.

The next night, Ayla sashayed into Judd's tattooed arms at that hole-in-the-wall bar and I learned, once again, that no matter how hard I focused on the future, the unwelcome present kept creeping up to bite me.

Chapter 9

Now

Saturday marks the end of our first week with Judd, and boy, is he in a good mood.

"Whoo-ee! Best week's payout in a long time, Ayla girl. You must be my good luck charm," Judd says and smashes his lips against hers. Standing in the kitchen drying the lunch dishes, I scoff and think, *Or maybe it's because you've had a live-in slave to do your dirty work all week.*

Judd spins Ayla around the living room while she giggles in this childlike way that pinches my heart, even though it shouldn't. Then he pats her butt and tells her to go dress up nice because he wants to take her out and show her off.

I am left behind with strict instructions not to set one foot outside the house. I nod like a good little drug mule but as soon as they leave, I walk out the front door and directly into the woods. Damned if I'm going to take orders from Judd when he's not around to enforce them.

I walk for about a mile, taking the left turn at every fork in the trail, until I'm on the fringe of some farmlands. Stumbling over the uneven ground, I venture off trail to pick a cluster of butterweed plants because they're pretty and I need some cheering up. As I'm tucking the tiny yellow flowers into my hair, I look up to discover a pond hidden by overgrown bushes and a stand of thick trees. Swaying along the water's edge are tall, willowy grasses— burnt orange with sprigs of green mixed in. Before I know it, I'm pushing my way through the foliage to reach the muddy bank.

The pond water doesn't glisten. It looks more goopy than anything. But there is a stillness here, a lovely stillness that makes me feel like life has been put on pause. A huge hickory tree leans out over the black water and lily pads, and I start climbing it. Once I'm nestled onto a high, thick branch with my back curved against the tree's trunk, I relax. I feel safe up here. Outside of Essex, it's the only place I've felt safe in weeks.

Several minutes later, while I'm perched up there listening to the wind, I hear something different—an unnatural rustling. At the far end of the pond, a girl pushes through the reeds onto a strip of dirt. She wears her streaky hair in two tiny braids on either side of her head, and she's built small, like me. It's not that warm today, not even mid-60s, so I'm surprised when she pulls off her clothes to reveal a light blue bathing suit.

The girl glances around as she dips her toe into the pond water, which must be freezing. She bravely wades in a few feet, then disappears underwater, barely making a ripple. The pond must be deeper in the middle because she doesn't surface for a long time.

When the top of her head breaks the surface, she releases a whoop of exhilaration, flips to her back, and floats there, arms stretched like sunbeams. I watch her, mesmerized. Curious. *Jealous.* It takes confidence to lie like that, eyes closed, exposed and trusting.

I watch the girl the whole time she's in the pond, diving down deep and bursting up through the middle again. She dog-paddles around the perimeter and I freeze when she passes below me. She treads for a minute, blows bubbles. After she's out of the water and has vigorously dried herself with a towel, she pulls on her sweats and a T-shirt. With her back to me, she loops the towel around her neck.

"I can see you up there, you know!" she calls over her shoulder, then saunters away. I freeze as her girlish giggle fades into the trees. I want to call after her, but I don't. I do smile, though.

The girl's innocent laughter sings in my head all the way back to Judd's place. It lightens my steps. When I arrive at his ramshackle house, I stand outside in the gravel driveway, feeling heavy again. I don't want to go inside yet and I'm sure Judd and Ayla won't be home until the bars close. I find a fallen log nearby and sit there in the waning light. The heat disappears with the sun, so I lie down on the forest floor where the dry leaves poke through my thin sweater but also insulate me. In the quiet, I stare up at the barren trees reaching their charred fingertips toward the sky. If I were a bird, I would fly right through those branches and launch myself into the clouds. I would sail to the sun and set myself free.

Free. Such a simple word, but a concept far more complicated than I ever realized.

Anyway, I'm *not* a soaring bird. I am a girl who is slipping, falling, sinking. I know exactly what I need. It's what I've always needed. School.

Just thinking about Essex Academy's bright halls, its library teeming with books, and the teachers who talk about the future gives me a jolt of energy. I love Essex, even though I'm considered a freak there. Even though I wear the same five articles of clothing in rotation and if the teachers don't notice, the rich kids sure do. Anyway, it's best if they view me as hardcore, with my dark eyeliner and darker expressions, with my vintage combat boots and long black vest. Those were the two items of clothing I bought after Gram's death, when I wanted to look like a bad-ass. When I wanted to *feel* like one.

I yank on those boots and that vest the next morning. Downstairs, I march toward the couch in Judd's living room and whisper urgently into my mother's ear, "Ayla, we *have* to get the car."

Ayla is lethargic from her night of partying, one skinny arm draped over her face, legs twisted like a pretzel. Judd is outside talking on his cell phone, which means I can badger her until he comes in and makes me shut up. He doesn't want us to have the car. He wants all the power.

"They'll tow it soon," I press. "Then when you want to leave, you won't be able to."

"Why would I wanna leave? Judd's shit is the best I've ever had," Ayla slurs, her milky white hand rising to pet my hair. When she does this, I can't help leaning into her palm a little.

"We can't stay here forever," I say.

"Why not? Sure beats that crappy apartment *you* found."
Her hand, so gentle a moment ago, jabs into my shoulder.

I force a calming breath because I'm still spitting mad that
she bounced the rent checks, that we got evicted after two measly
months. I'd *led* Ayla to that apartment because it was affordable
and in the right school district. As usual, she'd messed everything up.

But I have to focus on the car.

My mind searches for what will sway her. "The Buick's
worth a few thousand dollars, at least," I argue. "We can't give that up."

"Bones, you're startin' to give me a headache."

I pause, then say what I don't want to, "The police will
trace the car to Gram. They'll wonder where we are and come
looking. They'll take me away if they find you like this."

This startles Ayla into coherence. I haven't figured out
her motive, but she seems desperate to keep me. I've thought
about asking why, but I'm afraid bringing it up will cause her to
reconsider, and then I'll be on my own. Or back in the system. Ten
days in foster care was enough for me.

"Okay." She sits up, runs her fingers through her stringy
hair, and goes to splash water on her face.

"Put some clothes on!" I yell, because it's not impossible
that she'd forget. While I wait, my whole body tingles with
excitement, as if something good might finally happen.

Ayla emerges from the bedroom, dressed and pretty, her
purse on her shoulder. We find Judd outside and there's a short
argument, which Ayla wins. As messed up as she is most of the

time, my mother usually gets what she wants.

The sun is shining today, chasing the chill from the air. I feel light and hopeful as Judd drives us to the old supermarket complex in the neighboring town, a can of gas by my feet.

Please, please, please let the Buick still be there.

It is. Seeing her car near the lone lamppost is like reclaiming a piece of Gram herself. My heart sings with joy, but I try not to show it.

While Judd gasses up the Buick, Ayla hands me the keys and climbs into the passenger seat. "I'm tired, Bones. You drive."

The engine purrs under my foot as I snake through the parking lot. Glancing at the fuel gauge, I notice that Judd only put in an eighth of a tank. So I couldn't make a run for it, I guess. I wasn't going to. As long as I have Essex, I can handle Judd. I can handle anything.

I follow the black sedan all the way back to Judd's hideaway. But this time, I am not hungry or beat down. I am not powerless. This time, I memorize every turn.

Chapter 10

The instant I park Gram's car in the driveway, Judd yanks open my door and rips the keys from the ignition. I start to protest, but he slams the door so fast, I hardly have time to pull my arms inside. He stalks into the house while Ayla, wiped out by our thirty-minute excursion, follows him listlessly.

I climb out of the Buick and press my cheek against the slope of its roof, fuming. The cold sting of the metal seeps into my skin and spreads to my clenched jaw as the unfairness of my situation festers. This is *my* car, not Judd's. But he thinks he owns me and Ayla. He acts like he's king of the crap pile, and we have to bow to his commands. And maybe we do for now. I'll play his game. But I'm smarter than he is, and the tides will turn. I'm sure of that.

Right now, though, I can think only of school. Without the car, I'm screwed. There's no way Ayla's going to get up in the morning to drive me.

I bide my time all afternoon, but there's no opportunity to ask Ayla for the keys—Judd is always by her side. So later, when they're busy in Judd's bedroom, I initiate Plan B. I sneak the phone upstairs and call for bus schedules. The route is easy enough, but my heart sinks when I realize I'll have to ask someone for the fare.

As I'm returning the phone to the kitchen, I notice their clothing thrown haphazardly across the back of the couch. Sitting there on top of Judd's pants is his thick black wallet. A tiny smile curves up the side of my cheek.

The sun has not yet risen when I slip outside the next morning and begin the mile-long hike to the market. Dollops of snow are still scattered on the frosty ground. As I walk, it strikes me how isolated this area is, mostly farmland with an occasional house popping up way back from the two-lane road. Despite the blossoms peeking through the undergrowth, the woods near Judd's place are dense and dark, the trees tight like soldiers. We are completely hidden out here.

Judd's going to flip when he finds me missing today. I kind of wish I could be there to see the look on his face. Imagining it puts a spring in my step, even though crossing him now could bring trouble later. Who cares? I tell myself. Getting back to Essex is all that matters.

At the market, the plump lady at customer service sounds sugary sweet when she tells me where to board the bus, but she smacks her blue bubble gum too hard and her eyes seem insincere. I don't like the way she stares after me as I head outside, but I'm not letting anyone spoil my good mood.

I drop Judd's bills into the fare receptacle and slide into a rear seat. Once those big wheels are chewing pavement at fifty-five miles an hour, I feel invincible. I am light years away from Judd now.

The bus drops me in downtown Columbus. The air is charged with buzzing energy as people clip-clop their way to work. After a fifteen-minute walk, Essex slides into view. Four white stone buildings covered in ivy. A large green lawn. Clusters of students chatting in doorways. My heart swells. It looks more like a small college than a high school, and it's mine.

I'm too early for class, but the library is open. Flashing my ID to log onto a computer, I start pulling up maps. Haydon is the town where Judd lives, thirty-five miles southeast of Columbus. It's just a farming community—not much else there. I print out bus schedules going in every direction from the market, just in case. My finger traces the blue line that goes west to Indianapolis. On the map, it looks so close, like I could blink and be back in my old bedroom. I blink.

Still in the library, I open my email program and compose a note to Delaney. I write four versions of it before deleting them all. What can I tell her that's true? Only stuff about school. And then she'll type me ten paragraphs about her love life and Irish dancing and where the hell have I been. *If* she responds at all. She hasn't emailed in months. I never replied to her early messages, which were full of questions I couldn't answer.

My stomach rumbles, giving me an excuse to log off the computer, scarf down the peanut butter sandwich I planned to save for lunch, and settle into a soft plaid chair. I want to think my way out of this predicament with Judd, but the stress of the commute has caught up to me, and I'm soon dozing.

When the first bell rings, I shake myself awake and head for Building A. The students I pass ignore me, but the teachers say hello. I'm two chapters ahead in most of my classes, whereas the other kids are still shrugging off the fog of spring break. I wonder what my classmates did on vacation while I slaved away in Judd's shack. I was probably packaging the very "favors" they enjoyed at their parties.

In world history, we have to write an in-class essay on European imperialism. I finish mine super-fast and the teacher remarks that I must've been the only student who did the required reading over the break. Feeling prickly glares across my back, I mumble, "I had this unit at my old school." But inside, I'm gloating. This is where I thrive. No one can touch me.

At lunchtime, I go back to the library to study since I have nothing to eat and I need to save my money for bus fare. Some other sophomores meander in and decide to sit at the far end of my table. One guy from homeroom nods at me and says "hey" before continuing to talk with his friends. Without acknowledging him, I stack my books and stomp off.

"*Sorr-ee*," a girl named Madison mutters, but I ignore her. Most kids at Essex don't try talking to me anymore, not since my steel-eyed stares told them all to Go Away.

I blink fast as I leave, holding in the tears. I don't like acting mean, but it's safer to be a loner. Friends ask questions.

Chapter 11

"Where were *you* all day?" Judd's boot kicks sharply into the back of my leg as I stand at the kitchen counter making myself a tuna sandwich.

Gritting my teeth, I say, "School."

"School?" He repeats the word like it's a new concept, and I bite my tongue to keep from making a sarcastic remark.

All he's wearing are jeans, heavy work boots, and an unbuttoned flannel shirt with the sleeves rolled up. Out of the corner of my eye, I see him open the fridge and then the main cupboard, which I know is empty because I just scrounged for the last can of tuna. I cut my sandwich in half and quietly set the butter knife in the sink.

"How'd you get there?" Judd asks suddenly.

"Walked." My heart rate quickens, and I keep talking before I can chicken out. "But I'll need to take the bus from now on—"

"And how much is that gonna cost?"

"About twenty bucks a week." I hold the air in my lungs.

Judd's response is the hiss of a beer cracking open. When I turn around, his eyes are on me, suspicious. He takes a slow swallow and clucks, "Well. You'll have to earn that too, now won't you?"

Ugh. I don't have time for this! He better not take me out to the shed to work tonight. I'm exhausted and hungry, and I have a bunch of math worksheets to do.

Then Judd's eyes grow colder, less hazy. I see something in them that I don't like. Something sinister. He leans down into my face and commands, "Make me some goddamned dinner." Then he grabs my sandwich off the plate and squeezes it so the tuna oozes out the sides onto his grimy, nicotine-stained fingers. "And it better be something good. Not fucking tuna!" I wince as Judd shoves my sandwich down into the sink drain.

Incensed, I glare at him, my hands balling into fists. Judd chuckles at my reaction, but his voice is deadly when he whispers, "You don't ever eat before you serve me. Remember that." And to make sure I do, the back of his hand collides with my head.

His blow lands me across the counter and I stay hunched there, holding my head and whimpering in shock. Judd moves lazily back to the living room and pushes Ayla's legs off the couch to make room for his own. He fondles her while she sits there catatonic, gripping a bong.

A minute later, he hollers, "Hurry up, girl! I'm hungry."

I tiptoe across the kitchen. Tears blur my vision as I scan the meager contents of the freezer. In the silver plate of the ice maker, I don't recognize my own frantic eyes. They belong to a skittish animal.

I'm no chef. The routine at home was that I helped Gram cook and clean on weekends, but on weekdays my only "chore" was studying. Luckily, I spot a sack of frozen burgers and hidden behind it, a bag of peas. I can do that. My hands tremble as I drop the patties onto a frying pan, then fill a pot with water and dump in the peas. While I cook, Judd and Ayla pass the bong back and forth. I feel like I'm high, too, but it's probably just my head buzzing and throbbing through the stress of the day. I chew a handful of frozen peas when I'm sure Judd's not looking.

When his meal is ready, I set it on the table with a folded napkin and glass of water. All I want is to escape upstairs, but I force my feet over to the couch and announce in a tremulous voice, "Dinner's ready."

"Not hungry, Bones," Ayla slurs and reclines. No surprise there. Ayla doesn't eat much when she's using, which is just about always now. When Judd's eyes flick to me, his disgust is clear. He crosses the room, sits down at the table and begins chomping. I shuffle toward the stairs.

I get all the way across the kitchen, with Judd's eyes following me and his mouth chewing angrily, before his voice snares me. "Where do you think you're going, princess?"

My shoulders droop. I turn around.

He calls me back with a curl of his finger and tells me to wait until he finishes. So I stand to the side and wait. I keep my face masked, just like when I'm at school or in the crack houses. He finally sucks the burger juice off his fingertips, then balls up his napkin and throws it on his plate. "Now. You must be hungry after your long walk."

Judd dances his way to the sink, reaches into the drain and emerges with what's left of my mutilated tuna sandwich. He slops it onto a plate, then dredges up more bits of tuna mixed with God-knows-what. He smiles at me the whole time and I can't hide the horror on my face. He brings the plate over to the table and points at it. "Bon a-petit."

I lunge for the hallway.

But Judd is amazingly quick for someone who's been doping all day. His palm clamps down on my shoulder and pushes me into the chair. I claw at his hand, but he's like iron, with muscles that stretch across his wiry frame so that you can see each one ripple beneath his skin. I try biting his arm, but he just moves his grip to the back of my neck, two fingers extended like when we hike to the shed. He pushes me toward the tuna, mashes my face against it so that it smears into my eyes, my nose. I brace my hands against the table and push, try to raise my head, but his strength is beyond me. I sob, fitfully, and hate myself for it.

When Judd pulls my head up a few inches, tears and snot and tuna fall from my nose onto the plate. He sits down close by, his face inches from mine. "Now before you eat your dinner," he says slowly, "I'm gonna repeat my question, because I think you *must* have misunderstood it earlier. How'd you get to that fancy school of yours today? Huh, girl?"

My sobs stop abruptly as the realization hits. Judd nods. "Ah, it's all becoming clear now, isn't it?"

"Please…" I beg.

"Answer my question."

"I-I walked to the market and then caught a bus."

"I-I walked to the market and then caught a bus," his voice mimics mine. Then his left palm comes down on the table like he's slapping his knee. "Well, doggone it, you *did* know the right answer. Next question—why would a smart girl like you do something as stupid as *steal from me*?" he thunders.

"I'm sorry! I didn't know what else—"

"You steal my money? When I'm nice enough to take you into my home, give you shelter and food? That's how you repay my hospitality?" His fingers squeeze tighter on my neck and it's getting harder to breathe. I reach up to pry them loose, but it does no good.

"I'm sorry," I gasp again.

"I don't believe you're sorry enough," Judd rumbles.

"I am! I'm sorrier than you can imagine," I choke, tears flowing again.

Judd removes his hand from my neck and leans back in his chair. I suck in air as he pulls out his cigarette lighter and rolls it between his fingers. "If any of my dealers stole from me, they'd get a permanent reminder of that mistake."

An image of the kid with the scar pops into my head. I watch the lighter slide back and forth in Judd's large hand. He flicks it on and lets the flame burn, then looks at me.

Instinct kicks in and I start groveling. I apologize and assure him of my gratitude for his *hospitality* until my throat is too dry to speak. My eyes don't leave the flame until he snaps the lighter closed.

"Pathetic," he grumbles. "But seeing as you're new, and it'd be a shame to mess up that pretty little face of yours, I'll let you off easy this time. You eat up all your dinner now, and don't dare think of crossing me again."

My eyes move back to the tuna, nearly an hour old and warm and slimy from the drain. Little flecks of black are mixed in with everything. Coffee grinds from the morning or something worse. My stomach turns. I hear Ayla moan on the couch and wonder if she even cares what her sick boyfriend is making me do. Probably not. Hatred sears through every fiber of my body and I use that hatred to save myself.

Without shedding another tear, I eat every last bite.

Chapter 12

The next day in science class, *I'm* the student who's foggy. My mind turns over all the ways I can escape Judd. There's Delaney back in Indianapolis, but her parents barely make ends meet for her and her two little brothers. Every extra dollar goes to her dance lessons and costumes. The best they could do is hand me over to social services. And while I know there must be good foster families out there, I'm afraid to risk it.

Still. Last night, while I stayed awake, shaking with fury and fear, staring at my little barricade in front of the attic door, I told myself I couldn't stay here. Not for shelter. Not for Ayla. There is no way to please a tyrant. Even if I try to be Judd's perfect little assistant and cook five-star meals every night, he'll eventually find something unsatisfactory. And if last night was "letting me off easy," what will he do next time?

One of my classmates drops a beaker and it clatters to the floor. I jump at the noise, nearly falling off my lab stool. Then I scowl at my own clumsiness. It's Judd's fault I'm like this. Exhausted. Jittery. I think hard about how to make him pay. I could turn him into the police, easily. Today even. I'd like to see his face if I walked through the front door with a cop on each side of me. I know where he hides his drugs. If the police believed me, if they drove me around town, I could find some of the dealers' apartments. I could eventually find that shed in the woods. Judd would go down, and then…then what? Ayla would go down, too. And I would be sent into the unknown. I could end up with people worse than Judd, worse than Charlie. And in a crappy school district to boot.

No, thanks. The monsters I know are better than the ones I don't. At least here I have Essex.

Besides, who's to say the police *would* believe me? Judd has already painted me as a problem child to the people he knows in Haydon, shipped here by my mother 'to get a man's firm hand.' And then there's the Charlie incident, always lurking in the back of my mind, making me question myself.

He'd *laughed* after I shoved him off me that day. I remember his smirk and his words, *You sent the signals, Andrea. But I won't tell. Sometimes when girls your age lose a loved one, they look for affection in the wrong places. Everyone knows that.*

Do they? I'd thought. Either way, I had no energy for that kind of fight. I let Charlie and his threats go. And I can let Judd go, too.

If I could just convince Ayla to leave him, it would be the two of us again, and I could cope with that. That would even be easy. A flicker of hope rises in me. Ayla never stays in one place too long. She'll probably want to move on soon. And if not, maybe I *could* disappear and make it on my own…

That daydream lasts until the end of class. I know how most runaways end up—selling drugs or their bodies. Or dead. Anyway. It would be stupid to leave now, without a plan and some cash.

I've got neither.

Ayla is vomiting in the bathroom when I trudge into the house after school. From the kitchen, Judd barks at me to go help her. Sighing, I drop my bags at the bottom of the attic stairs. I want to fire off a snarky comment like, "how do you *help* someone throw up?" but I'm not in the mood for a smack-down. Anyway, I've seen Ayla through enough of these episodes in the past few months to know the drill. She shakes violently while I attempt to wash her face, clean her up. Then she vomits again. Rinse and repeat. Lovely.

After several rounds of this, Judd appears in the bathroom doorway. He holds out an unmarked bottle of liquid and says, "Pour some o' this down her throat."

"No!" I say automatically because I don't know what it is and I don't trust him. I brace for a blow, but he just pushes past like I'm an annoying gnat, grabs Ayla's jaw, and douses her mouth with the liquid until she sputters and swallows it. I glower as he walks out. But soon Ayla's stomach does seem to calm down and her convulsing lessens.

When I help her into Judd's bed, she clutches my hand and sobs, "I'm sorry, Bones. So sorry…" Tears waterfall across her cracked white lips.

There is a righteous part of me that wants to rip my hand away and leave her forlorn and scared, the way she leaves me. But there's something else, stronger, that makes me sit on the side of the bed and squeeze her hand back.

In the morning, she won't remember any of this.

I wait until she stops twitching and falls into a light sleep. With Judd's steady supply of drugs coursing through her lately, Ayla looks worse than ever. I've already concocted the story I'll tell if I ever have to take her to the hospital—that she's a homeless junkie who collapsed on the street near me. But right now I'm afraid she won't even make it through the night.

Gathering my courage, I head to the kitchen to confront Judd. He's working off a folded paper, making route notes as his cigarette leaks plumes of smoke above his head.

Keeping a safe distance, I demand, "What'd you give her today?"

He doesn't look up. "Nothin'. She needed a break. It's withdrawal."

"She looks bad."

"She'll be fine." His words are final.

It may cost me, but I have to say something else. "I think she needs a doctor."

No response. Just the firm set of his ugly little mouth.

"Judd, Ayla's gonna *die* if you keep on—"

His head whips up. "Your mama ain't gonna *die* in my care! You stupid, girl? You think I only take her off the junk to teach her a lesson? It's a process. Ayla's been usin' longer'n you've been breathing. You can't quit something like that cold turkey."

My head spins. "So you're trying to...get her *clean?*"

"I'm trying to teach her to manage her habit. A little can keep you going. A lot can kill you. She needs to learn the difference."

I ponder this for a moment. I know he withholds when he's mad at Ayla, but I never considered that Judd might truly want to help her. It's probably bullshit. "Well, I don't believe—" I start.

His chair scrapes the floor as he stands. Then he's in my face and I'm pressed up against the wall, silenced. "You think I give a *shit* what you believe? I'll take care of Ayla. What you oughtta be worryin' about is yourself. I got people lookin' now. Breaking my back to protect you, girl. You're just lucky *I'm* the one who found you living in that car like a dirty rat."

"Lucky. Right," I mumble. My riskiest move yet.

Judd cocks an eyebrow, amused. "Oh, so I should hand you over to one of my boys, huh?" He chuckles. "You'd be begging for me within minutes."

I hate his words with a blistering fervor, and all the more because I think he's right. As bad as Judd is, there's worse.

He releases me, sits back down, and sucks hard on his cigarette, then stubs it out on the tabletop. "Now listen up, girl, 'cause I'm only explainin' this once. I got a two-year master plan. By then I'll be ready to cash out. Ayla and I will disappear to a beachside bungalow, just like magic." He makes a "poof" motion with his wiry hands. "You're on your own at that point." He arches his brows, a warning. "But not until then. For the next two years, you work for me. Do what I say. Take orders from me only."

Two years? I try to swallow, but the lump in my throat is the size of a dinosaur and nothing gets past.

"What if I want to go sooner?" The words creak out.

His answer is choking laughter, and I don't need to hear why it can't happen—I know too much. I could do too much damage. I have to wait until they're ready to...*poof.*

"What if *I* just disappeared?" I say louder, stronger. A plea disguised as a threat.

His gaze is calm, sure, and scarier than anything else he's said or done today. Running his tongue over his teeth, he shrugs. "Me and my boys will hunt you down. You'd better hope it's not my buddy Donovan who finds you. He won't be as swift as I would."

I'm not sure what to make of that until Judd's gray eyes narrow. "I've put bullets in people before, Bones. Even people as pretty as you."

Chapter 13

The weather warms, and Judd's woods burst into full spring bloom. The trails are now dotted with purple cress and wild geraniums. They're also more populated, with day hikers and kids riding shiny mountain bikes along the trails. Judd and I move some of his equipment into the house to reduce the risk of being discovered on our frequent hikes to the shed. He doesn't hold the back of my head anymore. He thinks he has scared me enough, that I am no longer a threat.

I hate that he's right.

I may have lost my dignity, but at least I won Essex. Somehow I convinced Judd that a teenager not attending school would invite suspicion, that I could go to Essex and still work enough to cover room, board, and bus fare. I think he agreed just so he wouldn't have to watch me twenty-four hours a day.

I'll say one thing in Judd's favor—he's organized. There's never any waffling when it comes to business. Fridays are for packaging. After school, he tells me straight away where to hide the drugs, and he doesn't waste time. I've come to appreciate this. Our deliveries, which take place on Saturdays, are efficient and mapped out in a way that leaves me time to make dinner and complete my homework. Even when he makes me work on weeknights, I get to bed before midnight and that is a small victory. Believe me, I count every victory I can these days. It is amazing what a person can get used to.

When I'm not working for Judd, the woods belong to me. I hike to the secret pond and let my troubles fade away. It's sunny today, so I shuffle down the muddy bank, pull off my boots, and wade in up to my knees. Squishing the muck between my toes, I tilt my head back, spread my arms, and let the wind sway me from side to side. I feel light enough to be plucked up and carried away like a dandelion seed.

After my toes are good and numb, I climb my favorite tree and stretch out. Up in my nest, my body relaxes further. It convinces my mind to do the same. A band of sunlight falls across my face and plants a long, warm kiss on my skin.

Plunk! There's a splash below, like someone launched a big rock into the water. Peering down, I see that girl from the other day diving into the pond again. When she breaks the surface for air, she taunts, "Come on, you chicken!"

For a moment, I think she's talking to me but then I hear a boy's laughter from the bushes on the other side of the pond. "Nice try. You're crazy."

The girl flips to her back, indifferent.

I can't see the boy from my perch, but I have to agree with

his assessment of her mental state. Even though the sun is warm, that water is *frigid*. And I know she has been swimming when it was even colder.

"You're going to catch pneumonia," he warns. "This is Ohio, you know. Not Florida."

"You scared of a little polar bear plunge?" she mocks. "I thought you Southerners were supposed to be tough."

"Your tactics won't work on me," he scoffs, slightly annoyed. "Now, come on. I need to get back."

She stays where she is, treading water and blowing bubbles. "Why? The all-important homework gods are calling?"

"Just wait a few years. Life's not all fun and games."

The girl tilts her head back and laughs. "All the more reason for me to cut loose now. Run along and study then. I'll meet you at the house."

"Right," he says. "Like I'm going to leave you here alone to get hypothermia."

"Suit yourself." Grinning devilishly, the girl slips underwater.

I hear an exasperated sigh, but the boy doesn't leave. He starts walking around the perimeter of the pond, getting closer and closer to *me*.

I don't know exactly where the boy is, but I can see the pond clear enough. The girl has broken the surface again and is treading water, scanning the sandy strip where her friend was standing before. A small rock suddenly skips across the water four—no, five times. It's far enough away from the girl so as not to pose a threat, but close enough that she notices. She turns her head. "Jeez! You'd better not hit me with any of those."

The guy lets out a deep, hearty laugh. "Have a little faith," he says and that's the first time I hear the drawl. "You'll be safe if you keep to that side of the pond. Better yet, get out and dry off so we can leave. Your towel's over here."

"I'm not leaving yet." She doesn't say it in a bratty way, just matter-of-fact. Then she disappears underwater again.

I lean over a little and spot the boy. Or at least, the top of him. Brown hair. Broad shoulders. He's only a few yards from the base of my tree, standing on a large, flat rock. He keeps bending down to pick up more skipping stones while the girl floats.

After a few minutes of this, I start to feel restless. They could stay here for hours if the girl has her way! I glance at Gram's watch. It's almost six. If I don't show up at Judd's soon, I'm toast. Slowly, I edge closer to the tree trunk and start to climb down. If I'm quiet, I can probably sneak back into the woods without being seen.

As I near the lowest branch, there is sudden sloshing nearby. "I want to try," the girl says and scrambles onto the big rock. Wrapping up in her towel, she asks, "Got any more stones?"

The guy swivels to scan the ground and I freeze. I cling to the tree trunk, press my cheek against it.

"Hey," he says. "What's that?"

Oh great. He must have seen me. I peer around the edge of the trunk, but he hasn't seen me. He's seen my *bags*. Shoot! I forgot I left them by the log where I waded in earlier.

Perplexed, he starts walking toward my bags and she hops along next to him like some curious woodland nymph. Crap. Any moment now the girl will remember seeing me in the tree before and will look over this way. There's no escape. Besides, I don't want anyone pawing through my stuff. Or worse, *taking* it.

"Hey, those are mine!" I call out and scramble down the tree. In my haste, I completely miss the last foothold. I hear my jeans rip as they snag on a branch and I go tumbling toward the earth.

"Whoa! What the—?"

"Omigosh! Are you okay?" The girl cuts off her friend, then rushes toward me flapping her skinny arms in dismay.

I quickly climb to my feet. "I'm fine," I say, then glance down to be sure it's true. Aside from the torn jeans and a small scrape on my leg, I *am* fine.

The boy gazes at me and then up at the tree, more perplexed than before. "Were you watching us?" he asks slowly. Rather than accusatory, he sounds amused.

My face is suddenly five shades of hot. I don't want them thinking I'm some voyeuristic weirdo. "No," I say, flustered. "I was…resting."

Their eyebrows go up in surprise, in unison. Then the girl breaks into a delighted grin. I guess she thinks resting in trees is cool. The boy squints at me. "Are you sure you're all right?" Apparently, he is now worried about *my* mental state.

"Yes, I'm sure." My voice is clipped, out of habit. I walk over and hoist my bags onto my shoulders. "I have to get home."

"Oh!" The girl, who has followed me like a baby duckling, sounds excited. "Did you just move here? Where do you live? I haven't seen you at school. How old are you?"

God. Does she ask enough questions? I glance over and notice that her cheeks are still glistening with pond water. Her eyes look wide and hopeful, but I recognize another emotion hiding there—loneliness. I have to admit, I am drawn to this girl. And that, for us both, is dangerous.

I glance at Gram's watch, desperate for an out. "I really have to go," I say apologetically, turning away. I take two steps before stumbling magnificently over a root jutting out of the ground. The girl giggles as I fight to keep my balance.

"Careful," the boy says wryly. I can hear the smile in his voice.

"Hey, what's your name?" calls the girl just as I reach the path.

Without answering, I break into a run.

I don't slow down until I'm halfway back to Judd's and one hundred percent sure they didn't follow me. God, I am an idiot. An idiot who can't remember how to act around normal people. Or *walk,* apparently. I'm just glad I got out of there when I did.

When I reach the last clearing, I take a breath and compose myself. Thankfully, Judd's car is nowhere in sight when I emerge from the woods, but I open the front door quietly, just in case.

"That's *ridiculous.*" Ayla's voice echoes from the bedroom, strident. I roll my eyes. Judd must not have given her enough happy dust today. As I tiptoe past the door, she explodes again. "That amount wouldn't last *anyone* six months. She's a teenage girl.

Do you know how much crap teenage girls need?"

Puzzled, I stop in the kitchen and listen.

"Come on, Mr. Phipps. Surely there's something you can do? The whole *point* of my mother's trust fund is—" Ayla's voice goes quiet for a long moment. "No, no need to schedule any hearing. We'll get by somehow until July."

After she hangs up, a string of curses escape her lips. Dresser drawers slam against their frames. She bursts into the kitchen and I jump, afraid she'll know I was eavesdropping. But when her blazing eyes land on me, they light up with hope.

"Bones!" She hurries toward me. I step back until I bump the counter. Her hands squeeze my arms and she grins like I'm her savior. "You know where Judd keeps everything, don't you?"

I shake my head. No way am I giving her drugs behind Judd's back. I think of the tuna sandwich, the flame inside his silver lighter. I'll take anything Ayla can dish out before facing Judd.

"Don't lie to me," she hisses, and I grimace at her rancid breath. "He locked the door to the cellar, but you know where the key is."

"No. He doesn't trust me." That much is true.

"Where do you go in the woods? Show me the way." Her voice is pitchy and a layer of sweat sparkles on her skin.

"It's locked. Just have some wine or something."

"He took it all. Every last bottle, the bastard. Even my goddamn cigarettes."

"Drive to the market, then!" I yell, because her hands are pinching my arms harder.

"I can't drive to the market, you little snot. He hid my car keys!"

This scares me into a momentary stupor. I knew Judd had taken our keys, but I figured Ayla would have access. I feel suckerpunched. We are not just hidden out here—we're trapped.

Ayla starts shaking and swearing, and I know it's only going to get worse. It always gets worse until she makes it past the frenzy, then lies twitching and moaning.

I try to sidle away, but she clings to me like an anxious toddler, her eyes red and hysterical. "Listen, did you…did you look in the pockets of his flannel shirts?" I suggest. "Judd puts the keys in there sometimes."

This is a lie. Judd doesn't *ever* let me see what he does with his keys. But the lie serves its purpose. Ayla rushes into the bedroom to search his closet. As soon as she's gone, I grab the loaf of bread on the counter and sprint back to the woods. When Judd gets home, things will get worse. I'm afraid for Ayla, and I'm worried that the repercussions of the coming fight will spill over onto me. Best to stay hidden.

The pink sunrise streams in the rear window of the Buick. Thank God the doors were unlocked or I'd have been stuck in the woods all night. I sit up and stretch, feeling achy. I'm too used to sleeping in a real bed now. Judd and Ayla's little fight messed up my plans to shower last night, so my skin feels grimy. I peer at myself in the car's mirror and drag my fingers through my hair. It's a tangled mess, so I give up and pull on my ski cap. No boys will try to woo me today, that's for sure. Not that they ever do anymore.

My textbooks and papers are scattered all over, but I got my work done before the sun set. I scoop it all into my backpack. My bags feel heavier than usual as I hoist them onto my shoulders and glare at Judd's dark house.

Thinking about yesterday, I feel just as dark. At least now I know why Ayla wants to keep me so bad. It's not like I was expecting anything as outlandish as maternal affection, but I guess I was hoping to be more than her cash cow. Man, I wish I could get *my* hands on the money Gram left—apparently dispersed in installments to whoever "takes care" of me. What a joke. The worst part is, I know that as a minor, I can't cash in without Ayla any more than she can without me. We are linked, like two convicts chained at the ankles.

My walk to the market is miserable. As the sun glows hotter, I stop chattering from cold and start to sweat instead. On the bus, I smooth out my clothes and munch my bread and wish I had some water.

In the bathroom at Essex, I wash my face and brush my teeth with my finger. I braid my knotty hair and tie it with a rubber band since hats are not permitted in class. I slip through half the day before a teacher asks if I'm feeling okay.

"Yeah, of course." I give him a strange look.

"You look a little…tired."

I force a smile and complain, "Yes, because I was up late doing homework. I'm fine, Mr. Marsh." I say it in a tone that makes *me* sound like the authority figure. Like I'm telling him to run along and play. Grinning, he does.

After school, I wander downtown and look in shop windows. It's risky not to go straight back to Judd's, but I need a break. And if Judd and Ayla made up, they'll go clubbing tonight. That's their pattern.

I treat myself to a hot dog and Sprite from a vendor, even though it means I won't have bus fare one way this week. The guy selling the hot dogs smiles at me in a shy way, peeking up every few minutes. As he works, he shifts from one foot to the other, reminding me of the boys in elementary school who could never stand still.

Wrapping my food up in wax paper, he says brightly, "Here you go. One of 'Sam's Famous Dogs' for the girl in red."

I look down at my thin red sweater, fraying at the cuffs, and feel a little self-conscious. The boy keeps talking, explains that he's working for his uncle, who owns five of these vendor carts.

"Are you named after your uncle?" I ask as I pay.

He squints at me, confused, until I point to his nametag, which says "Hi, I'm Sam." Then he laughs. "Oh, duh. Forgot about the tag. No, I'm Doug." He wipes his hand against the apron and holds it out.

I shake it. "Andrea." My voice comes out like a bullet. It's because I'm so sick of being called *Bones* or *girl.* Or any number of cuss words. It's because I haven't talked to anybody but my teachers in so long. And I've been avoiding even them lately.

Doug must be bored because he rambles on about how he and his uncle are expanding soon. "I'm in my last semester at community college and then I'm taking one of the carts to

Lexington. I'll be a junior partner in the business," he says, puffing out his chest.

I really have to restrain myself from blurting, *Can I come with you?*

Doug keeps chatting so I stand there and listen, eating my hot dog and giggling at his jokes. They are lame jokes, but he's nice. And he's talking to me. And it's safe.

That night, after a much-needed shower, I spread out my books and papers with good intentions, but my mind keeps wandering to Doug the hot dog vendor, that brave mermaid-girl at the pond, and her no-nonsense friend. All mere strangers that crossed my path, nothing more. But there's something inside me that longs to connect with them, with someone. I have been too alone for too long.

Then my mind takes me to Indiana, to Gram, and I wish it wouldn't but I can't stop it. I double over, press my forehead against the papers. There's this battle waging inside me—the memory of Gram's love trying to push its way in versus my own raw energy, trying to think of anything *but* her. If she could see Ayla now, her eyes would fill with pity and pain. If she could see into *my* brain she'd call me a cuckoo bird, and that's exactly how I feel. My mind won't settle—I'm worried about Judd and his "two-year plan," about summer vacation, about our missing car keys. I feel like I'm going to burst into a thousand pieces and there's no one I can talk to.

Except…I haven't called Delaney since I left Indianapolis.

And the house is empty tonight.

In the dark, I tiptoe downstairs and pick up the phone. Slowly, I dial her number. She answers on the third ring.

"Hellooo?" she asks, impatient when I don't say anything at first.

"Delaney?" My voice sounds small, even to me.

Pause. "Oh my God, Andrea! Where *are* you?" I picture her bolting upright on her purple comforter. I love hearing her voice, the normalcy of it. But how do I answer? What can I say?

"I'm in Columbus."

"Ohio? Why didn't you tell me?"

"I think I was in shock or something," I mumble.

"It was so creepy the way you disappeared," Delaney says after a moment. "You didn't even say goodbye."

"Sorry. We had to leave pretty fast." So fast, I couldn't find out where they buried Gram. No one told me anything about her after I got dumped at the foster home. "Dee, do you know if…was there ever an obituary or anything? For my Gram?"

"No," she says quietly. "My mom looked for it. She heard from one of your neighbors that the house sold really fast."

My house. I wonder what the realtor did with all our stuff. And the money…I saw how Ayla squandered that.

There's a pause before Delaney asks in a low voice, "Are you with your mother now?"

The question throws me because I'd never told her much about Ayla, or why I lived with Gram in the first place. How can I fill in those details? Would it even be safe for her to know?

"Yes." That's all I offer. I feel the walls rising up as I slip into a resigned silence.

Across the phone line and the miles and the distance that is not just physical, I hear a sigh. A hint of exasperation. After a minute, she asks, "Did you get my emails?"

And there it is—the accusation. The handful of emails Delaney sent in January reflected her progression from shocked to worried to irritated, just like this phone call. Again, I don't have an answer.

"I got them...I couldn't write back," I say, hoping she'll assume it was a technical glitch instead of an emotional one.

"I thought maybe you were mad. That maybe you'd heard..." her voice fades.

"Heard what?"

Silence. And then her words come in a rush—"I didn't plan to like him. We just started talking about what could have happened to you and...we got close."

"Wait...what?" I sound so clueless because I don't want to hear this, to believe what she's saying.

"Ben," she confirms. "He's not as boring as I thought."

My first thought is genuine and I voice it quickly—"I don't care, Dee." Because, really, why should I? Ben and I never had anything, never *were* anything. But my second emotion is more confusing, so much that I can't name it except to say anguish, jealousy, and loss rolled into one. "I gotta go," I say abruptly.

"Well, can you at least tell me—"

"I'll call you later." I hang up the phone. Immediately

I regret this and pick it back up, but the connection is already broken.

I stand in the kitchen gripping the receiver for a long time, listening to the dial tone, then the flat beep, then the nothingness, until the silence grows so large and deafening I am sure it will blow out my eardrums.

Chapter 14

Almost every day after school now, I trek to the pond. Secretly, I hope the girl will show up again, but she doesn't. Today, this disappoints me so much that I walk around to the sandy side where she usually pokes her tiny head through the reeds. I collect a handful of stones and arrange them in the shape of one short word on the dirt by the pond's edge: **Hi.**

Maybe she'll leave me a message, too, I think. I *hope.*

I'm wearing the same jeans I tore when I fell out of the tree in that spectacular show of clumsiness, and the loose flap of material keeps getting stuck on bushes as I walk back to the trail.

Looking down at the denim flapping against my thigh, I groan. I have no summery tops or shorts, and what I do have is starting to feel threadbare.

I need new clothes, but who do I tell? I never had to ask Gram for anything. We weren't rich by any means—we cut coupons for groceries and stuff—but she always made sure I had what I needed. A year ago I had plenty. Trendy stuff, too. Outfits that get you noticed. Back then, I liked the attention. Now, I need to blend in.

Walking along the sun-dappled trails, I consider my options. Steal from Judd? Never again. Shoplifting is out of the question. I won't sink to that level and besides, I can't afford trouble with the police. Ayla is waiting until July to cash in on me, but she must have spending money because I see *her* wearing new clothes, and I see shopping bags in the trashcan. We are not compatible in size, but maybe I can convince her to share some cash at least.

When I get to Judd's, Ayla is alone in the kitchen with a cocktail tilted loosely in her hand. Speaking of new clothes, she's wearing some items I've never seen—skin-tight leggings, a low-cut top, and spiked heels. Probably waiting for Judd to take her clubbing again.

I stare at my mother, knowing she doesn't see me in the shadows. Her dark, layered hair lays limp. She's too thin, her pale skin scratched raw on her neck. Her auburn eyes are framed by swooping lashes on top and purple half-circles beneath. Her lips, once lush and pink, look cracked and dry. All my life, she was the most beautiful woman I'd ever known. She still sometimes looks beautiful, but the years of drug use are starting to show.

After two months with Judd, I know I'm different, too. But no one can see my scars. No one's even looking.

When Ayla finally notices me hugging the doorframe, she almost smiles, but it turns into a wry sort of smirk—like she forgot for a moment—and then suddenly remembered—that she hates me.

"Where's Judd?" I ask, coming into the room.

"He had something to do. Why?" she says in a mocking tone. "You miss him?"

My scoff is impossible to repress, and I don't try. Even Ayla laughs.

"I can't believe you're with him. He's so gross." I take a Coke from the fridge and sip it while she guzzles her own tonic.

"Don't hear you complaining about the perks," she says pointedly, eyeing my Coke and the box of raisins I'm opening.

There's no point in explaining that avoiding starvation is not what I consider a *perk* in life. Instead I ask, "How'd you meet Judd anyway?"

She jiggles the ice in her glass. "An old friend introduced us. We partied a few times back in the day." Her voice sounds wistful and I can't bear to imagine what her 'happy' memories must look like. "Judd always took good care of me," Ayla adds softly.

I want to scream. Judd fed her *drug habit* while Gram worried sick about her, helped her when she binged too hard, begged her to go to rehab, never turned her away! It's infuriating. Especially since not once in my life have I ever heard Ayla speak with such tenderness or gratitude toward Gram.

"What about the orders?" I ask, changing the subject before I lose my temper. "Judd said there was a lot to do tonight."

"We got 'em ready earlier. I helped." She tosses her hair like it's this big deal.

I can't believe I am going to get out of work! I was dreading another long night of packaging. The pressure on my chest lightens and the only thing that concerns me is how Ayla said *she'd* helped Judd. What if Judd decides he doesn't need me anymore? What if he wants me to disappear?

Then I remember who *does* need me—Ayla. For Gram's trust. Emboldened, I take a breath and ask for the money.

I expect to be shot down, but Ayla is half strung-out content. She sighs and sips her drink. "What do you need more clothes for, Bones? You're done growing."

"Yeah, but everything is worn out. I look like a freak at school." I realize this could backfire. What if she says I don't need to go to school anymore? "People are starting to notice," I press before she can think about it too much. "Teachers are asking questions."

"We don't want that." She frowns, puts down her glass, and reaches for her purse.

I watch her unzip it and start counting out bills. She hands me two hundred dollars in twenties, and I am stone-cold shocked. First, that she's giving it to me. Second, that she has so many more twenties in her hands, so many that she's now stuffing back inside her purse. *Where did she get all that money?*

"Thanks," I mumble. Backing away, I tuck the bills inside my jeans pocket and scurry to the attic. I sit on my bed and count the money three times. A day ago, I would've given anything for just one twenty dollar bill. Now I'm holding ten of them!

When Judd's tires crunch up the gravel drive, I pull the string to darken my room and scramble around for a good hiding place. I end up laying the money flat inside a children's Bible that I find on the bookshelf by my bed, a remnant from whoever occupied this room before me. No chance Judd will ever open *that*.

Judd collects Ayla quickly, not bothering with me. I watch from my hexagonal window as they speed away, kicking up a fine mist of dust.

Breathing easier, I think of the money hidden inside the pages of the Bible, protected by God's own words. I consider all the things I could do with it and thoroughly enjoy the imagining. Really, I'll just buy the clothes I need and maybe keep a little for treats. It's not enough to run away with. Still, it feels so good to have that money, that possibility, that *power*, at my fingertips. I almost feel free…like a girl who would swim in a secret pond.

Chapter 15

I'm sound asleep when Judd and Ayla stumble into the house, making all kinds of noise. I squint at Gram's watch—3:00 AM—and flop back onto my pillow. Downstairs, the lilt of Ayla's laugh is followed by the clomp of Judd's feet. I wonder if he ever wears anything but those horrible boots.

Judd is describing the island paradise where he wants to retire, and Ayla is eating it up. They are like schoolchildren with their fantasies, but I guess it's no worse than me dreaming of the Ivy League. Eventually they settle down and talk in lower tones until there is an abrupt silence that permeates the house. Judd says loudly, "You *what?*" Ayla's response is muffled, but I figure she flirted with someone at the bar again. After a moment, everything goes quiet and I slip halfway back to dreams.

I'm almost asleep when feet pound up my narrow stairway. I bolt upright as the door crashes open, my blockade useless. Judd's hand wraps around my throat before I can blink. He heaves me out of bed and shoves me against the wall, furious. My skull crashes into the wood three times until I don't know which way is up, and then he is squeezing my neck and his whiskey breath is in my nose. I sputter, prying at his iron fingers.

I'm able to breathe, just enough, but it hurts. Judd is calm now, patient. He's practiced at this. He waits until I realize I am trapped, my toes scarcely touching the floor. He waits until the tears are pouring down my cheeks, unabashed. He waits until I show all my fear.

Then he rumbles, low and noxious, "Did you forget who owns you? You don't ever ask your mama for money. You come to *me* for everything. This is my palace, girl. Not yours. Not your mama's."

I nod. *Okay, I got it. Just let me go!* His mouth is inches from mine. For an instant, I think he might kiss me like Charlie did, and revulsion sweeps through me. Instead, he gives my head one more crack against the wall before releasing my throat. *Too hard,* I think as I slump to the floor and watch the room turn splotchy. His boots echo down, down all thirteen steps. Everything fades to black. Curtain closed.

When I wake, every muscle in my body aches from sleeping crumpled, half on the floor, half against the wall. My neck is sore, my head blasting discordant notes. I manage to crawl to my bed and collapse on the pillow. I'm too worn for tears.

I lay there, waiting for my head to feel right again. Part of me is in shock over this. I wouldn't put anything past Judd, but Ayla *had* to know, had to hear him…*breaking* me. Yet she sat downstairs and did nothing.

It shouldn't surprise me, I know. All my life, she treated me like I was invisible—until she needed my piggybank money for her next score. Then I was her best friend. I think of Gram's trust fund and realize that nothing has really changed.

The crazy thing is, I might forgive Ayla.

After all, she was only fifteen when she got knocked up by some pimply-faced boy, and I'm only here because Gram found out and raced to the abortion clinic before they called her number. And I only know this story because Gram believed that if you were old enough to ask a question, you were old enough to hear the answer. Even if the answer wasn't pretty. That day at the clinic, she promised Ayla a thousand dollars to go through with her pregnancy and let Gram raise me. The bribe was enough to sway my mother. So here I am. I've always been nothing but cash to Ayla, from the beginning.

In my earliest memories, Ayla is a ghost flitting in and out of the picture, wreaking havoc on my life with Gram. The year I turned eight, she showed up on Christmas without a single present. She was trashed, of course, and ended up knocking over our tree, breaking ornaments and everything. I was boiling mad. Ayla got a big bloody gash on her forehead from the fall, but she just laughed. I remember screaming at her for ruining Christmas. I remember Gram holding me while I cried but also scolding me for thinking of the *tree* instead of Ayla's well-being. And I remember begging Gram not to let Ayla come home anymore.

Ayla *wasn't* home most of the time, but every few months

she showed up dog-tired and sorry as sin. Gram always let her in. Often, Ayla didn't last the night before slinking off in darkness, her pockets full of cash. Other times she stayed for days, getting sober, eating a ton of food, giggling and playing games with me one second, glaring like I ruined her life the next. And then leaving again without ever saying goodbye…

Lying on the pale pink sheets in the drug dealer's attic, I clasp my palms around my throbbing head. Rage bubbles against my throat.

When I leave Ayla, I vow, I won't say goodbye either.

Soon Judd calls for me, and I remember it's Saturday. Delivery day. I squeeze my eyes shut. When he hollers a second time, I lift my head and call back, "Be right down." I hate how my voice shakes.

Satisfied, he stomps away and I begin to pull on my clothes. When I shuffle downstairs, Ayla is at the kitchen table sipping coffee. Or maybe vodka in a coffee cup, who knows? When she glances at something on the TV, I see that she's sporting a black eye. At first I feel vindicated that I wasn't the only one who got a beating for nothing. Then I feel sick for having such a horrid thought. *What kind of monster is Judd turning me into?*

I head for the car. There's no reason to eat with them, and no point in waiting for Ayla's eyes to find mine and blame me for this. I stare at the pretty green forest behind Judd's house and think of Gram in her coffin. It's disgusting that I'm envious.

When Judd slides into the driver's seat, I shrink against

the passenger door. He looks at me like I'm the biggest nuisance, then his arm shoots out. I pinch my eyes shut and brace myself for whatever he has planned. But his hand lands lightly on my shoulder. He doesn't even squeeze. "Got my money?"

"No, it's upstairs," I breathe, opening my eyes.

"Go get it."

I stumble into the house to retrieve the money from the Bible, which did not protect it—or me. Back in the car, Judd shoves the cash inside his jacket, shifts the car into gear, and takes off.

Judd goes with me into the apartments today, pushing me up the steps and yanking me through doors. I am never fast enough for his long legs. When he drives through Kentucky Fried Chicken for lunch, he doesn't order me anything. The smell of the food and the sound of him smacking his lips together about drive me crazy. I get mad when my stomach rumbles—should have eaten breakfast. My mind takes me far away from this misery, mostly to the pond. Then I daydream about running away with Doug the hot dog vendor. With him, I reason, I'd never go hungry.

Judd's mood improves as his payouts increase, and by four o'clock when the deliveries are done, he's smoking and tapping the steering wheel to the music. Some hip hop crap. It's not bad, though. I might even like the music, if Judd didn't.

I assume we're going home so I rest my forehead against the warm window, feeling every dip in the road. I even shut my eyes, but they snap open when Judd makes a sharp turn into Walmart. He parks in the back, extracts the money I returned to him earlier, and thumbs through it. Silently, I count along. It's all there. Chewing an unlit cigarette, Judd elbows me to get my attention. When I turn, he holds out the wad.

What is this, some trick? I'm supposed to take the money, then get backhanded? I don't move.

Annoyed, he slaps the cash into my palm. "Go and buy what clothes you need. Bring me the receipt, and don't take too long."

I stare at the bills, confused. Why would he beat the piss out of me for taking this money from Ayla, only to give it back? Why would he pound on Ayla for doing the same thing *he's* doing now? It doesn't make sense.

Sighing, he removes the cigarette from his mouth and explains, "See, I take care of my girls. S'long as they remember who they belong to. You won't forget again, will you?" He pulls out his lighter, flicks the flame, lights his cigarette, and then snaps the lighter closed in front of my face.

"No," I whisper hoarsely because my throat is so dry. I squeeze the money and open the door.

Walking into Walmart feels like stepping inside a circus tent. I haven't shopped at a superstore like this in months, and I'm not sure where to look first. My stomach decides for me, as the smells of burgers and popcorn waft out from a small cafe near Customer Service. The idea of ordering food makes me insane with desire, but Judd told me to buy *clothes,* and he'll check every penny against the receipt I bring him. So instead of ordering a hot dog or fries, I grab a paper cup from the stack by the register, fill it at the fountain stand, and gulp water until my stomach doesn't feel so empty. Then I head to Juniors.

Gliding through the aisles, I grab several boxy T-shirts in neutral colors, a few pairs of shorts, a bohemian style skirt, and some sturdy sandals. I do the math in my head. I've spent a little over a hundred so far. Perhaps I should quit there and return the rest to Judd. But who knows when I'll have this opportunity again? Besides, I'd love to see the look on his face if I handed him a receipt for two hundred dollars on the dot!

After adding a pair of jeans, underclothes, deodorant, a toothbrush, and a lightweight cardigan to my pile, I linger near a rack of bathing suits. My mind drifts to the pond, though it seems silly to spend my last $25 on a swimsuit I might never wear. Then again, nothing else in my life makes sense. I select three suits to try on, and the bright orange one with a swirly yellow sun on the side wins—the only splash of color in my monochromatic wardrobe.

While I'm changing, I take a moment to study myself in the dressing room mirror. My legs are toned from all the walking I do. I'm skinnier than ever, but still curvy up top. Just what the boys like, Delaney always said. My body shape is exactly like Ayla's, I realize, but in miniature. I'm not sure how I feel about that.

I take my loot to the checkout and am elated when the total comes in at $198.17. In a moment of last-minute exhilaration, I throw a pack of gum on the counter. Judd might beat me blind for buying that gum, but I pop a stick into my mouth and decide, as the fruity flavors explode against my taste-buds, that it will be worth it. Besides, I like my new total better: $199.22.

On my way out, I stop at the fountain machine to refill my

cup. The cashier isn't watching me—he's busy getting slushies for a group of middle school girls—and my stomach is so empty that I decide to fill my cup with Sprite instead of water. I take my time walking out, mostly to prolong the inevitable return to Judd's car, to Judd's house, to Judd's strong, veiny hands that grab and smack and choke. As I loiter around the checkout area, a girl with white-blond stripes in her dirty blond hair bounces through the door. Our eyes latch and before I can pull mine away, her whole face brightens. It's the girl from the pond.

She's heading toward me now with a huge smile on her face and for some reason, this makes me incredibly happy. Maybe I could have a friend, I think. A secret friend. I could allow myself that. Couldn't I?

I start to raise my hand in hello, but as soon as my arm moves, the girl's cheery face pales. She's staring like she's seen a ghost. No, a monster. My whole body flushes hot. Did she think I was someone else and now realizes that I'm actually the freaky weirdo who spied on her from the tree?

But no. Her eyes aren't on *me* anymore, I realize, as a group of middle schoolers walks up the aisle behind me. The girl from the pond has halted at their approach, horrified.

The gaggle of girls stop directly between us, huddled like they'd blow over without each other for support. A tall, straight-haired blond with a huge purse slung across her torso, says loudly to her companions, "There's that little bitch. She probably buys her *clothes* here." The whole group laughs viciously.

What the hell? Are they *bullying* her? The girl from the

woods stares wide-eyed, then starts backing up on the balls of her feet. Before they can taunt her again, she whirls around and walks quickly outside, the automatic doors swooshing her out of sight.

The girls laugh harder as she retreats. They flip their hair and sip their slushies as the ringleader proclaims, "She's such a loser."

I stroll slowly past them toward the door, and they are so wrapped up in their nasty talk that they don't even notice me. They also don't notice the contents of my cup being dumped silently into the wide-open purse strapped across blondie's back.

Smirking, I swing my bags of Walmart clothes and toss the empty cup into the nearest trashcan. I pop another stick of gum in my mouth and walk outside, where the girl from the pond has completely disappeared. Still, I'm feeling so proud of myself for sticking it to that bitchy girl that I almost want to stick it to Judd too. I blow a huge bubble as I saunter to the back of the parking lot. I'm not as brave as I act, though. I spit my gum onto the pavement before getting close enough for Judd to see.

When I reach his car, I drop my bags on the backseat, then hand him the receipt and the 78 cents in change. I try not to smirk when he stares at the coins and then at me, his eyes cutting like claws.

"Have fun?" he asks.

I nod, keeping my face placid. But actually I did.

Unimpressed, he puts the car into drive.

Chapter 16

On the morning of the last day of school, I pull on my new clothes and eat a huge breakfast. I'm back in survival mode, stuffing myself every chance I get. For lunch, I pack three peanut butter sandwiches and everything else in sight.

I want to savor this day at Essex, so I ignore the dirty word that keeps circling my brain—*summer.* Spending three months cowing to Judd makes me want to rip out my hair. But it's not like I have a choice. I can't escape until I get into college and Judd's 'retirement plan' goes into effect. Two years. In the scheme of my entire life, I rationalize, it's not that long.

Escape feels closer when I spend my lunch hour perusing the *Best Colleges* book in the career center. There's a stack of fliers on the table announcing a new scholarship for promising Essex grads. I can't apply until I'm a junior, but I stick a flier in my backpack anyway. A little piece of hope to keep me going until Fall.

At the end of sixth period, as the teacher reminds us not to let our brains go to mush over break, a voice crackles through the intercom asking *me* to report to the school office. As I walk down the stairs, a million scenarios whiz through my mind...Judd got busted, Ayla OD'd, the little shed went up in flames.

As soon as I sign in at the main desk, a side door opens. "Andrea? I'm Ms. Cruz," says a young woman with smooth skin and pixie hair as black as mine. "Come into my office, please."

I follow her into a small room with large windows, half expecting to see Ayla or Judd waiting. Thankfully, it's empty.

"Am I in trouble?" I ask tentatively as I sit down across from Ms. Cruz.

"No, but we may have a problem," she answers, shuffling some papers on her desk. "Where are you living right now?"

I gulp and order myself to calm down. "With my mom's boyfriend."

"Can you give me the address?" she asks, pen poised.

I comply, but as soon as she writes it down, I get more nervous. Did Mr. Marsh tell her I looked unkempt that one day? Is someone coming to Judd's place to check on me? That would be bad, for all of us.

"When did you leave the apartment on Blake Street?"

I shrug. "A month ago? My mom wanted to move in with her boyfriend." I know I'm repeating myself, but I don't want to say too much.

"Well, that explains why a discrepancy arose when checking residency requirements for next year." Ms. Cruz puts down her pen. "Your mother didn't notify us of the address change, and we don't have open enrollment. You must live in Essex County to attend Essex schools."

"What?" I whisper, though I knew this. If I hadn't been so panicked earlier, I would have realized right away where this conversation was going. I would have lied.

I stare at her desk, crestfallen. My mask is gone. I must look as devastated as I feel, but I can't hide it anymore. *Everything I worked so hard for, everything I put up with...*

Ms. Cruz tries to make me feel better by saying, "Andrea, we'll be sad to lose you, but you're an excellent student and you'll do well at..." She swivels her chair and types something into her computer, then finishes, "...Belmont High School. When I send your transcripts, I'll write a personal note to ensure you get placed in every honors class offered. You won't have to re-test in any subject."

I know she's doing me a favor, and I *am* grateful, but Essex was the one thing keeping me afloat. And now, in a breath, it's gone. Just like Gram. Just like everything good.

I want to argue, to beg, but there's no point. Rules are rules. Laws are laws. People—children, especially—don't have a chance against them. Standing up, I force a small smile. "Thanks."

Instead of going back to class, I head straight to the library and google 'Belmont High School.' The picture on the homepage sure looks like Haydon—barren and dusty. Vast farmland surrounds the athletic fields and a meadow of high corn bumps up to one side of the lone brick building. The school is nowhere near as large as Essex. Or as prestigious. Clicking around the website, the myriad photos of smiling students serve only to depress me.

In slow motion, I return to homeroom. I turn in my school ID and clean out my locker like everyone else. It's hard not to notice how empty mine is when all around me kids are unfolding old notes or peeling off magnetic white boards, laughing at farewell messages scribbled by friends. I drop the scholarship flier in the nearest trashcan.

Outside, I tuck myself against the side of the white library building, where I'm mostly hidden by bushes but still have a good view of campus. I sit there all afternoon hugging my knees and memorizing the details. I wanted this so badly. And now that I've had it and lost it, I just want to remember something nice. Some*place* nice.

Later, I walk to the corner where Doug's hot dog cart was parked the other day. In its place is an Audi sporting an Ohio University bumper sticker. Slowly, I trudge to the bus stop, letting the tears roll down my cheeks and into the neck of my T-shirt. I don't bother to wipe them away.

My walk from the market to Judd's house is dreadful. I try not to think about the next three months, or the next two years. I just put one foot in front of the other in front of the other, until the sun starts to dip below the horizon, until the rhythm feels like a dance instead of a death march.

There's a blue BMW parked in Judd's driveway when I arrive. A man leans against the hood talking to Judd. He has dark, wavy hair that grazes his shoulders and when he catches sight of me, he does a doubletake.

"Wait for me in the cellar, Bones," Judd commands.

I make a beeline for the front door. Just as I'm stepping inside, the long-haired guy lets out a low whistle. "You sly little shit, Judd. You never said the daughter was hot, too."

"She's a kid," Judd replies, his voice tight.

"Old enough," the man counters with a laugh. "Hell, when you feel like sharing your toys, you let me know."

I shut the door, shut out his disgusting words. But then some other words jump into my mind—the ones Judd spoke to me weeks ago—*What you oughtta be worryin' about is yourself. I got people lookin' now. Breaking my back to protect you, girl.*

I didn't pay attention to his warning then, but now it's all I hear.

That night, after Judd and Ayla pass out on the sofa, I slip outside and pick my way through the cluttered storage area attached to the back of the house. It doesn't take long to find what I need. In the dark, I tiptoe to the Buick and pour the gas into the tank. Then I hide the empty red can under some pots, wipe my hands on the front of my shorts, and slip back inside, quiet as a mouse.

Chapter 17

Judd works me to the bone now that school is out. We spend long hours in the shed and cellar, make extra deliveries during the week. Sometimes we go as far as Dayton and Cleveland on special errands. My role is twofold—I'm Judd's cover and I always carry the drugs. I get it now—there's less impact on him if *I* get caught in possession.

I've visited the pond twice, but the girl wasn't there either time. I wish she would show up. I want to ask her about Walmart. I want to tell her about the Sprite I dumped in that blond girl's purse. I do find a stone message from her once. It spells **Saturday?** My heart sinks. Judd doesn't let me out of his sight on Saturdays. Defeated, I kick the stones so they scatter. I start to walk away, then come back, bend down, and rearrange the stones to say **Can't.**

It's true, in so many ways. I can't plan a meeting with her because Judd controls my schedule, controls *me.* I can't be her friend, anyway. What on earth would I talk to her about?

I won't come back to the pond again. It's for the best.

On a scorching June day two and a half miserable weeks into summer vacation, I'm listening to Ayla cuss Judd out downstairs. The two of them have never been averse to drama, but lately they're arguing non-stop. Fed up, Judd slams out the front door, hops in his car, and takes off in a cloud of dust.

Hope sparks inside me as Ayla grumbles about Judd's disgusting teeth and receding hairline. Planting those seeds in her head about his shortcomings lately has paid off, I think. She's ready.

My bags are packed, as always, and I've smuggled a bunch of food into them. They're super heavy, but I'd rather carry an elephant than starve.

"Ayla," I coax when I find her pacing in their bedroom. "Let's take the Buick and go. Aren't you sick of him?"

She pauses, her eyes infused with...something. Not excitement exactly, and it may just be the effect of whatever pills she popped today, but for once, for real, she's considering it.

"We don't need him." I pull her bags out from under the bed, then go to her drawers and start packing her clothes. She watches me obtusely, but she's not stopping me.

"We'll be better off on our own," I say.

"Yeah," she says slowly, testing the idea in her half-baked mind. "I *am* sick of him. Sick of him ordering me around, rationing my supplies. I don't need his crap!"

"Exactly. You're gorgeous. You can have any man you want," I flatter her. "Judd's not even in your league. He should be worshipping you."

Ayla's with me now, grabbing clothes off hangers and shoes

from the closet floor. I'm so excited at the prospect of getting away from Judd, away from Haydon, that I could burst into song. I've been waiting for this moment far longer than I realized. And now that I've lost Essex, it's worth the risk, it's worth everything, to run.

Then Ayla pulls a clear sack of pills from one of Judd's drawers and sticks it inside her bag.

"No!" I grab for it, remembering how Judd deals with people who steal from him.

Ayla snatches the baggie before I can. Holding it to her chest, she says lethally, "I'm not going without it."

I glance out the window, torn. "Fine, just hurry up." My heart is pitter-pattering in anticipation of our getaway and who knows when Judd will be back.

Then Ayla stops moving altogether.

"What's wrong? Come on!" I yell.

"We can't go anywhere." She slouches dejectedly onto the bed.

Panic clutches my chest. "Yes, we can. We *have* to! If we stay, he'll just keep pushing us around. We need to go now," I say, glancing out the window again.

"But he's got our keys, Bones." Ayla looks up at me with the disappointed eyes of a child being denied some treat.

Luckily, I haven't been a child for a long time, and I'm not waiting for someone to rescue me. "No, Ayla. *I* have our keys." I pull them from my pocket and dangle them in front of her.

Her face lights up. "Where'd you get those?"

"Found them," I say, pushing her off the bed. Now is not the time to explain how I've been secretly searching since the last day of school, memorizing the placement of clothing in Judd's drawers so I could put it all back the way I found it. After a few days, I discovered the keys in a cigar box under his dresser. "Now come on. You still have some money, right?"

She nods.

"Okay, then." I take Ayla's hand and pull her out the front door, my heart knocking against my ribs. I usher her into the passenger seat and toss our bags in the trunk. I don't stop to look back at Judd's house as I start the engine and hit the gas. Unlike Essex, this is a place I don't want to remember.

I have to force myself not to speed on the two-lane highway. Getting stopped by the police would derail everything. As we approach the market, the light turns red and I have to bring the Buick to a stop.

Sinking low in the driver's seat, I scan the lot. Judd's car is easy to find. He always parks in the back. "Oh no," I whisper when I see it. Thanks to his tinted windows, I can't tell if he's inside it or not.

"Oh no, what?" Ayla asks.

I spot Judd walking out of the liquor store gripping a brown bag. He stops on the curb to light a cigarette. *Don't look up, don't look up...* To Ayla I say, "Get the map out of the glove compartment."

She starts rifling around. Good. That'll keep her busy. The last thing I need is for her to see Judd and freak out.

After ten thousand hours, the light turns green and I ease smoothly onto the gas. I watch Judd the whole time, holding my breath.

"Aha!" Ayla pulls out the map, triumphant. She gets so proud of herself for the simplest tasks. I roll my eyes as we leave the market in the dust, but I can't help smiling too. She fusses with the map, turning it all different ways as if it's the hardest Sudoku puzzle. She's too high to read it but I memorized the route to the interstate long ago. As soon as we're heading east on it, cruising at exactly fifty-five miles per hour, I roll down my window and let out a victory whoop.

I don't really have a plan, other than to get far away fast. We can't go back to Indianapolis—Judd would find us there. I concentrate on driving, since I haven't done it in a while. And I refuse to stop for the first two hours, even though Ayla says she needs to pee. She probably just wants her bag of contraband in the trunk.

"Hold it," I tell her. "I don't want to risk running into anyone who knows Judd."

Ayla harrumphs, but doesn't argue. When we do stop east of Wheeling, West Virginia, I stay in the car and tell my mother she has five minutes or I'm leaving without her. I keep her purse. Normally she'd be irritated with my bossiness, but she's stoned and pliable, and I'm running the show.

After the pit stop, Ayla falls asleep and I'm left to navigate. A feeling of empowerment courses through my veins as I put more miles between us and Judd. He could be on our trail. But even if he discovered us missing soon after we'd left, he wouldn't know for sure which way we'd gone. If he guessed correctly, though, and he drove fast, he could catch us. Or he could send his cronies out in every direction.

I decide it's best to get off I-70 and onto a different interstate. The first one I come across is 79, so I head south toward Morgantown. The scenery is breathtaking and the towering mountains surround us like a fortress. I feel safer here.

Ayla is cranky when she wakes up, so we stop for an early dinner at McDonald's. Nibbling our fries, we regard one another warily, as if we are surprised by each other, and ourselves, and what we did.

I sigh so deeply I feel it in my toes. "I like West Virginia. It's pretty."

Ayla scratches her neck. She doesn't care about pretty—unless she's looking in a mirror.

"I thought we could stop in Morgantown," I add. "It's only a little farther."

"Whatever."

Ayla wants to drive. I hand her the keys, knowing that if she turns the car around now, we're too low on gas to get all the way back to Columbus. But she sticks to the plan and parks at a cheap motel on the edge of Morgantown, where she pays with cash and we settle into lucky Room Seven for the night. With the TV humming, we finally relax.

At least as much as two girls on the run possibly can.

Chapter 18

When I open my eyes, Ayla is drinking motel coffee from a Styrofoam cup, staring out the window at the mountains. The pastel hues of the mid-morning sun highlight both her profile and the dust motes floating in the air. It makes her look sort of like an angel.

"What time is it?" I murmur, rubbing my eyes.

"A little past ten."

I sit up and dangle my legs over the side of the bed. It is quiet and still—a heavy kind of stillness—because neither of us knows what to say. Ayla seems sober, and we've had so few moments together when she wasn't tripping or sleeping that I'm not sure how to approach her.

"I paid for another night," she says.

Part of me thinks we should stay on the move, but I don't argue. I can't tell if Ayla is happy we left or not, and that makes me uneasy.

"I was thinking we could eventually drive to the coast," I suggest, trying to sound upbeat. "Somewhere remote and warm. That way, we can camp on the beach."

She brightens a little. "I've never seen the ocean."

"Me, either!"

We both smile, delighted with this small similarity. Then the moment fades.

"We'll still need money," Ayla says.

"Yeah. So when does Gram's next check come?"

Ayla's eyes skirt over to meet mine. "How'd you know about that?"

I scoff. "I'm not stupid. Why else would you keep me?"

For the briefest moment, she looks ashamed, and I don't realize how badly I want her to deny my assumption until she doesn't. She purses her lips. "July first. I have to find a bank where I can get the money wired."

I swallow the hurt and ask, "How much do we have now?"

"Plenty," she assures me. "And I'm starving. Let's go eat."

Her words are a relief. Planning our next move is sure to bring conflict and stress, and I'd rather take a breather and enjoy my first morning of freedom, too.

"I need to shower first," I say, wondering if she'll wait.

She picks up the TV remote and leans back against the pillows on the bed. I select an outfit from my bag and head for the bathroom. The motel is nothing fancy, but it's clean and it's ours, at least for the next twenty-four hours. Stepping into the shower, I'm more than ready to wash away our life with Judd.

Like typical tourists, we end up in Morgantown's historic district at a place called Happy Pizza, which boasts colorful Rastafarian décor. Inhaling the aroma of freshly-baked dough and homemade tomato sauce, I attack the menu. I can't remember the last time I had the privilege of ordering a pizza topped with anything I wanted. When my spinach feta thin-crust pie arrives, piping hot and dripping with cheese, I realize that I'm leaning protectively over my plate, as if someone might snatch it away at any moment. I vow to relax as Ayla strikes up a conversation with a couple seated nearby—Morgantown natives eager to suggest "things to see" in the area.

"There's the university, with its beautiful grounds," they gush. "And Royce Hill in the park. You won't want to miss the arboretum…" They go on and on and on. By the look on Ayla's face, she is sorry she asked.

When the bill arrives, Ayla tosses way too much money on the table. I snatch back a ten before sliding across the wooden booth and following her out into the sizzling June sunshine.

Without discussing it, we start meandering through the gift shops dotting Main Street. Ayla fusses over the trinkets, looking at them from all angles. She wants to buy a paperweight in the shape of West Virginia, but I firmly tell her no. Pouting, she says, "You're such a buzz kill, Andrea."

My heart does this little shake. I can't remember the last time Ayla used my real name, if ever. It makes me feel…something like gratitude and heartbreak mixed together. I realize this is the first time I've come anywhere close to enjoying my mother's company, the first time I've caught a glimpse of the Ayla that Gram wanted me to know.

Instead of the paperweight, we buy a city map and study it on an outdoor bench, eating ice cream cones. "Look. We're near the park that couple in Happy's mentioned." I point to the tiny picnic table on the map. "Let's check it out." I jump up, excited.

Ayla shrugs and follows, sucking on her mound of butter pecan.

I lead the way to a winding trail, where we pass a placard marked 'Royce Hill.' Ayla is winded almost immediately, but I push on. We cross paths with some students wearing big smiles and WVU shirts who say, "Beautiful day for a hike!" and "The view's fantastic!" as they head down.

"Are we *hiking*?" Ayla asks after they've passed. "I don't hike."

I stifle a laugh. "We're just walking. You walk, don't you?"

"Depends on how far away the car is," she mumbles and falls into a hacking cough. But she keeps going.

I quickly lose myself in the rhythm of the hike. The sun is bright, the trees are lush, and the little blue wildflowers dotting the trail kindle something warm inside. I notice a fuzzy bee seeking the perfect flower to pollinate, stringy weeds poking through the dirt in search of sunlight. I take a deep, savory breath. I've always liked being out in nature, where every living thing single-mindedly pursues its purpose with clarity and devotion. What a relief it would be if *people* operated that way.

We're nearing the top of the hill when Ayla blurts, "You

ever had a boyfriend, Bones?" I bristle a little. She's never asked me anything personal like that. An image of Ben jumps into my head. Ben and Delaney.

"No. And I don't want one." As far as I can tell, boys—and men, for that matter—just complicate things. In a very unhealthy way.

"Oh…you like girls, huh? Me too, sometimes."

Shaking my head, I clarify, "I don't want a boyfriend *or* a girlfriend, Ayla. I don't need anyone."

"Huh. Maybe that's why Mama always said you were so smart."

I want to explain that Gram said I was smart because I pulled A's in honors classes, but it would be a waste of my breath.

"I was never smart," Ayla adds after a moment. It's not a sad sort of admission, just matter-of-fact. I don't respond, but now I'm thinking about Ayla falling in love as a teenager. I'm thinking about her and my father. Ayla never mentions him, but that doesn't mean she didn't love him. Gram didn't talk much about my grandfather either, and I know she loved him dearly.

After a few minutes, I glance back at Ayla and am met with a gorgeous smile—a full one, rare. Her eyes glimmer, looking past me. As I turn back to the trail, I see why. We have reached the top of Royce Hill and the view looks like something out of a travel magazine. Far below us, the shimmering Monongahela River snakes through rolling green hills that fade to a bluish brown in the distance. Farther off, puffy treetops blend together, creating acres of green cotton candy.

"Wow," I breathe. "I've never seen anything so beautiful."

"Me, either." Ayla staggers across the clearing and leans against a tree, sucking wind and coughing up phlegm. Still, her eyes sparkle.

I shuffle over, notice the same rattle in her chest that used to worry me so much in Gram's. Now I feel kind of bad for tricking her into the hike.

"The walk down will be easier," I say.

She nods, her cheeks apple red.

For dinner that night, we buy crepes at a sidewalk café, then wander around town some more. Neither of us wants to return to the motel. We don't want to think about moving on, or evading Judd, or building a future. The day has been too lovely to dismiss.

As dusk seeps in around the shops and restaurants of Morgantown, musicians trickle out to play jazz on the sidewalks. Street performers show off their tricks. Ayla and I stand shoulder to shoulder, wrapped in the warm summer air, giggling at a mime's impromptu show. There is this content, surreal feeling—almost an affection—stretched like a wire between us, and my heart is soaring because this, *this* is what I've wanted my whole damn life. And I never even knew it.

Chapter 19

The next morning in the dingy motel room, there are no more warm fuzzies in the air. We count what's left of our money and my chest tightens. It's not going to last two weeks—maybe not even one.

"What'll we do?" Ayla fumbles for her cigarettes.

I want to ask, "*Who* is the adult here?" But I know the answer.

"Let's talk to the motel manager." Squaring my shoulders, I stride outside and over to the office. Ayla follows slowly, unsure of my plan. Which is wise of her since I don't actually have one.

A bald, heavyset man with tattoos on his arms and one climbing up his neck stands behind the counter reading a magazine. He says good morning and asks how he can help us lovely ladies. I smile sweetly and ask if there are any discounts available.

"The rate is what it is. This is tourist season." He shrugs like it can't be helped.

"What if we pay for a whole week up front? Can you give us a deal then?" I plead.

Before he can shoot me down, Ayla pipes up. "Sir, we just need to get by until July first, when my husband's life insurance comes in." She lowers her eyelids. "He was killed in duty. Afghanistan…"

Unable to stomach her lies, I turn away. Ayla pats my shoulder and mumbles, "She's having a real hard time with it."

"Well, I'm sure sorry to hear that," the man says kindly, stroking his goatee. "I'm ex-Army myself. Maybe we can work something out this once."

"God bless you," Ayla gushes.

While they discuss the details of a payment plan, I notice a bunch of military magazines piled on a small table by the door and the one the man was reading when we walked in, titled *AMVETS*. Ayla must have noticed, too.

I push out of the office, disgusted and impressed.

"It worked, didn't it?" Ayla defends herself over brunch at the IHOP twenty minutes later. "Didn't hurt anybody."

She's right, though it makes me feel like scum. "I don't like lying. That guy was nice." The words sound ridiculous because, of course, I've been lying to plenty of nice people in one way or another all year.

"Fine." Ayla sighs. "I'll try not to lie anymore. What's next?"

I take a sip of water and lay out a short-term plan—stay here to save up some money, then head for the coast by early

August. That will leave time for me to get settled into a new school. My goal is to be able to stay in one place for the entire next two academic years, but I don't tell her that.

"Okay," Ayla says. I'm shocked that she's so agreeable. She doesn't even balk when I tell her she has to get a job. She glances around the restaurant. "Maybe I could waitress."

"Yes!" My whole face lights up. "Ayla, you'd get tons of tips. As long as you're friendly."

"I'm friendly," she assures me with a mischievous grin.

I swallow, trying not to think of her kind of friendly. "And sober."

She rolls her eyes and throws back her orange juice like it's a cocktail. "What do you think I am now?"

I'm still worried, but so far this is working out a hundred times better than I'd hoped. Ayla seems to be trying. I know she'll never be a mother to me, but if she just acts decent, we can make a life together. And then someday maybe I can help her. *Really* help her. Just like Gram wanted to.

We ask about jobs at the IHOP, but the manager just hired three new people. Ruby Tuesday is next door but the thin-nosed man behind the bar says he's not hiring, either. Ayla leans onto the counter, offering him an eyeful of her cleavage. Then she practically purrs, "Are you *sure* there's nothing you can do?"

The man takes in everything she's handing out. When he's had his fill, he raises his chin and smiles at Ayla. "No. There's nothing I can do, but *thank you* for stopping by." He turns away, grinning.

"Pig!" Ayla yells as we leave.

"Ayla. That's not okay," I chastise her once we're outside. "You can't just…flaunt yourself."

She laughs, then looks at me smugly. "Here's a tip, Bones." She twirls a piece of my long black hair around her index finger. "Learn how to use that gorgeous face and hot bod of yours to get what you want."

This is my mother's wisdom. This is what she has to offer me after years of life experience. I study Ayla, with her own gorgeous face and wasting-away brain, and know I will do just about anything to survive. Except that.

"Just let me do the talking from now on," I insist.

She puts on some lipstick and shrugs.

We hit every restaurant within five miles of the motel, but no one needs a waitress. Or a dishwasher. Or a hostess. A few businesses give us applications, but filling them out is more difficult than I anticipate, starting with the fact that we don't have a permanent address. We end up borrowing the motel's.

"What year did you graduate high school?" I ask Ayla, pen poised. I am sitting with my feet up on Gram's dashboard, using my legs as a desk.

"Never finished."

That's not surprising.

"Well, it doesn't ask specifically if you *graduated*," I say. "We just have to list the school and the last year you attended."

She tells me and I write it down, realizing she left school just before I was born and never went back. I push down the stirrings of guilt. That is not my fault.

"Job Experience," I read.

"Oh!" She raises her hand as if in school. "I answered phones for this guy Jamie once. Man, was he *cute*. He owned an auto parts store, a one-man shop."

"Perfect," I say.

"It only lasted a few months, 'til Jamie's wife caught us in the back room…her name was Viola. Like the instrument." Ayla remembers this detail, but she can't remember whether the shop was in Cleveland or Toledo, or even what it was called, so I make it up. I make up the dates, too. I feel like I am fabricating an entire person.

When I'm done with Ayla's applications, I fill out my own, listing each club and activity, every babysitting job, even the few times I subbed on the Essex debate team. A deep pity invades my heart as I realize I've accomplished more in my sixteen years on earth than Ayla has in thirty-one.

"Okay." I try to sound chipper as I cap the pen. "Let's go."

Job hunting is no fun. Rejection is hard, especially for someone like Ayla, who has never even tried. When I see her mood falling, I tell her everything will be fine and try to believe it myself. But beneath my calm veneer, I'm a wreck. When I think about Judd, my skin turns cold. Even if he was blowing smoke when he talked about tracking me down, there's no way he's not looking for his stolen drugs. If no job prospects come up tomorrow, I'm going to tell Ayla we should just move on.

That night, we eat half the food I smuggled out of Judd's

house for dinner. I work on a budget while Ayla watches TV. "We'll find something soon," I assure her as I turn out the light.

But I don't sleep well. Three times I'm chased awake by nightmares before I decide to splash some water on my face. When I flip on the light in the bathroom, I notice Ayla's bed. Empty.

My stomach plummets. This is it—she's abandoned me. But a sweep of the room shows her bags still piled on the chair and when I race outside, the Buick is parked where we left it, in the shadows. A neon sign across the street catches my eye. Most of the lights are burnt out, but I can make out the most important word—BAR. Of course.

Back inside the motel room, I realize Ayla's purse is gone, which means she could be spending all our money. And without an ID, I can't get into the bar to stop her.

I sit up stewing for a while, but fatigue eventually trumps anger. Ayla stumbles through the door at 4:00 AM, but my eyes don't pop open until I hear a man's voice, pleading, "Can't I come in, baby?"

My mother's silhouette in the doorway blocks the guy with the odd European accent. I grip the comforter and hold my breath. Ayla gently pushes him back, promising that she'll see him later. *Tomorrow for sure,* she croons.

Despite his protests, Ayla locks the door, strips down naked, and climbs under the sheets. She is asleep as soon as her head hits the pillow, hair spilling into her mouth.

"Where is it?" My voice trembles as I shake Ayla awake

four hours later.

"Wha-at?" she whines, flipping onto her stomach.

"Our money. Don't tell me you wasted it on tequila or something." I can barely breathe through my fury, so it's hard to get the words out.

Ayla's eyes are open now and amused because I don't often show this much emotion. She props up on one elbow and smiles like she's in the middle of a lovely dream. "I never spend money at bars, darling. I get all my drinks for free."

Unconvinced, I demand to see the cash since I've already looked through her purse and couldn't find a single dollar. "Don't get your panties in a bunch," she says, sitting up and grabbing her smokes on the bedside table. "I hid it, under the mattress."

I search there frantically until my fingers curl around the bills. I breathe a huge sigh of relief.

Giggling, Ayla flops back onto the mattress and proceeds to tell me about her "amazing" night at the bar. Feeling sheepish about my outburst, I sit cross-legged on the comforter, gripping the money and listening intently since Ayla rarely opens up to me. It's kind of nice. Her voice is giddy and expressive, like someone *my* age who just met the cutest boy in school…

Chapter 20

His name is Giovanni.

He's tall, dark, and handsome, I'll give Ayla that. And he's been glued to her side ever since she called him to meet us for lunch that day. I was against the idea at first, but Ayla looked so discouraged after another morning of fruitless job searching that I caved.

Mistake Number One.

Despite his name, I doubt there's an ounce of authentic Italian blood in Giovanni. That accent? As fake as his tan. His hair? Dyed black. And that first day, as we sat in the booth at Happy's, he remarked that his favorite pizza came from a little café in Venice. I almost choked on my cheese when he said he went there after touring the Pantheon.

"But, the Pantheon is in *Rome*," I blurted.

"Roma, Venezia…I get mixed up sometime," Giovanni covered. Flustered, he buried his cute, stubbled chin in his pizza.

My eyes narrowed.

"I'm sure Giovanni knows Italy better than *you* do," Ayla snapped, kicking me under the table.

Apparently I'd forgotten one of her rules: *Always let your man think he is smarter than you.* Rolling my eyes, I let it go.

A few days later, Giovanni moves us out of the motel room and into his sunny condo. The place screams "bachelor pad," all leather and steel. There's only one bedroom, but his couch is pretty plush so I'll take it. Besides, Giovanni has been paying for all our meals. I figure staying with him will allow us to save our money.

Mistake Number Two.

With Giovanni lavishing attention on Ayla, her eyes shine brighter. It doesn't take a genius to realize she actually *likes* the guy. One night, I find the lovebirds on the couch with their legs entwined, feeding each other noodles from red and white cartons. Could this be a good thing?

But then, between bites, Ayla slides a little white pill into her mouth. It's the first time I've seen her use since we left Haydon and my senses go on high alert.

Ayla offers a pill to Giovanni, but he declines.

I watch them closely after that. Even though Giovanni doesn't participate, Ayla doing drugs doesn't seem to faze him. He is the epitome of laid back. *That* trait feels authentically Italian, at least. But there is still one thing that bothers him—me.

The condo is small and Giovanni's resentment toward me sticks to every surface. Once, in the middle of the night, I flush the toilet, then cringe. Through the paper-thin wall, I hear Giovanni groan and say, "Why you have to have a kid, Ayla? It could be so perfect with us."

It is ludicrous that this hurts my feelings.

"I'll tell her to get out of the condo more," Ayla responds.

I'm not surprised by either comment, but still. How *dare* he waltz in here with his dimples and flattery and mess everything up! Things had been going well between me and Ayla. Now, once again, she thinks of me as a nuisance, a stick figure on a chalkboard that can be wiped away at will. The game has turned and there's nothing I can do. Giovanni is in. Andrea is out.

June melts into July, and I mean literally. Morgantown is *hot,* and I spend long sticky days in the park since I'm no longer welcome at the condo until dinnertime. I console myself by thinking, *it's better than Judd's shed.* But Judd still haunts me. Sometimes when I climb to the top of Royce Hill and stare out at the rolling hills, I feel like I can see clear to Ohio. And that's when I hear his voice in my ear, whispering, *Did you forget who owns you, girl?*

Despite Giovanni's generosity, the money in Ayla's purse dwindles. She doesn't confide in me anymore, but I know exactly when she cashes the next inheritance check because the purse is full again. The relief that money brings is indescribable. I start making plans for our next move. Unfortunately, Giovanni makes one first.

It happens on July fourth—Independence Day—and the

irony is not lost on me. Sunlight floods the condo and nudges me out of a dream filled with ocean waves and palm trees. Something nice for once. Sitting up on the leather couch, I realize I've slept half the morning away. Ayla is still curled onto her side of the master bed when I peek in. Giovanni is nowhere in sight.

"G must've run out to get breakfast," Ayla murmurs a little while later, shuffling into the kitchen wearing a silky bathrobe. I don't reply, just suck on a strip of beef jerky, the last of my stash. I know G won't bring *me* breakfast.

Half an hour later, I'm sprawled on the couch reading *Watership Down*. Even though I'm not returning to Essex, I still feel compelled to complete their summer reading list.

Ayla stares out the window with a creased brow, waiting. Personally, I think it's kind of nice being in the condo with Giovanni out of it. But when noon comes and goes, Ayla starts pacing like a restless panther, and I can't take it.

"Give me twenty bucks and I'll get us lunch," I say, exasperated. "I'll look for Giovanni while I'm out."

She shoots me a grateful glance. "Good idea." She scurries into the bedroom.

While I wait for her to return, I toss my novel onto the leather couch and stretch out long like a cat. I hear things being shuffled around in the bedroom, and then Ayla shrieks. "Oh no… oh *shit*. Bones!"

The panic in her voice makes me jump. I rush to the bedroom door, where Ayla stands in shock, her empty purse dangling in her pale white hand.

The realization of what has happened hits me fast, like a punch to the gut. I reflexively cover my mouth, lurch, and proceed to vomit jerky all over Giovanni's fake wood floors.

Chapter 21

"H-how could this h-happen?" Her words come out in hysterical hiccups.

We're back in the Buick, parked at the motel on the seedy side of town, and Ayla is a mess—swollen eyes and long lines of mascara painting zebra stripes down her face. Curse words explode from her lips as she hisses about killing Giovanni one minute, then collapses into heartbroken sobs the next.

I sit in the driver's seat, stunned. How *could* this happen? How could I have been so blind? Ayla was too enamored by Giovanni's charm to see the warning signs, but I should have. Now every dollar that was supposed to last us through the next six months is gone. The only thing Giovanni left was an eviction notice taped to his front door.

Ayla wept while I packed her bags. Mine, of course, were ready to go.

Anger boils inside me when I think about how we've ended

up right back where we started all those months ago—dead broke and living in the Buick.

I unstick my thighs from the hot leather upholstery and try to convince Ayla to come look for jobs with me at the gift shops. She's so distraught over Giovanni's betrayal, however, that she just sits there and swallows Judd's pills, one after another.

When she finally leans her head against the seat, eyes closed, I count silently to one hundred, slip the baggie out of her limp hand, and leave.

Every shop in Old Morgantown town is awash in red, white, and blue for the holiday weekend. Streamers and balloons adorn our land of opportunity. But there are no jobs to be had. All the store owners say I should check back in September when the college kids return and business picks up. Great idea, folks. By September, I'll have starved to death.

I spy a phone booth—the old fashioned kind that looks like it came from London—and slip inside. I dial Delaney's number, hoping she'll accept a collect call. I'm ready to tell her… some truths. And ask for help. But after seven rings, a recording tells me this phone number is no longer in service. I stand still for a whole minute, suckerpunched again. Could Delaney have changed her number to avoid me? I shake my head. Her parents probably got a better deal at a different cell phone company. Or something. I try the number again, to no avail. Sunlight pours through the glass, causing sweat to pool behind my knees and at the nape of my neck. The moist, thick air makes it hard to breathe. At least, I think it's the air.

I exit the booth, walk a few blocks, then lean dejectedly against a stone wall in a small alley. I'm hot and hungry, which is only one step up from being *cold* and hungry. I hate the way I feel—ready to give up—and what's worse is that I don't even know what "giving up" would entail at this point. In a cool square of shade, I take a steadying breath. A door jingles a little ways down and I notice the sign above it, and the tall steeple above that. My feet are moving before my mind has a chance to catch up.

"Do you have information on homeless shelters?" I ask the puffy-faced lady sitting in the church office as the AC blasts my sunburned skin.

She leads me to a shelf where dozens of pamphlets are stacked. They offer tips on everything from Family Planning to Midlife Crisis to Death and Grieving. A person could live her whole life in these pamphlets, I think. It would probably be a better life than mine.

"Here you go." The lady hands me the brochure, then takes in my appearance. I realize how I must look—messy hair, hard eyes, my whole life stuffed into the two bags on my back like a turtle.

"I'm doing a school project," I offer lamely. She doesn't mention the obvious—that it's July.

Smiling kindly, she wraps a bunch of cookies up in a paper towel and hands them to me. "Come back anytime."

A part of me wants to stay, to sit in the cozy little room and tell this woman *everything*. But of course I bolt. The last thing I need is her calling the authorities while I'm packing Judd's bag of goodies.

The cookies taste like heaven, but we still need cash, so I scour the sidewalk for loose change. It's obvious and humiliating, and I envy the people who can play musical instruments for tips. I find a crumpled five-dollar bill under a bus stop bench and feel like I've won the lottery.

When I climb into the Buick with our dinner—Taco Bell because it's the cheapest—Ayla jerks awake and starts slapping me silly, sending our meal flying all over the front seat.

I cover my head. "Stop it! I brought food!"

"I don't want *food*. Where the hell is it, you little thief! You're just like him," she shouts. "Did you sell it? I swear I'll wring your neck—"

"No, I didn't sell it," I hiss, though I wish I'd thought of that. "I just didn't want to find you dead!" Shielding myself from her blows, I fumble through my backpack for her precious baggie and hurl it at her. Clutching it to her chest, Ayla sighs deeply. Then she smacks me one more time, extra hard, and warns me never to touch her shit again.

Tears sting my eyes and I glare through them at Ayla's distorted face, hating her worse than ever. Hating her all the more because I fooled myself into believing she was capable of change. "You're the thief," I rumble. "Gram left *me* that trust money, not you."

My words have no effect. But I'm fired up now, my nerves jangling. "*Nothing* belongs to you, Ayla. This car is *Gram's*. Those aren't even your drugs," I point out. "They're Judd's."

"I earned 'em," she responds flatly. And I can't disagree.

While she paws through the bag of pills, I reach down to

salvage our dinner. I scarf it all down, even the tacos I meant for Ayla. Maybe we are stuck with each other, but I don't belong to her. She never did anything to *earn* me.

By the time I finish eating, Ayla's head is tilted against the seat, her eyes rolled back in ecstasy. I drop the church pamphlet into her lap, startling her. "What is this?" she slurs.

"A list of shelters. We're going to have to stay in one."

Ayla snorts. "Those places won't let me in. They don't give you a bed if you're using. Plus the rules they have, curfews…" Her mouth curls into a disgusted grimace. "So not worth it."

As I digest this information, a fresh sense of panic engulfs me. I'd always thought of shelters as our last resort. But as long as Ayla's an addict, she can't get a job. Or a life. Or even a bed in a homeless shelter.

A dull thudding starts behind my eyes. I look out the window at the bar and the seedy motel and the darkness that pervades our life. I am out of ideas.

But Ayla's got one. She mutters it, with words that leave me clammy and shaken. "We should go back to Judd."

"No!" The word shoots out like an arrow. Ayla looks at me funny, like she can't remember what she said five seconds ago or why I'm reacting so strongly. "We are never going back to Judd's. *Never.*" I point my finger at her face. "You are going to fix this. You are going into the bar tonight and picking someone who will help us. Someone who's not a monster and preferably not a thief!"

"Bones…" she objects, but I'm done listening. I still have a life to salvage. And if I have to start using her as she's used me, so be it.

"That's what you're doing, Ayla. So get ready," I threaten. "Or I'll be gone by morning."

She doesn't argue, and I know why I still have some pull here. Without me, once her drugs are gone, Ayla really has nothing.

The Buick is parked where I can see the bouncer admire my mother's body as he stamps her hand. She looks hot after I did her makeup and chose her sexiest outfit. I hate that I'm an active participant in this, but I have to survive.

After she disappears inside, I reach under the driver's seat for Judd's stash. Ayla will never be able to pull things together if she's constantly baked. I saw her slip a handful of pills into her purse earlier, but I have the majority of them right here. I push open the door, climb onto the hood, and launch the pills into the bushes, one by one.

As the last pill leaves my fingertips, I hear the random pop-pop-BOOM of fireworks down by the river. The display is miles away, but I can see the lights fan out in glorious technocolor before sinking behind the cityscape. *Happy Independence Day,* I think wryly.

Pulling my knees up to my chest, I wrap my arms around them. My mind conjures Delaney's coy smile, Ben's intense eyes, and proud Doug with his hot dog cart. Then I visualize those two kids I met at the pond near Judd's house, the girl who wanted to be my friend. Envy snakes through my veins as I imagine the normal teenage things they are doing tonight. I'll probably never see any of them again, I think miserably, stifling a sob. I did nothing to deserve this life. I did everything *right*. Look where it got me.

An hour passes.

Random people enter and exit the bar. Dance music pounds against the walls, a caged animal trying to break free. Couples laugh as they stumble through the parking lot.

Two hours.

I crawl back into the Buick and try to read. But there's too much static in my mind. In addition to a job, I'll need to find a high school to attend. And for that, we need an address. Camping on the beach really won't cut it. But I can only tackle one problem at a time.

A third hour passes.

I click off the light and curl up in the passenger seat. I'm almost asleep when I hear a ruckus and then Ayla screeches, "Open the door, Bones!"

Jerking up, I hit the unlock button. Ayla scrambles inside, slams the door, and turns the key. She looks disheveled. And pissed. I see two middle-aged men outside the bar, yelling obscenities.

"What hap—" I start, but Ayla hits the gas pedal so hard we both get thrown back. I fumble for my seatbelt. Ayla swerves onto the curb close to where those men are standing. More cursing ensues, along with some creative hand gestures.

She flips them the bird, guns the engine, and we fly.

We drive straight out of town, into the northern hills that now seem cold and ominous rather than comforting. Ayla's knuckles are white. I stare ahead at the jagged yellow lines.

We pass the Welcome sign for Pennsylvania and I somehow

feel better once we've crossed into a different state. "Ayla?" I ask, then stop. I'm not sure I want to know.

"What?" she hisses.

"Weren't you going to—"

"I tried! A bunch of bastards in there tonight. No one was offering anything but booze. So I slipped that dickhead's wallet out of his pocket."

"Oh, no," I whisper, rubbing my temples.

"Would have worked, too, if his friend hadn't seen," she grumbles.

"They could call the cops!"

"They're too drunk," she dismisses me. "Anyway, he grabbed the wallet back so there's no proof."

That, at least, makes sense. We don't speak for a while, but I watch anxiously in my side mirror in case those men decided to chase us down.

"Where are we going?" I ask quietly after a few miles.

"I don't know." Her voice is quiet, too.

She really doesn't know, because she circles back into West Virginia when she sees a sign for Cooper's Rock State Forest. Worried about gas, I demand that she keep going in one direction until we find a place to stay. She veers off the road so fast that my head clunks against the window. I cradle my skull as she pulls into a small dirt lot near a forested picnic area and slams the gearshift into park.

"Where the hell do you want to go? The Ritz?" she yells. "Do you have any money?"

I shake my head, trying not to cry.

"Well, that's okay. I've got two billion bucks." Ayla crazy-laughs until it turns into a groan. "Damn that Giovanni." She shivers violently and rubs her nose with the back of her hand. And that's when it hits me—Ayla has no more supplies, thanks to me. She's already starting to crash, and it will get worse.

Right on cue, she reaches under the seat for Judd's bag of pills. When she finds nothing, she reaches farther back, frantic. Then her eyes turn on me, cold as death.

Sliding against the passenger door, I say, "They're gone, Ayla. You've gotta stop."

I wait for her to hit me, to go ballistic. But all she does is close her eyes and grip the steering wheel.

"I'll get a job right away in the next town. Maybe if it's bigger..." My voice fades. The reality of our situation is just so daunting.

After a minute, Ayla opens her eyes and says calmly, "We can sell some stuff."

"What stuff?" We only have Gram's car, which we need as both house and transport. I follow Ayla's gaze, then clamp my right hand over Gram's silver watch. "We have *nothing* to sell."

Her expression hardens. I glance at the dense woods surrounding us. Gram's car is well hidden here. And it has been a very long day.

"Let's crash here," I suggest in a softer voice. "We'll decide what to do tomorrow, when we're not so tired."

Ayla rubs her nose again and nods. "Maybe head to the coast."

"Yeah..." But there's no conviction in either of our voices.

While I try to imagine soothing ocean waves, Ayla scrounges in her purse and pulls out a plastic water bottle, which she hands to me. "The bartender gave me this. I saved you half."

"Thanks," I say, surprised. I unscrew the lid and gulp. I had no idea how thirsty I was. When I'm done drinking, I shake the last drops into my palms and rub them over my sunburned cheeks.

"Move," she commands when I'm done. I climb into the backseat, grab the blankets off the floor, and toss hers over. She curls up in front, and I sprawl out in back, so exhausted that I don't even care about the sticky leather, the metal buckles poking my hips. As soon as I lie down, I can tell that I'm going to sleep hard.

Before I succumb, my eyes flutter a few times. Through the backseat windows, the crowded silhouettes of trees sway—too willowy, too fast—like living beings with faces and ragged fingers. They come at me, poking into the windows. Windows that are not solid glass anymore, but flexing like rubber, turning liquid, bending and soluble…until they become waves of clear water floating around me, encasing me in an enormous, translucent bubble. Finally, the water turns black, drowning me in slumber.

My dreams are fitful and strange. A giant appears, muttering, "Well, well. Look who came slithering back." My hand slides across the leather upholstery. The light and shapes around me are blurred and streaked, my mouth cotton-stuffed. Nothing feels right. I am floating, then falling, until my cheek lies flat against a rock and darkness folds over me like a sack.

Chapter 22

I'm not in the Buick. I'm underneath some sort of tent, and it's a thousand degrees. I push at the fabric and it slides away. Brightness envelopes me. I'm lying on something hard, twisted up in a pink sheet. I push onto my knees, but my head bobbles around my shoulders as if it weighs two hundred pounds in liquid form. I reach up to hold it still. Shut my eyes against the searing sunlight. I don't know what happened, can't tell the difference between my hallucination and reality. My brain ticks back the hours.

We were in the car, in the state forest in West Virginia. Were we abducted? Where is Ayla?

As if on cue, I hear a *whump* and then a long wail from below. "I said I was sooooorry!"

"Sorry don't mean shit."

The voice paralyzes me.

No. God, no. It can't be true.

I pry open my eyes and it is true.

I hyperventilate. Shake. Clutch my head as everything snaps into focus—the peeling wallpaper, the creaky bed, the flimsy door near the hexagonal window.

I am back in Judd's attic.

Downstairs, there's more noise. Crashing and cursing.

"Pleeeease, Judd. Just gimme *somethin'*. I came back, didn't I?" Ayla doesn't sound like herself. It's like she's pleading through a mouthful of food. Or blood.

My ears strain to make out their words while Judd's boots clomp and creak, a hunter circling wounded prey.

"Yer nothing but a whore," he growls. "Who were you with all these weeks, huh?"

"No one. I swear," Ayla insists, her words tumbling in breathless bursts. "Bones and I...we stayed in a motel in West Virginia. I wanted to come back, but she kept talking me out of it, telling me how worthless you were. Telling me we were better off alone, even though I knew in my heart I wanted you, Judd. So I...I slipped her something so she wouldn't fight me when I drove us back here."

I am frozen in horror. Ayla is blaming everything on *me*. She must know what Judd will do to me now. And...Oh my God, Ayla drugged me with the water bottle! That's why I feel like this. My fingers clamp around my skull in disbelief.

Why, why, *why* would she bring us back here? We were free, and she ruined it. For what? Not Judd's greasy hair and rotten teeth. No. She wants his drugs. If she thinks *he* doesn't know that, then Ayla is the dumbest person on earth.

Maybe I can get away before they notice. I'll hitchhike if I have to, back to that church lady in West Virginia. Or I'll take off on my own. Somehow I'll make it.

I crawl to the door, stand up, and twist the handle. It doesn't budge. I pull with all my strength, but nothing happens. I'm locked in. It takes all my willpower not to kick the door down. But Judd would hear that and then he'd come.

I slide to the floor, defeated. My face crumples. Burying it in my lap, I let the tears go, like little spiders running down my cheeks and spilling onto my cutoff jeans.

There is nothing to do but wait. I lay flat against the cool wooden planks because the room is seriously overheated. It reminds me of the sauna at the Y where I took swim lessons and Gram went for exercise class. Only the sauna door wasn't locked.

I watch the slow movement of shadows cross the walls. Several hours must go by. My mouth feels pasty, my throat raw.

Judd's methodical footsteps finally start echoing up the stairs. The knob turns and terror pops my heart. I scurry across the floor like a spider myself, pushing my back against the far wall.

When he enters, I avoid his eyes, staring instead at his steel-toed boots as they get closer and closer, step by menacing step. I brace myself for a kick, but instead there's a very deep sigh. Judd has settled onto the edge of the bed, a few feet from where I'm hunkered. I hear the click of his lighter. Still, my eyes stay on those boots.

"Bones, Bones, Bones," Judd finally says, like he's puzzling over something too big for his puny brain. God, I despise his voice—that gravelly twang that always sounds like a sneer. "Did you really think you could get away from me?"

I raise my eyes cautiously and press harder into the wall. The sight of his lean muscled arms inked with sword and flame, his smug, grungy face, and that familiar stench of whiskey, marijuana, and tobacco twist my stomach.

"I *did* get away." I spit the words. It's a stupid thing to say, but I figure it's better to die fighting than to just roll over.

He laughs, heartily. "You got as far as I let you. You think I don't know people in Morgantown?" Judd puffs on a lit cigarette held loosely in his hand. The red-hot butt dangles dangerously close to my face. "I got friends everywhere, girl. Eyes all around."

I stare at the cigarette, too scared to speak. *How does he know about Morgantown? Was he watching us? Or did Ayla just tell him the truth in exchange for a hit?*

"You know why you're alive right now? Because of me. All it woulda' taken is one word and…" he makes a gun-shooting motion with his hand.

"I don't believe you," I whisper.

"You'd better start," he growls. "I'm the best friend you got. Now, get up!" he shouts.

But I can't move. My limbs are frozen in fear, despite the sickening heat. When Judd sees that I'm not obeying, he grabs a fistful of my hair. He uses it to drag me down the stairs so fast I am flapping like a kite behind him.

My feet slam into the bottom step, my legs buckling. I'm still so dizzy from whatever Ayla slipped me that I have to steady myself against the walls to avoid toppling. We pass the door to Judd's bedroom and continue into the hallway. I'm afraid he's taking me out to the woods to lock me in the shed, so I say the first thing I can think of—"I need the bathroom!"

Judd grunts, pushes me inside and slams the door. "You got two minutes."

I really did need the bathroom. While I'm on the toilet, I look around for an escape, but there's nothing. No windows. No tools to use as weapons. I flush, then stand and retch into the sink. Some bile comes up—there's nothing else in my stomach. I scrub my hands and face with soap before gulping the faucet water. Then I vomit it back up. In the mirror, my reflection looks demonic, even after washing. My nickname fits now. I am a dirty, wasted pile of bones.

The door flies open and Judd squeezes my neck. He pushes me through the kitchen and over to the couch, where Ayla is curled up shivering, pale and red-eyed, and at least a day into hardcore withdrawal. My hatred for her is overpowering. I want to hit her, to drag her by *her* hair, to scream in her face, *What the hell were you thinking bringing us back here?*

But she's more a pile of bones than I am.

Judd throws me down next to her and mutters, "You two aren't worth the trouble you cause. Of all the times to take off and distract me from important business. Goddamn women!" He pauses, glaring. He chews his lip for a minute, like he's deciding something. "However, Ayla and I have a history, so I'll be gracious enough to take y'all back." He sighs like he's doing us a favor.

Like we should be *happy* about this. "But there's still the matter of restitution…"

We cost him, he claims. Money spent tracking us, money in lost deals and wasted time, money for the sack of drugs Ayla stole. Thousands, we owe him.

"So where'd you stash it? In the car?" he demands, looking to me for an answer.

"Stash what?" I mumble. "Your pills? I threw them in the gutter!"

Fump! His fist comes at me when I'm not braced for it. I cry out and fall into Ayla, my eye instantly puffing up to twice its normal size.

"Where'd you stash the mon-ey?" He articulates each syllable like I'm an idiot. "Don't tell me she ain't cashed her check."

I glare at him with the eye I can still see out of. Every nerve ending in my body is on fire. I feel like a monster held by a chain, ready to attack the first thing I can sink my teeth into. But I can't attack Judd and live. And he wants an answer.

Mentioning Giovanni doesn't seem wise, so I hiss, "We got mugged. Why do you think she came back here? For *you*?" It may be evil of me, but I take a small pleasure in throwing Ayla under the bus this time.

Judd's face turns crimson with rage, but instead of taking it out on us, he kicks the coffee table, and I wonder why he's so upset. Then I get it—*he* was planning to steal Gram's money when it came. Giovanni beat him to it. Maybe that's why Judd brought us here in the first place last spring. Why would Ayla even tell him about those checks? She is so stupid.

"Don't matter, I guess." Judd calms himself down so fast it's eerie. "There's more comin' in January. I'll take that, in addition to what you two will owe me for this little stunt."

I barely listen to his ramblings. While I try to assess the damage to my eye by feeling the size of the lump, Judd calculates my share of the debt to be seven hundred dollars. That's what I must pay him, on top of what I'll continue to pay for my room and board by helping with deliveries. "You have until the first of December to come up with it," he decrees. "If you don't, you'll earn it the hard way."

I don't even want to know what that means. I have no idea how he expects me to come up with seven hundred dollars, and honestly, I'm hurting too badly at the moment to care.

Ayla's debt is significantly higher than mine, but she doesn't care either. She just quivers and begs for a hit. Judd laughs harshly and says, "No way." She pulls a small pillow over her head and moans. I wonder how long he'll make her wait.

Then Judd sees how I'm trying not to even blink because the slightest motion hurts my eye. He sneers, "I'll be outside. Eat if you want."

Once he's gone, I snatch the pillow off Ayla's face and give her the most evil one-eyed glare I can conjure. "How. Could you. Do this?" I demand, my voice shaking.

She has the decency to look remorseful. Her red-rimmed eyes plead with me. "I had to, Bones—"

"I could've died," I rumble.

She shakes her head. "What I gave you wasn't that strong."

I scoff. Maybe not for *her.*

"We had a plan…the beach!" I say, clinging to the illusion of Ayla and me making things work, together.

She groans like I'm living in fantasy-land. "We weren't gonna make it. We were kidding ourselves."

She might be right, but I still would've preferred to try. "Now we'll never know! And he's still not giving you anything. So congratulations on your brilliant idea."

Unable to argue, Ayla goes back to sniveling on the edge of the couch. "At least you got food," she mumbles.

Without verbally acknowledging that truth, I realize that I'm starving. I fall over my feet to get to the kitchen, open the refrigerator, and chug the soda that almost seems worth the punch to my eye in trade. Then come chips and cheese and ham. Soon I'm so stuffed my stomach hurts and that's when I smell the smoke.

Peering out the window above the sink, I see that Judd has built a bonfire. I think of his threats of punishing me with flame, and the food I consumed threatens to reappear. I swallow it down, past the fear that is slimy and black and wending its way through my veins.

Before I can hide or think to grab a knife, Judd comes inside carrying my bags. He must have gotten them from Gram's car, which means he has the keys again. Wonderful.

Hurling the bags at me, he orders, "Get upstairs."

I scurry into the attic room, surprised that he follows. He strides over to the closet and yanks open the door, then points.

"Unpack everything."

Even with my brain functioning better, I can't figure out his plan. But I obey, funneling all my clothes onto the wooden shelves. Then I unload my backpack, dumping books and folders onto the closet floor. Compulsively, I reach down to straighten the books.

"Pick those up," he commands.

As soon as I do, he snatches them. I only have four books, but they are like old friends. It pains me to see them clenched in his gritty hand.

He shakes out both my bags to be sure they're completely empty. Then he thrusts them back into my arms, keeping my books in his own. "Bring those and follow me."

He leads me downstairs, outside, and across the yard to the bonfire, its flames licking the sky now. He points again and says, "Drop 'em."

I clutch the empty bags to my chest. While this is certainly better than him pushing *me* into the fire, I'm not sure I can do it. Of course destroying my bags won't stop me from taking off again, but he's making a point. He is searing it into me.

Hip lip curls as he whispers, "You ever try leaving here again, you won't be taking anything with you. *I* bought those clothes, girl. You remember that."

I have no choice. I fling my bags into the flames. He makes me watch until they have burned to ash.

I don't cry. I won't, in front of him. But those bags held my whole life after Gram died. They were as much my home as the Buick. Somehow, he knows this. *How* does he know this? How does he know what will hurt me most?

Grinning, he holds up my books. "You won't be needin' these anymore, either."

I open my mouth to say something, but before I can figure out what that should be, he tosses all four books into the fire. My lips tremble as the pages turn black and disintegrate into tiny glowing embers that float up to the clouds. I don't know if the agony I feel is for the loss of the books themselves, or the fear that his words mean I won't be going to school again. Ever.

Before he wrenches me back inside, I see victory in Judd's steel gray eyes.

PART II

Chapter 23

The new lock on my door clicks each night around ten, and that's when panic constricts my chest. I remember watching Gram twist the screws around the bottom of our Christmas tree every December, squeezing tighter and tighter until the big old pine couldn't wriggle loose and fall over. That's how I feel lying under the pale pink sheet—intense pressure coming at me from all sides, rendering me immobile.

My attic room is hot as a furnace, and the only window that opens gets stuck two inches down. Not much breeze squeezes through that tiny space.

Considering the torture I expected from Judd, the one punch he delivered feels like kindness. For the next three days, all I have to do is cook dinner. The rest of the time I lay in my little bed, wishing I had some aspirin and waiting for my face to heal. I spend the hours thinking about how I've always lived two separate lives. Childhood memories spent playing in leaf piles sit next to those of a ghost-white Ayla convulsing on the couch. I think about how I came into this world—unplanned, unwanted—and wonder how I will leave it.

Judd denies Ayla drugs for days. It is maddening to hear her beg for them. I remember these sounds from years past, when Gram put Ayla in the guest room and forbade me from going near the door. I'd be sent to sleep at friends' houses during the worst of it, which for Ayla came on day three or four. All those years, I never told my friends about Ayla, not even Delaney. Gram didn't ask me to keep secrets. I just did.

On day four, I'm back to work in the cellar and, crazy as it sounds, I'm glad. Glad to be out of the sweltering attic and the inane boredom that comes with isolation. Judd isn't even that mean. I think he's happy to have my help again. Just when I'm beginning to think day four is a decent one, Ayla loses it. She jumps on Judd's back, clinging to him with her skeleton legs and whapping him in the head, demanding a hit of some drug or other, then dive-bombing down the stairs to get at the goods we are packaging. Her physical attack is a joke, but annoying enough that Judd tosses her onto the floor of his bedroom and locks her in. Even muffled by the door, her ceaseless howls rub me raw. No wonder Gram sent me away.

On day five, I think I'll go insane if I have to hear Ayla screech and moan for one more second. Judd is working on delivery routes while I cook. After I set his plate on the table, I implore,

"Can't you give her something, to take the edge off?"

Amused by my emotional request, he says, "Didn't know it bothered you so much." Then he makes me sit outside Ayla's door for the rest of the night. I bury my head in my knees and try to block out her pleas, her hissing threats, her delusions of demons sucking her eyeballs. In between, softer, she sobs pitifully for "Mama." I want Gram, too.

By the time Judd sends me to bed, I'm bawling. For hours I hemorrhage silent, unwelcome tears. I don't understand why it affects me so much. Ayla has never concerned herself with my well-being. Why should I care about hers?

But somehow, for some reason, I do.

Chapter 24

The pond water is a little lower now, after two hot summer months. I watch a frog leap from a rock onto the muddy shore. With a stick, I write my name in the goo. ANDREA. But it looks more like ANDRE because the second "A" gets lost in the mush.

We've been back in Haydon for a month. It's early August and I still haven't worked up the nerve to mention school. It was only three days ago that Judd finally let me out of the house on my own, and I've spent all three afternoons at the pond.

Ayla and Judd are back to their original arrangement. On the surface, all is forgiven. On the surface, Judd doesn't care what I do as long as I cook, keep my mouth shut, and work as his runner. But he watches me for signs of rebellion. And thinks up new ways to keep me down. Like last Wednesday, when he didn't unlock my attic door at eight as usual. I knew something was up, but I had to observe it all helplessly from inside.

First I heard tires crunching up the drive, and then car

doors opening and closing, unfamiliar voices. I stood on tiptoe, peered through my hexagonal window, and watched in horror as a middle-aged couple poked around inside the Buick. With friendly smiles, they traded Judd a wad of cash for the keys—my precious keys!—and drove Gram's car away.

Tears spilled down my red-hot cheeks as I watched our car, our hope, our independence disappear in a cloud of dust. Judd stood outside counting the money, then turned and grinned at my window, fanning the bills.

I'd be lying if I said that didn't break me.

Since then, I haven't questioned or complained or schemed. I do my job and sprint to the woods every chance I get.

The woods caress my wounds. With their shady paths and myriad hiding spots—logs, bushes, tall trees good for climbing—I pretend that I'm not enslaved. But I'm no fool. I thought the mountains in West Virginia would protect me, too, and that turned out to be a joke. Still, it's all I've got.

"Who's Andre? Your boyfriend?" The chirpy voice comes from nowhere, from everywhere. I whirl around, but the wooded space behind me is empty. "Yoo-hoo," she says. Then I see the girl up in the tree, lying horizontal on a thick branch where she must have been watching me this whole time.

Before I can react, she swings around and drops down next to me. My eyes widen at her crazy stunt, but—unlike *me*—she lands intact on all fours. Her fingers squish the earth and she smiles, her face as bright and open as the sun.

"Nice...dismount," I say.

"Three years of gymnastics," she explains, standing up. Then her voice turns earnest, "Please don't run off."

I nod. There's nowhere safe to run, anyhow. Found that out the hard way.

"I'm Chloe." She extends her hand, dripping with mud.

"Andrea," I say, pointing to the smeared "A" with my stick. "Not Andre."

"Oh." She nods and scratches her arm. The mud sticks to it in a clump, then falls off. An awkward silence descends until Chloe says brightly, "I got your messages. The stones? That was cool."

"Yeah, I got yours, too. Sorry, I couldn't…" My voice fades.

A cloud of uncertainty passes across Chloe's face, but it's gone just as fast. "Well, it's too hot up in the tree." She begins pulling off her clothes to reveal the light blue bathing suit she always wears. "You came here yesterday, huh? I saw tracks last night, and no one else bothers with this place." She tosses her T-shirt on top of her shorts and shoes in a lumpy little pile. "Want to cool off?"

Without waiting for a response, she runs straight into the pond and disappears under the black water. I climb onto the big log to watch. It *is* really hot, but my orange bathing suit is back at Judd's and I'm not going in with just my underclothes on. At least, not with anyone else around.

Chloe's head pops up way out in the middle, where it is deep enough that she has to tread water. She waves, then flips to her back like always, face to the sky. I take the opportunity to study her. She is a tiny thing, even smaller than me. Her features are not proportioned or smooth—her chin is pointy, her forehead short.

151

And her eyes are like an owl's, protruding and innocent, the color of wheat.

After floating for a few minutes, Chloe dog-paddles over to my log, heaves herself up and leans back on her elbows to dry in the sun. "That felt amazing." She grins. "It's been *so* hot." She shakes the water out of her hair and some lands on me. It feels good.

In the next awkward lull, I glance sideways at her, feeling like a complete moron. I barely remember how to speak to kids my age, it's been so long. Chloe doesn't seem to mind my silence, so I go with it. I learned long ago that keeping quiet is far better than saying something stupid that you can't take back.

"I'm going to miss this pond when school starts," Chloe says eventually, her eyes closed and her face tilted upward. "I like coming early in the morning, before the woods wake up. You know?"

"No, I...haven't come that early," I fumble.

"You should. It's so peaceful. But I'll have to settle for the weekends now because my cousin's driving me to school this year and he's one of those annoying people who has to be thirty minutes early for everything," she says with an eye roll.

I start fiddling in the mud again with my stick. I don't know what to write. Or say. Or think. She hasn't mentioned anything about seeing me at Walmart, so I don't mention it either. Maybe she's embarrassed.

Chloe shakes her hair out again. "I looked for you all summer. Thought I'd see you more after—"

"I was out of town," I explain, cutting her off.

"Oh. Well, I guess we're even now. We've both spied on each other."

"I didn't spy on you!" I protest, but Chloe just smiles.

"I'm not mad, *Andre*. I don't own the trees," she says with a laugh.

"Right." But I can't tell if she's laughing at me or she's just one of those giggly girls.

"Do you go to Belmont?"

Her question brings back images of the high school's website—the tan building, the sports fields, the corn stalks. When I lost Essex, Belmont seemed like the worst alternative. Now I will do anything to attend. "I will this year," I say with resolve. "I'm transferring there from Essex."

"Ooh, snazzy school." Her eyebrows wiggle, and then she says, "I'll be new at Belmont, too. It's my freshman year. Are you a sophomore?"

"Junior."

"Do you know anyone who goes there?"

"Not a soul," I respond and suddenly feel a little sick. I was nervous starting at Essex too, but last January when Gram's death scraped so raw against my heart and life with Ayla was so unpredictable, I didn't have the energy to stew on it. Back then, life was still happening in a sort of haze. Now everything seems razor-sharp.

"My cousin's giving me a tour of the school tomorrow. He says that way I won't be so overwhelmed next week."

"That's nice of him," I say mildly.

"He's the one you met...or sort of met, anyway." Yes. The rock-skipper who knows that life is not all fun and games. I remember.

"You could come, too. It'd be fun to check things out together. The last thing I need is to walk into the wrong classroom on day one. That would be just like me." She snorts. "So, you wanna come?"

My first instinct is to decline, to push away from this effervescent girl, but I'm tired of being alone and if I'm stuck in Haydon now—which it seems I am, since we have no money and no car—then maybe having an ally would be smart. Anyway, tomorrow is Tuesday and Judd won't need me for anything except making dinner.

"What time?" I ask.

"After lunch. I'll meet you here at noon, okay? Then we can walk to my house. It's not far," Chloe promises.

I hesitate. Then I nod slowly.

"Yay!" she squeals, delighted. She wraps her arms around my shoulders and squeezes. "You're my first high school friend!"

You're mine, too. I don't have the courage to say that aloud, but I need to give her something. So I offer half a smile, and judging by the happiness smattered across Chloe's face, it's enough.

Chapter 25

It is ridiculous how nervous I am, pacing the bank of the pond waiting for Chloe to show up. Worried that she won't. Afraid that she will.

I spot her skipping—yes, *skipping*—through the woods like some modern-day Little Red Riding Hood. Her hair is in two low pigtails, sprouting from the back of her head. The blond streaks glint in the sun. She has broken out overnight across her forehead, and I wonder if she's nervous, too.

"Hey, Andre!" she calls, practically knocking me down as she approaches. "Whoops, sorry." Chloe laughs and grips my arms to steady us both.

I resist the urge to pull away because even though it feels nice, I'm not used to all this touching. And giggling. And I wonder how I'm going to fit in with Chloe at school. She must have a slew of bubbly little friends who will take one look at surly old me and ask her what the hell she's thinking.

"Let's go," she says, pulling me by the hand. "Brick's waiting, and I swear he's the most impatient boy in the world."

I let her lead me. "Brick?"

"Yeah. Weird, I know. It's a Southern name," she explains as we walk through a section of the woods I have never explored. "He lives with us. It's kind of nice, but also kind of annoying. Mostly because he's three years older and thinks he can boss me around."

Having zero experience with siblings or extended family of any kind, I'm not sure what to say. Which doesn't even matter because Chloe changes the subject like lightning. "Do you have your schedule yet? If so, we can find all your classrooms."

Schedule? "No. When did they send yours?" I ask, wondering if mine was mailed to Judd's house over the summer. He would've trashed it anyway.

"About a week ago, via email."

"Oh," I say, relieved. "I haven't checked my email all summer."

"You can check it at my house before we leave," Chloe offers. "And print your schedule."

"I don't want to hold up your cousin," I say, but I *really* want to get my hands on that schedule.

Chloe smirks. "Brick will just have to learn some patience. Besides, good manners have been bred into him since infancy. He won't complain, at least not in front of you." She laughs.

"Okay," I say and take a breath. Somehow being with Chloe makes my whole world seem lighter.

Brick is leaning against his car with his arms crossed when

we emerge from the woods. He stands up straight when he spots us, and his frown turns into a smile. I'm suddenly glad I chose to wear simple shorts and a gray T-shirt today instead of my leather.

"So the girl in the tree *does* exist," he teases as we approach. I cringe, remembering that embarrassing fall and how I stumbled away like a crazy person afterward.

"Hi…again," I say, sounding stiff.

"It's a pleasure to meet you, Andrea," Brick drawls politely in his thick accent.

I finally get a good look at the guy. He's stocky, athletic-looking, not too tall. Except for his hair color, he doesn't resemble bird-like little Chloe one bit. I like how his soft brown eyes look directly into mine when he says hello, as if talking to me is actually important. But this also makes me nervous. People used to look at me all the time, but I've spent so many months trying to be invisible that I'm no longer used to such scrutiny. Chloe is right about his manners, though—when she explains that I need to print out my schedule, he acts like waiting doesn't bother him at all.

My new friend tugs me through her garage into a sprawling country house. We thump through a mudroom and enter a large kitchen, where a heavyset white-haired man is peering at the stove. "Dad, this is my new friend Andrea," Chloe says as the man glances up, surprised. He has red cheeks, kind eyes, and a smile he's not afraid to use. He reminds me of Santa Claus.

"Well, hello there," his voice booms and I half expect him to finish with a jolly little "ho, ho, ho."

"Nice to meet you, Mr., uh…." My voice trails as I realize

I don't know Chloe's last name.

"Pete Masterson," he supplies, enclosing my small outstretched hand in both of his. "Oy, sorry about that." He pulls his hands away and I realize mine is now covered in flour. Handing me a towel to wipe it off, he says excitedly, "Baking day. Want to try a plum raisin cookie?"

"Sure!" I respond because I never turn down free food, but Chloe drags me into the other room.

"We'll get it on the way back," she yells. Once out of his earshot, she whispers, "My dad's a farmer. He's great with food in the ground, but when it gets to the kitchen? Not so much." She shakes her head solemnly.

I laugh out loud, then gasp at the tickling sensation the laughter makes in my throat. It feels so foreign, but so nice. We cross a wide-open great room and attached foyer. The house is beautiful, but not in a fancy way. There's lots of wood and colorful pillows on overstuffed furniture. Everything has a cozy, country feel. It's the most homey I've felt since...home.

"Computer's in here," Chloe says as we enter an office with an L-shaped desk. I sit down at the keyboard and pull up my email. There are exactly two messages, both from the school. The first subject line reads WELCOME and the second CLASS SCHEDULE. Boy, a whole summer and that's all I got? I hope Chloe doesn't notice.

Because Brick's waiting, I don't even look at the schedule. I just hit PRINT and close the program. While Chloe grabs the papers from the printer tray, I am drawn to the bookshelves like a hummingbird to sweet nectar. I'm wondering whether she'd let me borrow a book when my attention is swiftly diverted. Propped in front of a tattered volume of *War and Peace* is a photo of Santa/ Mr. Masterson with his arm around a woman who is a carbon copy of Chloe, about thirty years older. "Wow, you look just like your mom," I say, peering at the photo.

Chloe looks up. "That's my Aunt Stacey, actually. Brick's mom. My dad's sister." Her voice sounds different, not so chirpy, but when I look back at her she's shuffling out of the office, my schedule in her hand. I follow on her heels, without the book, but graciously accept a warm, lumpy cookie from her father on our way out.

"Thanks, Mr. Masterson," I call as I'm pulled toward the garage. "It looks delicious!"

"Hope to see you again soon, Andrea," Santa responds.

I lift the cookie up to my nose. It smells heavenly. I hope Brick won't mind me munching in his car because I am *not* giving it up.

"All right, this is the quad," Brick explains as we circle the parking lot in his green Ford Explorer. My eyes follow his outstretched finger to a large grassy area bordered on three sides by a squat tan building. "See the section in the far right corner, where the trees are thickest?"

"Yeah?" Chloe leanis forward to get a better look.

"Stay away from it." Brick's voice is firm.

"Why?"

"That's where all the burnouts hang. Low-life druggies," Brick explains in what I assume Chloe would call his bossy voice. "Those losers will harass anyone in range."

My cheeks feel warm and I'm grateful to be in the backseat. The embarrassment irritates me. I've never taken drugs in my life— at least not knowingly—but I'm too close to all that stuff with Judd and Ayla. Sometimes I feel like one of them.

Pursing her lips, Chloe demands, "Is *that* why you wanted to give me this tour? To warn me about all the bad influences lurking around?"

Brick grins and drawls, "Yeah, partly." He pulls into a spot in the near-empty lot and shoves his gearshift into park. "What does your schedule look like?" While Chloe shows it to him, I unfold my own printout and glance down the list. AP U.S. History, Honors English III, Advanced Trigonometry, AP Chemistry, French Composition, Gym, and an elective, Musical Masters.

"Musical Masters," I mutter out loud. "What the heck is that?"

Brick and Chloe stare back at me through the hole between the front seats. "Why'd you pick that elective?" Brick asks with disdain.

"I didn't. They must have assigned me to it, since I'm transferring."

"So *that's* how they fill it." At my sudden look of concern, Brick backtracks. "It's not so awful, Andrea. You're supposed to learn about all the great musicians, from Mozart to Dylan, but the teacher just geeks out and plays music the whole time. A lot of people use it as a study hall. What else do you have?"

I hand him my paper and lean back against the seat, disgruntled. What kind of school is this, with junkies loitering the lawn and teachers who don't teach? God, I wish I was back at Essex.

"Whoa." Brick is staring at my paper. "Honors English. AP Chem?" He laughs. "I think you're even in Advanced Trig with me. That's a senior-level class." He hands me back the paper. "Impressive."

"She used to go to Essex," Chloe offers.

"Oh yeah?" Brick looks at me with interest, like I'm supposed to start quoting Shakespeare or something. Then he teases his cousin, "Maybe you can learn something from your new friend, Chlo."

Chloe whips her head toward him. "Lay off, Brick. School hasn't even started." This is the first time I've heard Chloe sound anything close to angry. Obviously academics are a sore spot with her.

"Yeah, but I'm the one who's going to hear about it from Aunt Lil if you start falling behind again," Brick fires back.

I hold my breath. The tension is so thick, it's like they forgot I'm in the car.

Just as I'm about to break the silence and ask for that tour, Chloe says, "I'm going to walk around." She opens her door and heads toward the building. Brick closes his eyes, obviously regretting his words.

I jump out of the SUV and jog after Chloe, falling into step beside her. She opens her mouth, and I'm seriously expecting her to start bitching about Brick, but instead she blurts, "Eighth grade was tough, and I don't mean the schoolwork. Bad grades were just a byproduct of an all-around bad year." She shoots me a quick glance. "I should probably tell you—I'm kind of a social leper. You might not want to be my friend once school starts."

It's amazing to me that someone so fun-loving could be any kind of outcast. We walk on, side by side. I take a deep breath, and decide to open the door just a crack, "Well. I'm kind of a social leper, too. So I guess we're even again."

Chloe looks at me and smiles. *Really* smiles. I almost smile back.

"I see what you mean about Brick being bossy," I add after a minute, hoping she won't take offense.

She snorts. "Ya think? But he means well. He just tries too hard. He feels like he owes my parents for taking him in, which is so stupid. We're family." She shrugs. "Anyway, he's fairly popular here, so that may help us fit in. The girls drool over his accent, and all the guys think he's cool. He's pretty picky, though."

"About the girls or the guys?"

"About everything."

We have reached the main entrance and somehow Brick beat us here. He must have sprinted. He opens the door and holds it for us both, but once we're inside I pretend to be fascinated with the bulletin board on the wall, and let the two of them walk ahead.

Brick mumbles to Chloe, "Sorry I gave you a hard time. I know you'll do well this year."

"It's okay." She tosses him a forgiving smile.

He pulls her into a playful headlock and she laughs, shoving her elbow against his ribs. Chloe may not have friends, I think, watching them walk down the hall together, but at least she has Brick.

The rest of the tour goes smoothly, and I find myself enjoying being with people my own age. I find myself not wanting the afternoon to end, not wanting to leave their world. But I have to be home before dusk to serve Judd his evening meal, so I decline their invitation to dinner. Chloe jokes that I'm probably better off because her mom's working late and who knows what experimental delicacy her dad will concoct. Brick offers to drop me at my house, but I casually say, "No thanks, I'll just walk home from your place."

Before I leave, Chloe orders me to meet her at the pond tomorrow, like there is no question about us being best buds from here on out. Then she hugs me tightly, leaving me breathless, and I am reminded of everything, everything I've been missing.

"School fees are fifty dollars," I tell Judd quietly on Sunday morning. I figure acting meek is the best approach.

"You don't need school," Judd retorts, sipping his coffee. "You need to start workin' off your debt, girl. Thought I made that clear."

"If I don't go to school, how am I supposed to support myself when my two years are up?" I ask desperately.

"Not my problem."

I look away, distraught. I know that arguing with Judd will bring trouble, but school is the one thing I won't give up. I will fight to the death on this one.

Before I can figure out how to explain this in a way that won't result in my head getting bashed in, Ayla saunters into the kitchen wearing a long silky nightgown. "Give her the money, Judd," she says flatly.

Judd slams his coffee cup down and looks at Ayla like she must have a death wish. I look at her the same way. Is she actually sticking up for me?

Ayla pours herself some coffee. "It's the only way I can prove she's with me, taken care of. They look at the school records before they send my checks," she explains. "My mother set it up that way. She has to be attending regularly."

My heart deflates. Of course it's about the money. Any connection I thought we'd made on the road is…roadkill. But when Judd agrees to let me go to Belmont without any more fuss, I shrug off my disappointment in Ayla. Who cares why they're doing it, as long as I get what I need?

Five ten-dollar bills are laid out flat on the table next to the paper Judd uses to keep track of my debt. I swallow hard and force myself to speak again, despite Judd's scowl. "I won't be able to carry all my books. I need a backpack."

Judd storms over to the pantry. A moment later, he slaps a black plastic garbage bag on the tabletop in front of me. "There's your backpack."

Jaw clenched, I take the bag and the money and jam them into my shorts pocket. I stand up to make my breakfast, but Judd halts me by gripping my neck.

"Your new total's seven fifty. Figure out how to come up with it yet?"

"I'm working on it," I lie.

"Tick tock," he whispers, lips close to my ear. His hot breath repulses me, and my body reacts by wrenching away from him. Judd's grasp keeps me in place, though, his fingers squeezing tighter until I stop resisting. Then he glances around and says, "The goddamn house is filthy. Needs to be cleaned, top to bottom."

"Fine," I mutter, gritting my teeth.

"*Before* you eat," he snarls. I close my eyes. That means I may not get a bite until dinnertime.

As I pull out the cleaning supplies from beneath the sink, I realize why Judd's in such a foul mood. Even though he's got Ayla back on her pills, he hasn't been nearly as generous as he was before we left town, so she's grouchy from the time one buzz starts to wear off until she gets her next dose. It's a chain reaction of meanness— withdrawal to Ayla, Ayla to Judd, Judd to me.

I shouldn't have asked him for that fifty dollars, should have just clicked the link for financial support on Belmont High's website. But I was worried that someone from school would need to meet with Ayla about it. I can't trust her to be sober long enough to have a normal conversation with a school official.

Having no good options, I chose Judd. And now, as always, I'm paying for it.

But at least I'm going to school next week. At least there's that.

Chapter 26

The woods look different in the dark—producing longer shadows and distorted shapes. They sound different, too. Each twig breaking, each tweet of a bird, each rustling leaf echoes in my ears. A year ago this trek would have spooked me. Now I have bigger things to be afraid of than the coo of a mourning dove.

I don't let the darkness slow me down because it takes fifteen minutes of brisk hiking to reach the pond. The first rays of sunlight are poking over the horizon when I scramble up the hickory tree and join Chloe on a thick brown branch. I settle in next to her and we wordlessly watch the sky transform from the darkest indigo to the color of salmon before it settles into a pale shade of blue.

Chloe opens a satchel that's hooked around her neck, pulls out two small baggies, and hands one to me. Inside is an assortment of nuts, berries, granola, and M&Ms.

"I brought something too." I pull out a peanut butter-and-honey sandwich and give her half.

"Ooh," she squeals. "My mom made these for me when I was little."

"So did my Gram," I say without thinking twice.

We listen to the woods come alive as we munch our breakfast. A feeling of contentment sweeps over me. For once, I refuse to worry it away.

"Last day of summer vacation," Chloe murmurs and leans against the tree trunk.

I think about all that happened this summer and sigh heavily. Despite my efforts, I ended up back where I started. Well, not exactly. I have Chloe now, and that's a huge improvement.

After a moment, Chloe says, "Brick said you could ride to school with us if you wanted. We can pick you up."

The idea of Brick pulling into Judd's driveway and tapping his horn for me sends my heart racing. No way will I let Judd anywhere near my new friends. He would find some way to use them against me.

"Well," I say slowly, stalling. "A ride would be great, but I'll just meet you at your house each morning."

Chloe shoots me a strange look. "Okay, if you want to walk that far. You'd better be on time, though," she says, giggling. "Now that he knows you better, his manners won't be so impeccable."

I nod, feeling warm and fuzzy at the idea of Brick knowing me better.

But he doesn't know me, not really. And neither does Chloe—even though I've spent every free moment with her this week. For all the prattling she does, Chloe doesn't ask dangerous questions. Brick asked a few, but I dodged them. When he pressed me, I pulled out my tough-girl look and that stopped him easily enough. Now he sticks to lighter topics.

It's so weird. The hours I've spent lounging in Chloe's canary yellow bedroom or tasting her dad's odd recipes in the big country kitchen exist in stark contrast to my depraved reality with Judd and Ayla down the road. I've played my role with Judd perfectly, though, working late nights in the cellar and acting extra grateful for every bite of food just so I can keep my small freedoms. I'm living a double life—and I'm not even sure which one is the sham. But I'm determined to make it all last. Maybe, if I'm careful, I can make it last until I finish high school and get released from my contract with Judd. One day at a time.

"To a new year," Chloe says, raising an orange M&M in the air for a toast.

I tap her M&M with a blue one of my own. "To new beginnings."

Instead of knocking on the Mastersons' door, I sit down on one of the steps leading from their driveway to the side entrance. These steps are long and shallow so my knees almost touch my chin, making me feel like a little girl on a big couch. I arrived early, and now I'm seriously questioning my choice of clothing. I yank down the edges of my gray T-shirt and tug at the top of my black combat boots. They stick out from under my bohemian skirt like a soldier in camouflage.

The door opens and a cheerful voice floats through the dewy air, "What're you doing out here all alone, Andrea? Come on in. The kids are finishing breakfast."

I twist around and look up into Pete Masterson's twinkling eyes, peeking out beneath bushy white brows. He's impossible to refuse, so I stand up, duck under his arm, and follow the voices into the kitchen. Brick, Chloe, and her mom are all seated at the table prodding their forks at what looks like scrambled eggs mixed with...kale?

"Help yourself." Mr. Masterson gestures to the table.

"Yes," Brick says wryly, pushing back his chair. "Please help us out, Andrea, and eat as much as you can stomach." Before he walks away, I see that his plate is still full of the green stuff. I suppress a smile.

Mr. Masterson waves him off. "Oh, don't listen to him. He's too used to fried chicken and pork sausage. His mother ruined him with all that down-home southern cooking."

I grin, but Brick keeps walking, deadpan. I watch his back disappear into the great room. When I return my gaze to the table, the atmosphere has changed. Chloe stares fixedly at her plate and her dad shakes his head, his smile erased. My eyebrows crease in confusion. That's when Chloe's mom, Lillian, perks up. "So, Andrea, are you all ready for your first day?"

"I think so. I'm just glad I don't have to walk in alone." I glance at Chloe.

"Me, too." She stands up and carries her plate over to the sink. Then she snatches her bag and calls over her shoulder, "Tell

Brick we'll be in the car!"

Before we can slip away, Mrs. Masterson rushes over and gives Chloe a tight hug and a kiss on the forehead. Chloe shrugs off her mother's affections, but I watch it all closely while an ache of longing riddles through my body. "Make it a great day, you two," she says as we leave.

Chloe seems subdued as we walk to Brick's Explorer. "We have the same lunch, right?" I ask, even though I know we do. I'm just trying to bring Chloe back from wherever she went because it doesn't look like a happy place. It bothers me—Chloe and sadness don't seem right together.

"Yeah. Let's meet outside the cafeteria so we can walk in together."

"Okay. I'll be coming from trig, right down the hall," I tell her. "With Brick?"

"Um, yeah," I say, but I doubt Brick will sit with us. He's a senior, after all, and apparently Mr. Popular. I hope Chloe doesn't get upset when he chooses to hang with kids in his own grade. I'll just have to distract her again.

We climb into the car and I lean over the front seat. "Are you nervous?"

She turns sideways to face me. "No. Yes. I don't know. What to expect, I mean. I was ostracized for most of last year."

I'm about to ask what exactly made her so unpopular when Brick opens the driver's side door and slides in. He seems pensive as well, and I'm totally confused. *I'm* supposed to be the moody one in this trio.

About halfway to school, Brick snaps out of it and slaps his hand down on the seat. "First day of high school, Chlo. It's a big deal," he says cheerfully.

"Yep." Her voice is significantly less cheerful.

"Hey, don't be nervous. Just be yourself. Trust me, it's not like junior high. And if any of those kids from last year bother you, they'll answer to me."

Chloe doesn't reply, but I think it's sweet of Brick to try and pump up his cousin like that. I don't expect him to turn the charm on me, though. "You'll do fine, too, Andrea. I was new last year, and everyone was real friendly."

That's because you've got that cute Southern accent, I think.

"Just watch out for the football players," he warns. "Some of them like to make bets on who'll snag the new girls first."

"I'll keep that in mind," I say, but what I think is, *No one will be betting on me.*

And of course, I'm right. As soon as I'm away from Chloe and Brick, I make my eyes cool and aloof, my gait purposeful and disinterested. Body language is a powerful tool. Nobody bothers me for long. Anytime one of the arrogant guys struts toward me, I fix him with a glare that could turn blood to ice. And if that doesn't work, I slip out my middle finger. They all turn away, either in surprise or anger. One guy whispers, "bitch" under his breath.

It's not until trigonometry, when Brick plops into the desk next to mine, that my eyes soften. "How's it going so far?" he wants to know.

"Good. But you don't have to look out for me. I'm not

your cousin," I say, letting him off the hook.

Brick gives me a strange look and says, "No, but you're my friend."

His *friend*. The word throws me. I mean, really throws me, since it's coming straight from his mouth and not from my imagination, and because Chloe told me Brick was picky about people. It throws me so much that I miss the first few minutes of what our teacher is saying. I look stupid when she stops at my desk to ask me a question and I have to stammer, "Uh, sorry, I was lost for a minute. Can you repeat the question?"

"Your *name,* dear?" Ms. Sampson enunciates carefully, and the room ripples with laughter.

Flustered, I mumble, "Andrea. Hathaway."

She looks down at her clipboard. "Ah, yes. Says here you're a junior. And new to Belmont."

"Yeah. I went to Essex last year."

She nods. "Well, I'll have to ensure that you find our curriculum every bit as challenging as what you're used to."

"Great," I say with all sincerity. "I'm counting on it."

I don't realize how pompous I sound until I see the open mouths of the students around me. Someone on my right stage-whispers, "Suck up."

Ms. Sampson chooses to ignore it. "Nice to see a student with some gusto on day one," she says with a smile. "But try not to get lost again, Miss Hathaway. Trig can be tricky."

I nod, then glance at Brick. His mouth is pinched closed, but if eyes could laugh, his would be rolling on the floor. I blow out a deep, humiliated breath and flip open my book.

Trigonometry *is* tricky. And I do have to pay attention because Ms. Sampson teaches at lightning speed. I'm dizzy by the time class ends and, judging by the frazzled faces around me, so are the other kids. As the bell rings, Ms. Sampson writes our homework assignment on the board—pages 4-10, odd numbers. There are many grumbles about so much homework on the first day of school, but I don't mind.

As Brick and I pack up, Ms. Sampson says to the most vocal whiner, "Mr. Barnes, if you would like something to complain about, I'd be happy to assign you the odd *and* even numbers tonight." The guy's face turns as red as his hair as he mumbles that that won't be necessary. The rest of the class falls silent.

Once we're in the hallway and out of earshot, Brick groans and says, "Sampson's gonna be so tough."

"What's her deal?" I ask.

"She figures if you're in this class, you'd better be ready to do college-level work."

"Perfect," I say and mean it. Brick shoots me an amused glance. He's never seen this hardcore side of me.

"Oh, and I've heard she hates it when students are late," he warns. "So be careful."

"I'm never late," I assure him.

"Knew there was a reason I liked you," Brick says.

We walk briskly toward the cafeteria, where Chloe is waiting. "She looks happy," Brick whispers.

"Chloe!" I call out. Her face lights up at the sight of us,

and she half-skips over. I decide I'm going to have to talk to her about all this skipping.

"Hey guys, how's everything going?" Before we can answer, she gushes. "I can't believe I'm in high school! You're right, Brick. It's so much better than junior high. I mean, even the classes seem more interesting. Also, score! My homeroom teacher, Mr. Cavanaugh, is super cute."

"Try to keep your priorities straight," Brick chides light-heartedly and bumps Chloe's elbow.

"I totally am." She elbows him back. "Hot teachers, new friends, and much better food options," she says with a sniff and a dreamy glance over at the deli counter.

"Beats kale, at least," Brick mumbles.

As we maneuver through the cafeteria, several people slap Brick a high five or call hello to him. He introduces me and Chloe to a couple of his friends, and I realize that I might have to tone down my attitude. I don't want to mess things up for Brick by association. Or for Chloe.

"So how was your morning?" Chloe asks as we find an empty table. To my surprise, Brick sits down next to me and across from Chloe as if he's planning to stay.

"Well, I don't know about the rest of her classes, but Andrea made quite an impression in trig," Brick teases.

Ignoring him, I pull out my bagged lunch and start setting out my food.

Chloe's eyes flash from me to Brick and back again. "What do you mean? Because she's so smart? You probably blew everyone out of the water, huh?"

"Something like that," I respond coolly while Brick shakes his head and smothers a grin. "Chloe, do you want some pretzels?" I ask, changing the subject.

"No, thanks," she says. "I'm buying today. I'll be right back." She jumps up and makes a beeline for the salad bar.

"She's going to be disappointed. The food's not that great," says Brick. "Thank God she's having a good day, though." As he pulls a sandwich and thermos out of his backpack, his eyes follow Chloe protectively. I can't help feeling protective as well. She looks like a baby kangaroo hopping from one spot to another, all smiles.

"What happened with her last year? She never said," I ask Brick, my eyes still trailing my friend.

"Typical mean-girl stuff. She was at a slumber party and got blamed for talking trash about someone. Chloe said she wasn't even in the room when it all started flying around—which is probably why they pinned it on her. Anyway, the rumors went viral and the victim set out to make Chloe's life hell," he explains ruefully. "I guess it got pretty nasty."

A vision of that blonde girl from Walmart pops into my head. Now I'm even happier that I doused her purse with Sprite.

"Didn't Chloe tell anyone what was happening?" I ask. She and Brick seem so close.

He frowns. "She didn't want to burden us. It was my first year here and everyone was focused on me and my transition. Her folks and I heard bits and pieces, but we didn't know how bad it was until her grades tanked." Brick takes a huge bite of sandwich

175

and looks away, and I get the hint that he's done talking about it.

"Junior high sucks," is all I say.

It's not all I feel, though. I keep picturing sweet little Chloe, who wouldn't kill a moth, hiding in the school bathrooms, waiting until the halls emptied out before wiping her tears and heading home. I imagine her trying to appear normal in front of her family after being tormented by her classmates day after day. I'm not nearly as fragile as Chloe, but even I feel overwhelmed by my situation sometimes. Like Charlie hijacking my first kiss. Or being forced to deal with low-life druggies on a daily basis. Or owing Judd hundreds of dollars for no reason. The injustice of it all is maddening. How can there be pure souls like Chloe sharing space in this world with despicable human beings like Judd? It's not right.

By the time the three of us depart for our next round of classes, my insides are simmering so hot it feels like my organs are on fire. Musical Masters and gym are a shared block, alternating days of the week. Today I have gym. It's my last class, and we're playing dodge ball. Which is perfect, because I totally feel like throwing something.

Chapter 27

Brick is right about Ms. Sampson, except that calling her "tough" is like calling a killer shark "moody." She doesn't explain the classroom rules (they're available on her website), she adores pop quizzes, and she appears to enjoy making our heads spin. After Ms. Sampson's second-day speech about how only the top four students will receive an A—a fact she seems proud of—I vow to ace every homework assignment, quiz, and test. I *will* be in that top four. Because the first step to getting a full ride to the Ivy League is having straight A's, no matter what high school I attend.

The rest of my classes are pretty much a cake-walk, but teachers at Belmont give more busywork than they did at Essex, and it cuts deeply into my already scant free time. Still, I spend every unscheduled moment hanging out with my new friends since I know that ride could end any minute.

They're an interesting pair. Where Chloe is an open book, Brick is one big contradiction. He enjoys a healthy social life with his classmates, but I can tell he keeps some distance, both physically and emotionally. He rotates his way around the lunch room each week, sometimes eating with me and Chloe, other days sitting with random groups of seniors. Never the same ones twice. I wonder why he's like that, so noncommittal, when any one of those cliques would happily claim him. But I know better than to ask personal questions.

Chloe is nice to everyone, so it seems like she already has a hundred new friends—or at least acquaintances—but for some reason she prefers my company. Maybe she's still wary after what happened last year, although those mean girls seem to have dropped their crusade. Selfishly, I'm glad Chloe likes hanging out with me best. All in all, life at Belmont isn't so dreadful.

Life at Judd's is a different story.

His demands are increasing and his patience is close to extinct. He doesn't tell me this, but I'm pretty sure Judd is expanding his business. The Saturday deliveries take longer than ever, and we often return home midday to reload supplies. I do what I'm told, always afraid he'll take school away from me again, despite what Ayla says about the inheritance checks being tied to my enrollment.

One moonless night in September, I wake to find Judd standing over my bed. It's chilling to open my eyelids and see his gristly face looming, knowing he entered my room and I didn't even hear him. Instinctively, I open my mouth to scream. Before I can draw a full breath, his tobacco-laced fingers are on top of my lips and he's hissing, "Shut up or I'll knock your teeth up your nose."

I shut up.

When he removes his hand, I pull the covers up to my chin, even though I've never really been afraid of Judd in that way. He instructs me to get up, dress in black clothing, and meet him downstairs. That night, we make three trips from the cellar to the shed in the cover of darkness, carrying the canisters silently through the woods. They are cumbersome and heavy with their toppings of rock salt, and Judd warns me not to spill any. All the muscles in my arms quiver, but I don't drop a thing. It's not until I collapse back into bed a few hours past midnight that I think about the date. September 15. My birthday.

After school that day, I find Judd's cellar filled with a large shipment of new goods—clothing, small appliances, children's toys—indicating an increase in distribution. Boxes are stacked high against the walls. Even though it's a Wednesday, I'm put directly to work. For three evenings straight, I rip the lining out of bomber jackets, stuff the drug-filled baggies inside, then sew them up. It's not easy to sew through leather with a needle, and my fingertips are soon red and raw. My eyes start to match them because I'm up until dawn finishing my homework.

The moral implications of what I'm doing with Judd continue to creep in. How many people, how many teenagers at some out-of-hand party, will become addicted like Ayla? How many lives are we ruining?

To complicate matters, Ayla is acting like my new best friend. She curls up on the couch while I'm studying and plays with my hair, tries to persuade me to sneak a little off the top of

Judd's canisters. As if I would risk my own life for her nasty habit! If I were going to steal cocaine from Judd, I would sell it on the side to pay back my debt—not slip it to Ayla. Still, I accept her soft, motherly touches for what they're worth.

There is only so much of me to go around. Soon Chloe questions why I can't hang out, why I spend so many lunch periods in the library. I explain that I'm swamped with schoolwork and leave it at that. Brick offers to do some of my trig problems, but I'd never let him. I'm going to escape from Haydon, from Judd and the whole hellishness of my adolescence, on *my* terms. On my own. I refuse to owe anyone anything.

Brick seems to understand this—and my evasiveness— better than Chloe, who acts hurt when I brush her off. But I always save Sundays for her. On Sunday, Judd is too tired to care about work, and too busy enjoying his profits to terrorize me.

So it has become a ritual for Chloe and I to meet at the pond and watch the sun begin its day. She never brings Brick to our sunrise meetings, but sometimes we go back to her house later and cajole him into spending the afternoon with us. He refuses to swim in the pond—says the water looks foul—so we ambush him, try to drag him in. Of course, we're no match for his strength. In the end, Chloe and I jump back in while Brick stays dry, skipping rocks. Sometimes we get pizza or see a movie. When I explain that I can't pay, Brick shoves me in jest and says he wouldn't let me anyway. He's a Southern gentleman, after all.

One Sunday I walk into Judd's living room after a blissful day with my friends to find Ayla stretched across the floor, moaning in ecstasy and staring at the ceiling like some hottie is up there performing a striptease. Judd must have given her a topper.

As I step over her twiggy form, Judd says, "Get over here, Bones. I got somethin' for you." He's holding a box. Full of surprises today.

Inside is a cell phone that's meant to dial one number only—his. "Keep it on at all times," he says gruffly. "Whenever I text, call me back within two minutes, or else."

I look at the little black phone with loathing and ask, "Or else *what*?"

His answer is a hard smack to my head. "That, times ten."

I hate this new phone. My two lives are now intersecting. On Thursday, as I'm heading to trig, I feel the vibration in my pocket so I duck into the girls' bathroom and dial Judd's number.

"Not fast enough," he growls.

I sigh. He's been testing me randomly over the past week and I seem to be failing.

"What do you want?" I ask impatiently. I can't be late.

"I want you to do as you're told, and call me back within two goddamn minutes!"

"I did! I just got the text."

"Don't argue with me, girl." His tone shuts me up.

After an agonizingly long pause, Judd says, "Need you here after school today. Don't forget."

I want to snip, *Do I ever?* But that would probably constitute arguing. So I simply say, "I won't."

After hanging up, I sprint down the hall and walk into trig just as the bell stops ringing. I think I'm in the clear until Ms. Sampson strides over and hands me a slip of yellow paper.

"What's this?" I ask, shocked.

"Students must be seated in my class before the bell rings, Miss Hathaway," she says curtly.

I take the paper from her, crumpling it up as I plunk into my chair. I don't even care how she reacts. I'm never late and I'm one of her best students—that should count for something.

"Hey, cool it," Brick warns quietly. "You'll make it worse."

I whip my head around angrily, but the sincere look of concern on his face melts the fight out of me. He's only trying to help. "You're right. I just can't do detention today. I have to work."

"Work? Where do you—?"

His words fizzle as Ms. Sampson strides down the aisle toward us and slaps a detention slip onto his desk. "Awfully chatty, Mr. Mason. You can join Miss Hathaway after school."

"Yes, ma'am," he mumbles and leans back in his seat.

While class resumes, I un-crumple my paper and write a note on the back, *Sorry I got u in trouble. But…Brick MASON? Didn't know your last name. Funny.*

When he reads it, he snickers softly and sneaks a look at me. Encouraged, I write, *Do you come from a long line of stoneworkers or something?*

Brick smiles at my joke, but a faraway look has crept into his eyes.

Just kidding! I scribble, feeling terrible. *It's a nice name.*

Perfect for a Southern boy.

On his own detention slip, he scrawls, *It's OK. It is a funny name. Not upset with you.*

But I don't believe him. Maybe no one else would see it, but I'm better than most at reading facial expressions—a survival skill. Then I remember that I don't know anything about his parents or why he's living with his aunt and uncle, and feel like an idiot. I never should have mentioned his family.

"Are you okay?" I whisper, abandoning the notes.

"Yeah. Perfectly fine," he whispers back, but he's a terrible liar. Still, I won't press him. I know the signs for "back off." I invented half of them.

I turn toward the front of the room, but it's too late. Ms. Sampson is already standing between our desks. "Since the two of you have no interest in class today, you may now take your conversation to the principal's office." She dismisses us with a flick of her wrist.

Ever the gentleman, Brick apologizes to Ms. Sampson as we pack up and shuffle out of the room. In a state of shock, I follow Brick's shoes down the hall. I've never been kicked out of class. I've certainly never been sent to the principal's office for being disruptive! I *have* seen the kids that frequent the office, though, slouching so low in their chairs they might as well be sitting on the ground. I wonder what happens once they go through the door. Can a principal dock your grade for bad behavior?

Noticing that I've fallen behind, Brick makes his way back to me. "Relax, Andrea. Everything will be fine." I look at him skeptically. "*Unless* we take too long getting there," he says and links his arm through mine, pulling me along.

I must still look dubious because he smiles. "I didn't think anything ruffled your feathers."

"It doesn't," I retort, yanking my arm free and walking faster. Brick laughs softly behind me.

It's the assistant principal who takes care of discipline problems, but that doesn't make this any less terrifying. At least we are called in together. That helps. It also helps that Mr. Greeley seems nice and apparently knows Brick.

"Okay, what happened?" he asks, reclining in his chair.

"We were just talking for a minute," Brick explains. "Ms. Sampson didn't even give us a warning."

Mr. Greeley chuckles a little and says, "No, I bet she didn't." Then he turns to me. "Andrea. How are things going for you here at Belmont? Everything okay?"

"Yes. Everything's fine. I'm sorry about this. It won't happen again."

"Oh, I'm not worried," he says, frowning. "New school, new rules…it's not an easy transition. Eh, Brick?"

"No, sir," Brick agrees sheepishly.

Mr. Greeley turns to me again. "When I pulled your file, I noticed that we don't have a phone number on record for you. Your mother must have missed that line on the registration form," he says, peering at his computer screen.

Phone number? Is he planning to call? Ayla won't answer. But Judd might, and then what? He might not care at all, or he might be furious that I brought attention to myself. He might forbid me from going to school, despite what Ayla said about my enrollment being a condition of Gram's trust. Or he might decide that I need some discipline. *His* variety.

"No, it's not a mistake," I explain, flustered by this whole day. "We don't have a phone."

Both Brick and the assistant principal stare at me as though I've sprouted a third ear. "No phone at all? Are you pulling my leg?" Mr. Greeley asks.

"No, sir. It's…a religious thing. My mother doesn't believe in technology, really. She's very different," I say with just the proper balance of tolerance and irritation.

Mr. Greeley raises an eyebrow. "Huh. Well, since you two aren't exactly troublemakers, I'll let you off with a warning. Just don't let me see you in here again."

Brick and I take our time going back to class, since neither of us is in any hurry to deal with Ms. Sampson. We sit down in the hall to kill a few minutes. "No phone?" Brick nudges me. "Can't believe he let you off after that lie."

"He believed me," I insist, but Brick just laughs.

"He did *not* believe you, Andrea. I know Mr. Greeley—he and my uncle grew up together. They play golf and poker on the weekends. Ten bucks says the two of them are laughing about this by nightfall."

"Shut up," I tell him, worry gnawing me.

"Mr. Greeley's not stupid. He acts cool with us kids, but he's got his shit together. Trust me." Brick is still laughing, but I feel sick. Could I have made things worse?

"He wouldn't, like, show up at my house or anything, would he?" I ask.

The nervous note in my voice stops Brick's laughter. "Not for talking in class."

"Are you sure?" My eyes burn. I blink several times. "I mean, if he thinks I lied, he might…"

Brick's face sobers, and I realize I'm freaking out, giving away too much. "Andrea," Brick says, his sure brown eyes staring right into my pale blue ones. "He won't go to your house. He's got kids dealing drugs at lunchtime. He's got bigger things to worry about."

"Okay." I shudder in a breath and try to compose myself. "I'm just not used to this. I've never been in trouble before."

"Yeah? You lied pretty smoothly in there." Brick's voice holds the hint of a challenge.

"Not smoothly enough, apparently." I jump to my feet. "We'd better go back to class."

I don't wait for Brick because I don't like the suspicious look in his eye. All afternoon I curse myself for acting so scared in front of him. The last thing I want is to give up my friends. But if they get too curious, that's exactly what I'll have to do.

Chapter 28

"Wasn't sure you'd show," Brick drawls as he sits down next to me in the back row of after-school detention. "Thought you had to be somewhere."

"I do," I mumble. "I'm going be late." I dread facing Judd, who expects me home right after school. I'd fretted about my situation all afternoon, finding myself once again with no good options. In the end, I decided that missing detention could cause more problems than just being late to meet Judd. Either way, I'd have to face his wrath. At least this way I won't have the school administration tracking down Ayla on top of it.

Detention lasts an hour and I watch the minute hand slowly tick its way around the clock, my stomach in knots. When it's over, Brick offers me a granola bar as we walk out to the parking lot, and I accept it gratefully because I doubt I'm getting dinner tonight. He insists on driving me home, but I ask him to drop me at the market instead.

"Is this where you work?" he asks, idling his SUV outside the door.

"No, I'm meeting my boss here. We have to make some deliveries."

"Should I wait to make sure he's—"

"No. Thanks for the ride." I hop out of the car and rush inside before Brick can ask anything else. I wait until he drives away, then I dart back outside and start jogging down the road. I look at Gram's watch as I run. I'm almost two hours late.

Judd is waiting.

I've barely stepped inside when his voice bellows from the kitchen, "*Shut* the goddamn door and *get* your ass in here!"

He's leaning against the counter when I slink in. His eyes are red slits and he holds a whiskey bottle in one hand. His knuckles look pink from gripping it so hard.

"Guess I've been too easy on you, lettin' you run off all the time. Now you think showing up to work is *optional?*"

"I got hung up," I murmur. "I'll work extra to make up for it."

"There's no goddamn *extra* work to do. I needed you here for somethin' specific. Now you fucking cost me more money!"

Fed up with his baloney debt, with his mandates and his menacing, I glare at Judd with all the hatred I have suppressed over the months and yell back through gritted teeth, "So add it to my tab, asshole!"

I barely have time to recognize the danger I'm in before he

hauls back and pitches something at me. Luckily, my reflexes are quick and I duck instinctively. The whiskey bottle whistles past my left ear and shatters against the wall.

I screamed at some point, but now I'm speechless. He threw that bottle with all of his strength and if I hadn't ducked just right... The realization turns me cold. He really *doesn't* care if he kills me.

When I look at Judd, his lip curls. "What're you waiting for? Clean it up."

I pull the wastebasket out from under the sink, grab the hand broom and dustpan. The glass is everywhere, crunching beneath my shoes. My hair falls into my eyes as I survey the mess, trying to figure out where to start. I go for the biggest pieces first, bending over to pick them up and drop them into the garbage can. Judd circles me, watching. I keep turning my body toward him so he can't launch a surprise attack. Squatting down, I brush the tiny shards of glass into the dustpan, working frantically.

"Where were you?" he barks as he paces. "Off with some boy? Gettin' busy in the back of his Explorer?"

Shit. How does he know about Brick? I remain silent and continue to sweep up the glass, assuming his questions are rhetorical. Until I realize my mistake.

"I asked you a question. *Answers* aren't optional either!" He plants his boots, bends his knees, and lunges at me so fast, I yelp. It is nothing but a fake-out, meant to scare me. And it works. I recoil and lose my balance. I manage to catch myself before sprawling face-first onto the glittering floor, but my palms press into the tiny pieces of glass and it hurts. It really, *really* hurts.

While I crouch there in agony, Judd continues, "Yeah, I'll bet you and lover boy got 'hung up.' Didn't realize you were a slut, too, Bones. Just like your mama," Judd sneers.

My long hair hides my face, but it doesn't mask the thin lines of blood trickling out from under my hands. Tears are coming and I'm not going to be able to stop them, so I turn everything—my pain, anger, fear—into venom. I look straight up at Judd and hiss, "If my mama's a slut, know what that makes you? An ugly little troll who can't keep her satisfied."

It happens so fast. I barely feel being lifted into the air and thrown across the room. I do feel the thud of my body hitting the wall, and his hands on my neck as he shoves me to the cellar, and then his steel-tipped boot cracking against my backside as he kicks me down the steps. I fly and land hard. Then I writhe on the cellar floor like a yowling cat, unable to suppress the pain radiating down my tailbone. It's the worst pain I've ever felt. Much worse than the glass still embedded in my palms.

The door closes and the light goes out.

As night falls, the temperature drops. It's always cool in the cellar, but it's too cold now, in my shorts and thin T-shirt. My body hurts way too much to curl up for warmth, so I lay flat on my stomach and shiver, my breath coming out in little puffs. I focus on a box of toys across the room. Mr. Potato Head stares back sadly, like he's sorry. I must be delusional. Every time I try to move, pain grips me and I give up.

In my delirium, I curse myself for being so small for my

age. If I were bigger, like some girls at school, Judd couldn't whip me around like a rag doll. I could fight back and have it make a difference. Even Ayla, skinny as me, has her height as an advantage—and not just for making clothes fit her like a supermodel. Gram was tall, too. Maybe I get my short stature from my father, whoever he is…

The next morning, Judd's boots clomp-boom-clomp menacingly down the stairs, but I don't lift my head from the dusty cement floor. When he hauls me to my feet, the sound that escapes my throat is a cross between a whimper and a moan. Tears drip down my dirty cheeks as Judd guides me upstairs and into the bright light of the kitchen. He's gentle for once, and I can't help feeling thankful.

At the sink, he allows me to pluck out the glass shards from my hands and wash my cuts. I know this is necessary to avoid infection, but it hurts like hell and brings on a surge of fresh, silent tears. Judd perches on the counter smoking, watching as I tend to my injuries. When my hands are clean and patted dry, he holds out a box of bandages, which I take with trepidation.

After my palms are bandaged, Judd hops off the counter and cups my chin in his hand—the one holding the cigarette. It trails smoke right into my eyes so that they burn. He tilts my filthy, tear-streaked face up to his and sighs. "This is gettin' tiresome, Bones. You're here because I'm fond of your mama and she asked me to take care of you. Don't I give you everything you need?"

I nod.

"Now I don't want to have to keep reminding you who's running this show. But I will, if need be."

I swallow, but I'm not afraid at this moment. Just utterly defeated.

"You knew you had that coming, didn't you?"

"Yes," I say in a raspy, regretful voice.

"Good. Glad we understand each other." He smiles—or at least attempts to.

I wish he'd let go of my chin, but it's a power tactic. He holds onto it for a minute before releasing me with a jerk. "Get some food, then take a shower. You stink."

The food, I'm all about. I open cupboards and eat everything within reach so I don't have to move too much. When I'm full, I hobble into the bathroom. It takes forever, since each step is excruciating. I don't look at myself in the mirror. There's no good reason to face what I've become.

After I'm clean, I realize that it's Friday, and I flinch at the idea of having to work tonight, when the tiniest movements hurt my hands. Luckily, Judd's not around when I crawl up the steps to my room wearing nothing but a towel. The exertion makes my rear-end bloom with pain. It makes the stinging in my palms feel like a mere annoyance. When I reach my bed, I ease myself onto it and fall into a thick sleep. I fall so far and so fast that my prayer is left half-whispered on my lips, *Help me, Gram.*

Chapter 29

Just when I think there is no end to his cruelty, Judd lets me off all weekend—no preparing orders, no deliveries. I'm left to doze in bed instead of tackling the hundreds of steps up and down all the dealers' apartments. It's no act of kindness, though. Judd knows I'd slow him down in my current condition.

Pretending to be Ayla, I email in sick to school Friday. On Saturday when she and Judd are doing deliveries, I inch my way downstairs to dial the Mastersons' number. Brick answers, which is perfect because he's the one I need.

"Hey. Can you tell me what trig problems Sampson assigned yesterday?" I ask, making my voice neutral.

"Yeah, sure." Brick rattles them off.

"Thanks. I'll see you—"

"Wait, are you sick or something?"

"Yeah. I have the stomach flu," I lie.

"Oh, that's too bad," he says with sincere regret. "Do

you need anything? I could have my uncle whip up some chicken noodle soup. Of course, it might end up tasting more like corn and eggplant."

A quick laugh escapes, causing a spasm in my ribs. "No, but thanks. Tell Chloe I won't make it to the pond tomorrow morning."

"She's right here, I'll let you talk to her."

Before I can protest, Chloe is lamenting into the phone, "Oh, Andrea! Why don't I come hang out with you tomorrow? We could play board games and listen to music. Or talk about boys…"

My eyes widen in horror at the thought of Chloe stepping one impish little foot anywhere near Judd's rat-hole. I moan and try to sound pathetic. "No, Chlo, I don't want you to catch this. It's pretty nasty. I'm sure I'll be better by Monday. I'll see you then."

"Alright." She sounds dejected. "I hope you feel better." Then she adds, "Hey, how are you calling me anyway? Brick said you guys didn't even have a *phone*."

In the background, I can hear Brick snorting with laughter. I close my eyes and remind myself to murder him on Monday.

While Judd and Ayla are out, I slip into Judd's bathroom to inspect myself in the mirror. Despite the pain radiating from everywhere, I find no bruises on my body. The only visible marks are the cuts on my hands. Even drunk, Judd knows what he's doing. I paw through the medicine cabinet until I hit the jackpot—Advil. Then I hesitate, wondering if he might've put something more potent in the bottle as a cover-up. But a closer look reveals the stamp on each pill, so I'm safe. I pour several of them into a baggie and take them upstairs, along with as much food as I can carry.

The Advil eases the soreness in my tailbone and soothes my throbbing hands enough that I can hold a pen and bust out my homework. I work through mid-afternoon, until I hear a car spewing gravel outside. Assuming Judd and Ayla are back for more supplies, I'm startled by sudden, urgent pounding on the front door. I tiptoe over to the window and peer out. A short, bald man is pacing back and forth on the front step in that jerky, agitated way of junkies. He bangs on the door a few more times and yells, "Judd, if you're hiding in there, you better get our money! You don't want Donavan to pay you another visit." Cussing some more, he circles the house and looks in a few windows before kicking an old piece of pipe laying in the gravel. Then he climbs into his car and disappears in a swirl of dust.

I crawl into bed again, my heart beating a staccato. So Judd owes some thug named Donovan money. Maybe that's why he's been increasing his dealings lately. Perhaps that's why he slapped that crazy debt on me and Ayla. But *who* is Donovan, and how much money does Judd owe? Realizing that I may have found a flaw in Judd's armor, I savor the idea like candy in my mouth.

Judd and Ayla are back by dinnertime, and I feign sleep when Judd pokes his head into my room to check on me. His gaze makes the hairs on my neck prickle. Soon, his big black car pulls out of the driveway, but I can still hear Ayla clattering around downstairs.

Gingerly, I head down and find her standing at the kitchen

counter, mixing a drink. She looks nice in a flippy black skirt and coral-colored tank top. The black sandals on her feet expose some chipped pink toe polish. Except for her bloodshot eyes, Ayla could pass as any normal woman—a mom, even—after a long day of work. Something lurches in my chest. Why *couldn't* she be normal? Why couldn't she change?

"Ayla?" I speak softly, knowing my voice will startle her.

"What?" she says without looking up.

I take a breath. "What do you know about Judd's business?"

"It's pretty straight-forward. Doesn't take a genius like you to figure it out."

"No, I mean. I think…" I lower my voice. "I think he owes someone money."

Ayla's head is down by her knees so fast I almost miss the arc of it. Laughter fills the corners of the kitchen. "Oh, yeah, that's a surprise!" she gasps. My eyebrows crease. "Bones, these people always owe each other. That's what it's about for them—money. Profit. Power. It's not pure, like it is for me—" She abruptly stops laughing, straightens up, and takes a long sip of her drink.

"Don't you ever want to quit, Ayla?" I don't know where the question comes from, but I wish I didn't sound like such a pleading baby when I ask it.

My mother's eyes fix on my face for a long, lingering moment, and I would give anything to know what she's truly thinking.

Then she sighs so deeply it's as if she sucked in all the light of the world, and with one breath, extinguished it. "What the fuck for?"

She throws back her remaining drink and shuffles over to the sagging couch, the stained carpet, the cheap coffee table. The flat screen TV that she turns on is, however, state of the art. Soon the voice of some sleazy talk show host is rambling on about which of these three men is the real father of blah blah blah.

Slowly I back up, climb the stairs to my attic room, and close the door. I gaze out the hexagonal window at the leafy green woods, dull in the twilight, and hear my mother's question reverberate in my mind.

I whisper a sorrowful answer, "For me."

The Harvest Dance is a few weeks away and it seems to be all anyone at school can talk about. The teachers even take time out of their lectures to let students sound off on themes and clothes and music. It's getting on my nerves. If I didn't care about making waves, I might raise my hand and ask if we could please stay on track and actually learn something. Ms. Sampson is the only one who refuses to allow any dance-related gossip to pervade her classroom. This week alone, four senior girls were sent packing because they couldn't stop whispering about the big event. Ms. Sampson is growing on me.

"You're *going* to the dance, Chloe."

"Shut up, Brick. You can't make me do anything."

As I sit in the cafeteria listening to my friends bicker, I begin to wish I was spending my lunch hour in the library.

"Your parents are going to worry again if you don't start

socializing," he warns.

"I socialize. I hang out with Andrea."

"Slinking off to the woods every weekend isn't their idea of being social," Brick argues. "No offense, Andrea."

"Just keep me out of this," I mumble and rub circles into my temples. I'm careful to conceal my palms, which are almost healed but still a little blotchy.

"I don't have a date," Chloe reminds him. "And I'm not asking anyone. And you're not asking any of your posse to ask me. I won't be a charity case."

"I'll take you then," Brick says simply.

"Oh, great. Just the popularity boost I need—to show up at my first dance with my cousin! No one would think *that* was pathetic." Chloe launches a raw carrot onto Brick's tray. He scowls as it plops into his chocolate pudding. I smother a grin.

"Look, I promised them I wouldn't let you disappear again." Brick's voice deepens into an annoyed growl. "And I keep my promises. Besides, I know you want to go," he adds, digging into his mashed potatoes.

A mutinous silence descends and I secretly agree with Brick on that last point. I saw the way Chloe's eyes lit up when she spotted the first Harvest Dance flyer in the hallway. But then she realized that the dance was scheduled for a Friday night, when I always have to work, and her enthusiasm dwindled. In a way, I wish I *could* go, to keep her company. But mostly I'm glad I have an excuse to opt out. Dancing is not my thing. Even Gram and her sore toes knew that.

After school, Chloe says she doesn't want to ride home with Brick and asks if we can walk to my house instead. I don't blame her for wanting to avoid Brick and his bossiness, but I certainly can't have her skipping into my mess of a world.

"Um, that might not be a good idea," I say, trying to ignore the hurt that flashes behind her eyes.

"Why not?" She tugs at her hair.

"My mom isn't feeling well. She caught my stomach bug. But we could walk in the woods. Go to the pond?" I suggest, dreading the pain this extra walking may cause.

"Okay," she agrees reluctantly, so we set out.

I've been spoiled getting rides home from Brick all semester. Halfway to the woods, my books feel insufferably heavy, their bindings cutting into my arms. Casually, I pull the detested garbage bag from my pocket, shake it open, and dump the books inside. Then I twist the bag up and heft it over my shoulder. Chloe has the grace to keep talking, to pretend like this is a perfectly normal book-toting method. *Who cares?* I think. By now, Chloe and Brick are well aware of my financial issues since I can never even spring for my own ice cream cone.

At the pond, we scramble up to the big log where we first spoke that scorching August afternoon. There's a wide, flat area where we can sit cross-legged comfortably if we face each other. Automatically, this is what we do, not feeling awkward in the silence that descends.

"We've been friends for two months," Chloe says after a minute, brightening.

"Yeah, almost." It's early October. Thinking about the date doesn't remind me of time passing idly, however, but of time running out. Judd gave me until December to pay off my debt, which swelled to eight hundred and fifty dollars after I missed that weekend of work. A methodical thumping begins in my right temple, and Chloe catches the stress evident on my face. Suddenly her hand clasps my fingers.

"What's wrong, Andrea?" Her wheat-colored eyes are full of concern. "You look so worried. Not just now, but all the time lately."

I'm about to brush her off when my throat catches. "It's just…" I begin. "If I tell you something, promise me you won't tell Brick. Or anyone?"

Chloe hesitates, then shakes her head. "I can't promise. You'd better not tell me."

I glare at her, disappointment and anger sizzling on my tongue. "You're my best friend and you can't keep a simple promise?"

"Not from Brick," she says. "I already did it once and… well, I can't keep secrets from him anymore."

"This isn't your secret. It's mine," I quip, annoyed.

"It doesn't matter. If he asked, I'd have to tell. And he does ask about you sometimes."

"Unbelievable," I huff.

Chloe looks miserable. "I'm sorry. But he was so upset when he found out what was happening to me at school last year. So hurt that I didn't confide in him," she explains. "He wouldn't speak to me for two days, and then out of the blue he caught me in the woods and just started unloading. He said I had to make a decision—we were either going to be polite cousins who made small talk and kept all the important things to ourselves, or we were going to be the closest confidants. Like brother and sister."

As she speaks, my eyes fill with tears, and I'm surprised that half the reason for them is simple jealousy. Not just because of the special bond they share, but because it means she can't be *my* closest confidant. It means I can't tell her any secrets. I don't know what Brick would do with them.

Still. I'm too close to bursting not to let something out now, so I say what I can. "My mom has issues. She's sick a lot. It's... hard sometimes."

I lean forward, putting my head all the way down into the space between my knees. I rock there for a minute and let Chloe rub my back just like Gram used to. "I'm so sorry, Andrea," she says. "Can I help?"

My nose is too clogged to answer, and there's nothing she *can* do anyway. So I keep rocking, back and forth, trying to remember what it feels like to breathe without a weight pressing against my chest. I go on like this until Chloe's tiny fingers grip my shoulders and she makes me sit up. "I know what you need," she announces and begins stripping off her clothes. "You need to float. Just float. It's the best therapy, I promise."

She's wearing a T-shirt and her underwear now, completely at ease standing half naked in the woods in the middle of the afternoon. I look around at the deserted forest, shake my head. "I can't float. I always failed that part of swim lessons."

I assume that will be the end of the discussion, but she reaches down, grabs my hands and pulls me to my feet. She is surprisingly strong for one so tiny. "C'mon. The water's only getting colder. This will be our last swim of the season. Be brave, Andre. Be a warrior." Then she strikes the warrior pose, totally serious. I snort.

She straightens up and looks at me, hands on hips.

"Fine," I say. If she can do it, I can, too. I yank off my clothing until I'm wearing the same few garments as Chloe. We stand on the edge of the log and count to three. Even before we jump, we are laughing.

Our bodies splash into the pond and we emerge breathless from the cold, but the shock feels wonderful. We swim out to the deep part and Chloe flips onto her back, floating with ease. I try to imitate her, but my legs immediately sink until I'm vertical in the water.

"See? I told you," I gurgle. "I could never pass level four at the Y. I'm a sinker."

Chloe rolls her eyes and makes me try again, tells me to puff out my chest this time. I humor her, but the same results ensue. This time her eyes crinkle in concentration. "Hmm," she says after a moment. "Try raising your arms straight above your head. Don't hold them out at your sides."

"That's not how you did it."

"Everyone's different," she responds, treading beside me.

"You are ridiculously persistent." But I flip onto my back, kick my legs to the surface, and extend my arms up past my ears.

I am sure this is a major waste of time and energy...until I realize I'm *not* sinking. My legs are bobbing on the surface of the pond, ebbing and flowing with the movement of the water. I'm floating for the first time in my life!

Chloe lets out a whoop and I can't help grinning. "I can't believe it. You were right, Chlo."

She laughs. "Don't act so surprised."

I laugh, too. I stare up at the hazy sky, feel the sway of the current moving me any way it pleases, feel my body relax, my tension drift away. I could stay like this forever.

I am floating. My best friend is floating, too, and giggling, right beside me. I have a best friend. It is mid-October and I'm freezing and exhilarated and filled with energy, and I've never felt so alive.

Nothing, nothing, nothing can bring me down from this high.

Judd's black sedan is parked in the driveway, but the house seems deserted when I tiptoe inside. As soon as he hears me pulling pots out of the kitchen drawers, though, Judd is in there and in my face.

"Cuttin' it close tonight," he remarks, smoothing down his wiry hair and eying my damp locks.

"Yeah," I respond, because if I don't say something he'll accuse me of ignoring him.

"Make double. I'm having company."

I glance around the empty house. "Where's Ayla?"

"Out." He walks through the kitchen and sits down at the

table. "Get me a beer."

A beer he could have gotten himself while he was passing the fridge two seconds ago, I think bitterly. Outwardly, my face remains a perfect stone mask. I grab a bottle from the fridge and set it on the table in front of him. Before I can get away, his fingers clamp around my wrist. My eyes dart up, startled.

"I got you something today. It's on your bed. Once you get dinner started, go put it on."

I don't like the way he's got his fingers wrapped around Gram's watch. When I try to take my hand back, he lets me, but he smoothly unclasps the watch and slides it over my knuckles, and now it's in his grimy fingers. I lunge to snag it back, but he's too quick. He leans back, holding the watch high, teasing me. I reach for it again, and once more am disappointed. Judd's evil laughter fills my ears, but the blood is rushing to them so fast that all I can think is, *No, no, no. With the Buick gone, Gram's watch is all I have. He can't take that too!*

But fighting him outright never works in my favor, so I feign subservience. I swallow and ask, "Can I have it back?" My voice is shaking, my eyes frantic.

Judd frowns and examines the watch up close. While he does so, I hold my breath—and all my instincts—tightly inside.

"Please, Judd?"

After a long, agonizing minute, Judd answers, "Nah. Think I'll keep hold of this little trinket for a while, to make sure you do *exactly* as you're told tonight."

The first step in "doing as I'm told" requires me slipping

into the red tube dress I find laying across my bed. It's totally inappropriate, something Ayla would wear clubbing. After I pull it on, I keep tugging at the fabric, hoping for some give, but it clings to my bony hips, my breasts, my butt, like a cocoon to a caterpillar. I wish I were inside a cocoon.

With the image of Gram's silver watch clear in my mind, I give the dress a final frustrated tug and head downstairs to finish cooking. Judd's "company" has arrived, and I flinch a little when I see the man who was chatting in the driveway with Judd all those months ago sitting at the table. Even seated, he's intimidating. His eyes pierce me from beneath the dark hair that is a little longer than before, slicked down to his chin.

"You remember Bones," Judd says.

The man looks me over, smiling appreciatively. "How could I forget?"

I cross my arms. Then my eyes skip to Judd, who cocks his head slightly in warning. I know what he wants. I drop my hands to my sides and produce a tight smile for the guest, thinking only of Gram's watch.

"Ain't she pretty all dressed up?" Judd asks.

The man stares and says, "Mmm."

I turn to the stove and continue making dinner, acutely aware of Judd's friend watching my every move in that tight blood-red dress. The tension is so thick, it makes me sweat. As they begin to talk business, I feel my hands trembling. I want to be anywhere but in this kitchen. I wish with all my heart that Ayla were here, too, though I don't know what difference she could make.

"How'd the rounds go?" I hear the man ask Judd, and then after Judd's recap he says, "Good. Call Louis tomorrow and set up the next drop. I've gotta go to Dayton on other business…"

I work quickly so I can serve dinner and get the hell out. No one speaks directly to me again, except when the big man drops his fork and Judd instructs me to pick it up and bring Donovan a new one. My eyes bulge at this. *Donovan?!* If this is the guy Judd owes money to, I can think of only one reason for him to parade me around in this dress. I push down the bile that threatens to rise in my throat, but welcome the resolve that accompanies it. I will not become Ayla. I will not be someone's *payment.*

While the men eat, I position myself near the countertop where I've left a sharp knife within reach. I am ready to grab it the moment Donovan makes a move. But he's lost interest. He doesn't look at me during dinner or even after, when I'm cleaning up. He doesn't speak to me or touch me, lucky for him. Judd also ignores me, chatting instead about delivery schedules and pricing options. To hear them talk, you'd think they were accountants!

When the meal is over, I serve them after-dinner drinks. Instead of dismissing me, Judd tells me to wait in the kitchen in case they need something else. He's never had me do this before, and I'm positive he is just trying to give Donovan more time to view my ass.

After forty-five long minutes, they wrap up their business. Judd snaps more orders at me and I jump, thinking only of my reward. I walk Donovan to the door and hand him his jacket.

Donovan's coal-black eyes rake me over from top to bottom

before he smiles, slow and lazy, then disappears outside. It's not until I hear the roar of the Beamer's engine that my heart starts to slow down. I turn around in the hallway and face Judd. "Good?" I ask in a shaky voice.

"Good enough," he grumbles, looking troubled. He pulls Gram's watch out of his pocket and flings it at me. "Get outta my sight. You look like a whore."

I run upstairs and throw off the dress as fast as I can.

Chapter 30

"What pose are you going to do?" Chloe turns around in line to ask me.

"Huh?" I say without looking up from the notes I'm studying.

"For your portrait," she says in exasperation. "You know, you could totally pull off some dramatic over-the-shoulder gaze," she suggests and models it. "Or there's always the sweet girl-next-door look. Just fold your hands under your chin and try to appear demure."

I grunt. Hate Picture Day.

"Have you thought about it at all? You're up in, like, two minutes."

"I have a history test in ten minutes that I'm more concerned about," I tell her.

"Ugh. You and Brick are too much alike," she mumbles.

Soon Chloe takes her place in front of the fake blue

background set up in the library and smiles sweetly for the camera. As I watch, I feel a surge of pride, followed by uneasiness. It's nice being Chloe's friend, but sometimes I feel sorry for her. She's the only bit of cheerful relief between my surliness and Brick's intensity. It must take its toll. She really should be hanging out with a bunch of giggling freshmen.

Instead, she's waiting for me on the other side.

It's my turn. I trudge up to the platform, sit on the bench, and face the photographer—an older gentleman with a cheerful expression who prods, "Smile pretty, now" when I give him my serious-portrait pose.

"I'm all out of pretty," I say, my voice as flat as my face.

The photographer frowns but takes the shot. "Nice one, Andre," my best friend mutters. I clutch Chloe's arm and we bolt into the hallway.

We walk side by side down the hall to the place where we have to part for our respective classrooms. "I'll see you after school," I tell her.

Chloe shakes her head. "No. My mom's picking me up early for a doctor's appointment today. So you and Brick can go be boring and…oh, let me guess, *study.*" She grins, sticks her tongue out, and bounces off into the sea of students. My heart swells as I watch her go.

Chloe is always cheerful, always looking for the good stuff. Just the opposite of *me*, I think wryly. I realize I don't really like this about myself. Even my preoccupation with grades and stature in school, which once seemed like an admirable trait, now makes me feel...unbalanced. I glance down at my meticulous history notes and remember Delaney once asking me why I obsessed about my grades so much.

"I'm not obsessed," I'd retorted lamely. But she was right—my desire to excel was compulsive. "I just want to go to a good college," I'd tried to explain. "Anyway, *you* should understand. You're the same way with dance."

Delaney let it go after that. But later, I thought about her question and searched for a deeper answer. Sure, I wanted a shot at getting into an Ivy League school. And of course I needed a scholarship. But there was more. Acing tests and collecting academic accolades was something I could control, and it put me in a different league than Ayla. If I was an exceptional student with a bright, promising future, then no one could say I was anything like my deadbeat mother. And Gram could never, ever compare us.

I'm almost at my classroom when I pass the picture windows facing the east side of the quad. Outside, the brilliant rust and ruby leaves catch my eye. Trying to embrace the moment like Chloe would, I pause to admire the scene. Then a shadow steals my gaze—it's a guy, half hidden behind the maple tree talking with one of the regulars in the quad. A guy with scruffy red hair and a scar above his eyebrow. A guy who looks a little too old to be a student, but who seems familiar. I try to place him, but nothing registers, and then after a quick glance at Gram's watch, I'm sucked back into the wave of students. It doesn't hit me until twenty minutes later, halfway through my history test. Recognition slams into me so hard I gasp.

The guy in the quad is that junkie who came to Judd's house my first day there. The one Judd marched into the woods. But why would he be *here*? The answer pushes its way past all the history lessons I've stored in my brain—the guy with the scar must be supplying the kids who deal at Belmont. And Judd must be the one supplying him.

I'm not sure why this surprises me. Haydon is a small town—surely there's not enough room in it for two suppliers. But I never see the kid with the scar on our Saturday deliveries. Maybe he's an indirect link to Judd. Or maybe Judd makes extra deliveries when I'm at school. To acquaintances I know nothing about. Maybe they know *me,* though, and they're watching. Suddenly, my skin feels itchy, my senses heightened. As if I'm realizing for the first time how messed up my life truly is. This distraction almost causes me to flub my test, which absolutely *can't* happen, so I force it all from my mind. I build a mental dam and push it away, like I do when dreams of Gram sneak past my defenses. It works for now.

If only I knew how to keep them all from flooding back.

"Want to come over and study?" Brick asks as soon as I slide into the front seat of his Explorer after school.

I burst out laughing.

He shoots me a quizzical look, so I explain, "That's what Chloe predicted we would do today. We really are boring, huh?"

A grin meanders up the side of Brick's face. He leans forward and rests his arms on the steering wheel, thinking. "Well then, how 'bout we go downtown? Walk around the OSU campus. Grab some dinner?"

"That's not boring," I agree, sitting up taller, enraptured with the idea.

Brick cranks up the radio and swings his Explorer onto the road toward the expressway. The wind crashes through the open windows and a euphoric feeling of freedom rushes through me, just like when Ayla and I escaped from Haydon all those months ago. But a shadow dims my elation as I also remember the glass stuck in my palms and that miserable night spent in the cellar after coming home late.

I glance uneasily at Brick and yell over the music, "Let me see what time I have to be back."

He nods as I pull Judd's phone from my pocket and send a text, *What time do u need me tonight?*

The answer comes quick, *I don't. Stay away.*

"Stay away" means Judd has company. The last time he gave this order, I hung out at the Mastersons' all afternoon and then accepted their invitation to dinner—pickled bratwurst and fried green tomatoes. Interesting. The apple pie for dessert was made the traditional way by Chloe's mom. Yum! Then the five of us played Hearts until I won by shooting the moon, and everyone accused me of being a hustler. I really hated to leave their house that night. And when I got back to Judd's, there were still cars parked in his driveway. I'd waited in the woods until I saw the men leave. They were a sleazy-looking crew, even in the dark. Donovan was probably one of them, I realize now, a shudder zinging down my spine. After seeing him the other night, I am more than happy to follow Judd's order today.

"I'm free for the night," I report to Brick, who smiles. A moment later, he turns up the volume and starts belting out lyrics as *Song of the South* comes on.

"Country music fan, huh? I should've guessed," I shout.

He throws his head back and laughs, looking more carefree than I've ever seen him. He squints at me. "It's in my blood, baby!"

I grin and bop my head along to the music, and then we are both singing together at the top of our lungs and I'm not even self-conscious. It's one of those moments—one of those perfect moments when your heart swells so big it feels like a balloon expanding, and if the earth exploded in that nanosecond you know, you just *know*, you would die happy.

We settle down as we approach the city, take the Lane Avenue exit, and start looking for a parking space around the crowded campus. After circling for a while, we snag a metered spot on a side street and take stock of our surroundings. Ohio State University is *huge,* with massive buildings that stretch on and on. Students scurry every which way, like ants attacking a slice of watermelon. Neither Brick nor I know our way around, but we have fun wandering, getting lost, walking through large academic halls and smiling at professors as if we belong. Being on a college campus is invigorating—a good reminder of what I'm working toward. And why I'm putting up with Judd.

"Did you apply here?" I ask Brick, thinking how nice it

would be if he were close by next year.

"Yes, just last week."

"Where else are you looking?" I venture, wriggling my fingers into my pockets as we shoulder past a chatty group of students on the sidewalk.

Brick sighs. "I have a list of reach schools and safety schools to choose from...I've applied to eight so far. Haven't really decided where I'll go yet. Hell, I might even take a year off and help my uncle on the farm."

"Oh." It's all I say because that would be *awesome*—for me. But I know that isn't likely to happen. Brick will be long gone next year, moving forward into a new, amazing life. I imagine how Chloe and I will send him videos and write him emails. And miss him.

Brick and I eventually find ourselves on High Street, which appears to be the epicenter of student social life. Lined with restaurants, shops, bars, and an array of colorful people, High Street is an assault on my senses. After spending the last few months mired in corn stalks, vast farmland, and, of course, my serene woods, the activity level here sets my head spinning in a good way. It seems to give Brick a boost as well.

"Let's do something crazy," I suggest, giddy. "Look. Let's get tattoos!" I grab his arm and point to a shop named *Ink Me* that's housed above a Chinese restaurant.

Brick laughs. "Andrea, you're not old enough. *I'm* not even old enough."

"You think they care? Let's go," I say boldly and pull him

across the street. "At least have a look."

He lets me drag him up the wooden steps and into the store, where a twenty-something girl behind a large desk that has been scribbled on a hundred times over waves us in. We sit on tapestry-covered futons and page through the design books, giggling about what we would tattoo on our bodies and where.

"How about a brick wall with your name graffitied on it?" I suggest, cracking myself up.

"I wouldn't stamp myself with my own name," Brick says. "But you're more than welcome to."

I purse my lips. "In your dreams, cupcake."

"Now *that'd* be a statement," he says, poking me. "Right above your belly button." We crack up.

In one of the idea books, there are pages and pages of quotes. I pore over them, trailing my fingers down the list and lingering on any relating to courage and strength. Then my hand falls on a word that is simple and perfect. Something lodges in my throat.

"That's the one," I whisper. "Someday, I'm going to have 'unbreakable' tattooed around my wrist."

My voice has taken on a kind of demented intensity, but I can't help it. After a moment, I glance at Brick, my eyes potent with passion. He's looking at me kind of funny, but he nods in his calm way. "That's a good one."

Then we leave because I don't have the money for this. Or the ID, which the sign clearly states is mandatory. Back outside, my stomach growls and I start thinking about dinner, which leads my mind back to money, and how I have none, and how I don't want to mooch off Brick again. Embarrassment colors my cheeks when he asks where I want to eat.

"I'm not really hungry." I stuff my hands into my jeans pockets.

He stops in the street, turns me to face him. "Look, I'm taking you out to dinner. I invited you, remember?"

I look past his shoulder. "I'm sorry, I just…"

"There's nothing to be sorry about," he says curtly. "Unless you're planning on making me eat alone."

When my eyes find their way back to his, I spot the twinkle buried in the depths of soft brown. "Okay," I admit. "I'm starving."

We end up at a tavern that makes the greasiest, tastiest cheeseburgers either of us has ever consumed. The seasoned steak fries practically melt in our mouths, and we shovel the food in like we haven't eaten in months. "Oh my God," Brick says around a mouthful. "See what you almost missed?"

"Would have been tragic," I agree, stuffing my face.

"Dreadful," he says.

"Appalling," I one-up him. Our eyes meet challengingly over our burgers.

"Abysmal." He grins. "What else you got?"

"You know we could go on like this for eternity," I tell him.

"For eternity," he repeats, then his eyes dart away and he nods as if he's decided something. "There's this quote I heard once, *What we do in life echoes in eternity.* If I got a tattoo, that's what I'd want it to say…" His voice fades.

I nod, but try not to think about the quote too much, since the things I'm doing in my life with Judd are not things I'm proud of. They are certainly not things I want following me into eternity. But I tell Brick, "That's cool. Where'd you hear it?" The question is innocent, but his eyes dance away from mine.

"I...don't remember," he says with a shrug, and I back off. We eat in silence for a moment.

I decide to pick a new topic. "So where in Mississippi are you from?"

"Jackson," he answers, crunching a fry. "Also known as The City with Soul."

I smile. "I like that. Do you miss it?"

He pauses a moment to finish chewing. "I don't miss the heat." He laughs. "I do miss my friends, my football buddies."

"I didn't know you played football," I say, surprised, though now it seems obvious. He has the build for it—stocky, strong. "Last time I checked, Belmont High had a decent team. Why don't you join?"

"Not interested," he says curtly, then elaborates. "I wasn't that good anyway. I mostly played to make my dad happy."

He's never mentioned his parents before and I'm not sure where to take the conversation from here. Luckily, Brick decides for me. "How about you? Any hidden hobbies? You look like a ballerina."

I smirk. "A lot of people think that, but no. Born with a dancer's body and two left feet."

His eyes lock onto mine with the unnerving intensity they

sometimes carry. "I'll bet you're not so bad."

"You have no idea," I argue. "My Gram tried to teach me some classic dances, like the waltz and the tango? Yeah. It was more like the tan-*gle* where I was involved." As soon as the words are out of my mouth, I wish I could suck them back in. By mentioning Gram, I fear I've opened a door that I desperately need to keep shut. I glance down at my plate.

"I'll bet if I asked your Gram, she'd tell me a different story," Brick teases.

"Well, she's dead so you can't ask her." I blurt this out to shut him up, but then I regret that too. The thing is, when you tell someone your grandmother died and they offer condolences, there's this underlying implication that it's *just* a grandparent…that it's less important because it's supposed to happen. That it's natural. They don't understand. My Gram wasn't some feeble old lady who showed up at holidays with tacky sweaters and butterscotch breath. She was more than a mother to me. She was…everything.

Brick seems to get it, though. He reads me pretty well. "I'm sorry. I can tell you really miss her," he says softly.

My heart squeezes. "Yeah."

"And do you miss living in Indianapolis?" Brick asks, filling the gaping silence.

"Not really," I lie. Just then, a waiter walks by carrying a bowl of chocolate mousse. "Ooh, should we get some dessert?"

Brick's way too perceptive to miss my abrupt change of subject, but he doesn't pry. Instead, he leans back in his chair and pats his stomach. "If it's anything like their main course, I don't see how we can pass it up."

We are still raving about the food twenty minutes later as we step out of the tavern onto the crowded street and smack into a small commotion. A pack of college students surrounds us, several of them visibly drunk or high. Or both. One guy is slurring his words and staggering, but whatever he's saying must be hilarious because his friends can't stop laughing. At the edge of the group, two people are bickering. It's impossible not to overhear the argument between the glassy-eyed guy and the girl he's with, since they're not exactly being quiet. The guy keeps insisting he's *fine* while the girl tries to grab his car keys.

As we maneuver our way through the crowd, I hear the guy slur, "Stop being so paranoid, Julia. It's like a two-minute drive. I got this."

"It's ten minutes, and you've had too much," she insists weakly, trying to keep her voice down. Their conversation dwindles as we break away from the group. It's not hard to figure out who's going to win.

A few stores down, Brick stops walking, shoulders slouched. I turn to see if he forgot something and notice a pained look on his face. "Are you oka—"

Abruptly, he wheels around and heads back the way we came. I follow as he strides right up to the girl who was arguing with the drunk. Does he *know* her?

"Don't let him drive. Definitely don't get in the car with him," Brick says to her in a low, quiet voice. I've never seen such intensity on his face, and that's saying something where Brick is concerned.

It startles the girl as well. "What'd you say?"

"Please. My mom was killed by a drunk driver two blocks from our house. It's not worth it."

I suck in air at the same time as the college girl. Brick and the girl stare at each other for a long moment, and then she nods and Brick swings around and starts booking back down the street again. His strides are long, his pace fast. I have to jog to keep up.

When we reach the Explorer, he unlocks the doors and holds mine open without looking up. Then he walks around the car and climbs in, but instead of inserting the key into the ignition, he leans back against the seat and closes his eyes.

"I didn't know," I say quietly. "I'm sorry, Brick."

From the corner of my eye, I see the rise and fall of his Adam's apple as he swallows. His voice scrapes like sandpaper as he says, "It was my dad."

"What?" I ask, confused.

With his eyes still closed, Brick explains, "My dad was the drunk driver. He's in prison in Mississippi. That's why I'm here with my aunt and uncle."

I don't breathe or speak, have no idea what to say. After a long minute, my hand reaches across the seat and wraps itself around Brick's, lying flat against his thigh. He doesn't push me away. He doesn't squeeze tight. He just curls his fingers the tiniest bit and lets me hold on.

Chapter 31

We drive home in silence. After parking the car in front of the Mastersons' big country house, Brick starts walking toward the woods. I hesitate, unsure if I should follow. Maybe he wants to be alone. But when he reaches the tree line, he looks over his shoulder and seems surprised that I'm not behind him. "Aren't you coming?" he calls.

He waits for me to catch up and when he sees the grim look on my face, slides an arm around my shoulders and squeezes. "It's okay, Andrea. I wanted to tell you."

"Why?" I ask as we slip into the shadows.

"First, to see how it felt," he says. "I always imagined when I told someone, it would…I dunno, deepen the pain or something. Make it worse." His voice is soft, like he's whispering forbidden secrets. I stay silent, but I understand. It's why I don't talk about Gram, why I try so hard not to even think about her. Memories like that…they make any kind of physical pain seem like nothing.

"But you're not like other people in Haydon," Brick continues. "You don't try to make a joke or slap a smiley face on everything. I mean, if I told my guy friends, they'd just get uncomfortable, mumble that they're sorry, and revert back to talking about sports. They'd talk about it later maybe, when I wasn't around. And I'd be left wishing I never said a thing." He pulls a piece of bark off a tree as we pass it. "I've been here over a year and you're the first person I've told."

I find this amazing, with the way he attracts people. "What about Chloe?"

"Her parents explained what happened, of course, but she understands it's private. I've never worried about her telling anyone around here. She knows I'd kick her butt." Brick smiles crookedly to show he's kidding.

Worse, I think. *She knows you'd never forgive her. And she adores you.*

I decide to say that part out loud. "She adores you, Brick."

"The feeling's mutual." Then he adds, "She adores you too."

I snort. "Don't know why."

We step around a log, almost missing it in the darkness. I'm glad I can't see Brick's face when he says carefully, "She understands people with secrets."

I stiffen, then decide to play it lightly. "You think I have secrets?"

"Oh, I know you do," he plays back, but there's a hint of something solemn underlying his tone. He tugs me over to a small clearing where there's a log bench wedged between two trees. Brick and I sit down on the bench and look at each other.

"Do you ever see your dad or talk to him? Can you visit?" Half the reason I'm asking is pure selfishness. I want the conversation diverted away from me, and whatever secrets Brick thinks I'm keeping.

He turns his head away, tilted down so I can barely see the look of raw pain. But it's there. I bite my lip, abashed. I crossed the line. The air between us drips with heaviness.

"Would you?" He's not being sarcastic. He really wants to know.

I remember Gram on our kitchen floor, her heart deflated at fifty-eight. Imagine if Ayla had directly killed her in some reckless accident.

"No," I answer. But I'm a hypocrite because I forgive Ayla too easily all the time. "I don't know," I say, more honestly.

Brick swallows and looks at me. "I haven't spoken to my father in a year. Chloe thinks I should go see him. At least once for closure, if nothing else. Aunt Lil thinks I should go, too."

"What do *you* think?"

"I think...I don't want to go until I figure out how I feel about him. He writes me letters, but I don't read them anymore. The first few were just him apologizing in about fifty different ways. I know he means it. I know it wasn't what he wanted to happen. But he put her in that car. And now she's dead. Sometimes sorry doesn't mean shit."

I hear Judd's voice in my head, talking to Ayla after she brought us back here: *Sorry don't mean shit.* I guess he was right.

"My dad, he drove drunk all the time...thought he was

223

invincible," Brick whispers and I can hear the quiet anger beneath his words. "Well, my mom wasn't."

I place my hand on his arm, feel the warmth of his skin and the muscles twitching beneath it. He takes a deep, calming breath. I know, because I recognize the technique. "Chloe gets upset when I talk that way," Brick admits. "She doesn't want me to be bitter."

"But Chloe believes in sunshine and smiley faces," I remind him with a shrug. "You and I know life's not like that."

His eyes burn into me. "That's why I get you, Andrea. I know you keep your secrets tight, too."

I bristle at his words. I can't have Brick knowing too much about me—for his own good. "Look, stop saying that about me, okay? My life is no field of daisies, but it's not as mysterious as whatever you're imagining."

He waits, gaze steady. So I start lying.

"My mom's sick. Like, mentally." When I say this, it doesn't seem like a lie at all. "And her boyfriend, J—" I stammer, not sure I should use Judd's real name. "—Jason...he's a dick sometimes, but at least with him we have a place to stay, I get a decent school to attend. I mean, he makes me work every Friday and Saturday, which sort of sucks, but he pays me so I can't complain."

"He pays you?" Brick sounds surprised, and I suppose it's because I never have any cash on hand.

"It goes straight into a trust for college." The lies fly out, easy as pie. It's disturbing how much I've learned from Ayla. "He says someday I'll be glad he didn't let me waste it on clothes and movies."

"Hmm," Brick says, chewing his lip. "This Jason, he's a decent guy?"

"Well, he's not that *nice* about anything. But he takes care of Ayla—er, my mom. Like I said...no field of daisies, but it could be worse. I mean, I couldn't take care of her and go to school too."

"Does your mom get help? Counseling or something?"

I shrug and look away. "She takes medicine." Again, I'm not technically lying. Some of those pills she and Judd play around with are prescription narcotics.

"I'm sorry, Andrea. That's gotta be hard."

Nodding, I say, "I'm sorry for you, too." After a moment, I ask, "Can you please not tell Chloe that we talked about this? I already mentioned something to her and...I don't want her worrying about me."

"Sure, of course," he says easily.

"Really? Because...she said she couldn't keep secrets from you. You'd disown her or something. I thought it was mutual."

"What? Like she has to tell me everything?" Brick moans and rakes a hand through his hair. "Oh, that girl. I should've known she'd take it that way. Jeez, I don't want her thinking she can't have any privacy. I just want her to come to me when she needs help. Am I that overbearing with her?"

I raise my eyebrows and press my lips together.

He sighs and rubs his forehead. "I'll talk to her."

There is nothing more for us to say. We're both spent and a little edgy. We stand up and I give Brick a hug. It seems like the thing to do, after all we've been through in the last five hours.

"Thank you for dinner," I say. "And everything."

"Hey, I'll walk you home. It's pitch black out here," Brick insists, eyeing the woods.

"No, I'm fine."

"Come on, Andrea. I'm a Southern gent, remember?" He grins, teasing.

"Yeah, and I'm a big girl who can take care of herself," I snap too sharply. "I'll see you tomorrow."

His mouth falls open. Before he can speak, I take off down the path toward Judd's. I sprint the whole way, crunching leaves under my tennis shoes. Tears seep from the corners of my eyes, slither across my cheeks, and trickle into my ears. I don't want to be mean to Brick, but he needs to know when to back off. I already told him way, way too much.

Chapter 32

On Monday, there's no school because of some district-wide education conference—the teachers' turn to get smart. While the rest of the student body rejoices, I wake up worried about being home all day. When Judd finds out I'm off, he makes me work in the shed for three hours, but at least he's in a decent mood. In the afternoon he lounges around reading his *Island Travel* magazine, caressing Ayla, and dreaming of Fiji. Guess I'm off-duty.

Right now Ayla is asleep on the couch and Judd has been occupied in the bathroom for the past half hour. I'm sitting at his kitchen table inhaling sliced peaches and reading a novel for English when I hear a knock at the front door. Before I can get up, Judd flushes and goes to answer it. I assume he's talking to one of his desperate junkies out there—until the visitor's voice carries into the kitchen and makes my food stick in my throat.

Chloe!

I almost knock over my chair scrambling down the hallway,

where I find Judd leaning against the doorframe, chatting into the sunshine like he's Mr. Congeniality. On the doorstep, Chloe looks so cute with her little pigtails and innocent eyes. She has no idea that she's talking to the local drug lord. When she sees me rushing up behind Judd, her shoulders pop up in excitement.

"Surprise!" She beams. "Can you believe this weather? It's like summer again."

"What are you doing here?" I demand.

Chloe's face falls. She glances at Judd, embarrassed. "I stopped by to say hi."

"Don't be rude, girl." Judd gives me a little shove. "Miss Chloe and I were just gettin' acquainted. She lives over on the Masterson Farm." He is smiling and playing dad, or stepdad, or whatever. But I know better. He's telling me that he knows where to find her—he's warning me.

My heart pounds as I slip past Judd. "Let's talk outside," I say to Chloe, who looks confused by my less-than-ecstatic reaction to her arrival.

Pulling the door closed, I lead her to the pile of firewood across the driveway. "How'd you know where I live?" I ask, perturbed.

"I followed you home the other day, since you're always so secretive." She says this proudly, like she's some genius spy.

Now I'm *really* annoyed with her. She has no idea of the danger she's in, or how she has messed up my world. "Wow," I say. "That's so…stalker-ish."

Chloe stares, her mouth open and her eyes hurt. "I'm not

stalking you. But you never invite me over, and you block your phone number when you call—"

"I told you my mom was sick!" I explode. And then things get real quiet.

"Doesn't look like she's around. And your stepdad doesn't seem to care that I came by," she argues quietly.

I cross my arms. "He's not my stepdad. He's just Ayla's boyfriend, and he can be a real ass."

"Seemed nice to me." She crosses her arms right back.

I want to pull out my hair. My voice is downright nasty when I snap, "Look, I like my privacy, okay? I don't like having friends at this house."

"Right." Chloe laughs harshly. "All those friends of yours, beating down the door. Sorry I *bothered* you."

She turns away, flipping her little brown-and-white-striped pigtails indignantly and stomping into the woods. I'm still so flustered by her appearance in Judd's domain that I just want to let her go. I want her far, far away from him. But I can't. I *can't* let her think I'm turning on her like everyone did last year.

"Wait! Chlo…" I call out, but she doesn't stop. I jog up behind her and catch her in the first clearing. "I'm sorry," I breathe, touching her shoulder. "You just caught me by surprise."

"I thought we were friends," she says, dropping her arms. Her eyes are wet and my chest tightens. "Friends go to each other's houses. Are you embarrassed by me? You only want to associate with me in the cover of the woods?"

"No!" I'm about to point out that we eat lunch together

every day, but she isn't done raging.

"What, then? I'm too young? Too ugly? You don't want me around because you're so darn pretty and I'm not?"

"Don't call me pretty," I snarl, and it startles her into silence. I know I must tread very carefully with my words now. I glance back at the house. "Listen, my mom's boyfriend…he's not always that nice."

Chloe's face sobers and she waits for me to say more.

"It's like, he thinks we owe him for letting us live here. And I've only been here a few months. It just doesn't feel like home. So it's weird to invite people in, you know, like I'm imposing on his space. It has nothing to do with you," I assure her, grabbing her hand.

She lets me squeeze her fingers, but she's still miffed and wants me to know it. Angry Chloe is almost adorable, like a fluffy bunny trying to scowl.

"And stop saying you're ugly, Chlo. You have no idea… You're beautiful." I mean this, even though she complains about her pointy features and skin problems. But on her, it doesn't matter. She *is* beautiful—she's like an angel. She's the best friend I've ever had.

Chloe pulls her hand away and makes a circle in the dirt with the toe of her shoe. "You don't have to suck up *that* much," she says. Then she moves in for the kill. "I'll forgive you on one condition—you go to the dance next weekend."

My expression hardens, but Chloe pops up and down on her toes, begging, "Please, Andrea. Brick is threatening to drag me there by my nose, and he's got my mom and dad backing him. He's, like, the most annoying cousin ever. Just because he's all charming and popular at school with his little southern accent, he thinks I'm his goodwill project. Like he's got to save me from spending my entire adolescence hiding in the woods. Well, maybe I *like* the woods!"

While she rants, a smile spreads across my face. It still feels foreign, but I'm getting used to stretching my cheek muscles more often. "Brick's right," I tell her. "You should go."

"And so should you. And now you have to because you really hurt my feelings."

I stare at her pleading face, but know I can't commit. "It's not that I don't want to. I really can't."

"Why not? Give me one good reason."

"You know why. I have to work Friday night. If it were any other day—"

"Stop right there." Chloe's hand shoots up. "The DJ had a scheduling issue so student council moved the dance to Saturday night. Ha! You have no excuse now!" Her eyes practically dance with victory.

My eyes narrow. "You tricked me."

"Yep," she says proudly.

I consider what she's asking me to do and whether or not I can pull it off without Judd knowing. Then I decide I owe her. I owe her so much more than one stupid night at a dance.

"Fine, I agree to your terms," I say. "But only if you promise not to stop by again unless I specifically say so. Trust me on this, okay?"

"Okay," she agrees reluctantly.

"And don't pick me up on Saturday. I'll walk to your place after Judd and Ayla go out."

"Yeah, they'd probably be annoying, huh? Taking pictures and stuff? My mom will surely have her camera ready to document *this* historic event." Chloe growls, which comes off as comical.

I shake my head, but refrain from telling her she couldn't be more off-base. "Just don't come to the house. Or I won't go to the dance at all." I squint so she knows I mean business.

"Okay. Deal, deal, deal. Yay! And Brick will be so happy you're coming with us!" Chloe sings out and dances around in a circle. I watch her in dismay and wonder how someone like me ever became best friends with such a quirky little sprite. Then I allow a laugh to escape my lips.

Judd ruins the moment. The front door opens and his voice scrapes out like gravel against a chalkboard. "Almost dinnertime! C'mon inside now."

Chloe stops dancing to wave at Judd—a little less enthusiastically than before—and gives me a quick hug before skipping off into the trees. I walk back to the house and slink past Judd's body looming in the doorframe. "Want anything special for dinner?" I ask, keeping my voice mild.

"Lasagna," he replies, following me into the kitchen. I hate how he walks so close, his footsteps echoing in my ears, his tattooed arms within easy reach of my hair, my neck, my wrist.

Good thing we buy frozen lasagna. All I have to do is tear off the wrapping and stick it in the oven. While I get things ready, Judd leans against the counter and watches me. "So you made a friend," he states.

"Not really. She's just some freaky girl who clings to me because no one likes her." I hate saying the words, even though I'm doing it to protect Chloe. But Judd sees through my bluff.

"You just be sure that she don't come snoopin' around here again. And no sharing secrets about your dear old stepdad, either. Sure would be a shame if somethin' happened to the little Masterson girl." His threat seeps through my veins like ice.

"Don't worry, she doesn't know anything. And she's not smart enough to figure it out, so leave her alone," I snap.

Judd doesn't take kindly to my tone, and he lets me know it by grabbing the back of my head. His fingers press painfully against my skull. "Just you be sure," he whispers softly, then releases me with a jerk. He gives me a menacing look before settling onto the couch to watch TV. I resist the urge to spit in his lasagna, but only because I want to eat some too.

While the lasagna bakes, I go upstairs and lie down on the pale pink sheets to fret. It's almost November now, but the attic room is hot again, due to this Indian summer we're having. The heat makes me languid and drowsy, and before I know it...I'm eleven years old, riding my bike home alongside my new friend Delaney. It's late August—a warm, sunny day. We have plans to make lemonade, pull out the slip-n-slide, and spend a blissful afternoon on the lawn deciding who to invite to my upcoming birthday party.

I vividly remember the day—the balmy breeze, the way my insides felt like they were filled to the brim with sunshine. We dropped our bikes in the driveway and raced inside Gram's house. I scrambled to the top cupboard for the lemonade powder while Delaney grabbed the pitcher from under the sink. My body froze when I heard the retching noises coming from downstairs. Delaney missed them because she was talking, but I knew immediately—Ayla was back.

I left Delaney in the kitchen to finish the lemonade while I ventured downstairs alone. Our basement had a bathroom, a pull-out couch and a sitting area in it, along with stacks of my toys and games. Ayla knelt in the small bathroom, hunched over the toilet, while Gram perched on an upside-down garbage can and rubbed her back. No one saw me in the shadows.

"It's just the flu," Ayla told Gram, wiping the sick off the side of her mouth.

"Are you sure? You said you've mostly been sick in the mornings. If there's any chance you might be pregnant, you have to tell me," Gram insisted.

"Why, Mama?" Ayla said scathingly. "So you can buy this baby too? There's no price tag big enough to make me go through that again."

"Oh, Ayla, what made you so bitter?" Gram said and started to cry.

Seeing this, my eyes went wild with anger. How *dare* Ayla come here and upset Gram again! I charged into the bathroom, startling them both, and began slapping Ayla on the head and shoulders. I screamed at her to leave, to leave and never come back, because I hated her...we *all* hated her! She only made people sad and she should never have been born.

Gram wrapped her arms around my flailing little body and pulled me out of the bathroom while Ayla laughed viciously. "*I* should never have been born? That's the pot calling the kettle black," she hissed and turned back to the bowl, heaving again.

Gram dragged me up the stairs to calm me down, and I didn't even think about Delaney until we got to the kitchen and saw the pitcher of lemonade leaking all over the floor and only one bike out in the driveway—mine.

"Ayla ruins everything," I sobbed. Gram held me tight as tears poured down my face.

"She's *sick,* baby. She's just sick. She'll get better one day." Gram's voice was soft, but firm. And I knew that no matter how much I wanted it or wished it or willed it, Gram wouldn't send Ayla away. She would never give up the fairytale.

Somehow I miss the oven buzzer that signals the lasagna is ready, but I don't miss Judd's voice at the bottom of the stairs hollering, "Girl! Get your lazy ass down here before I belt it!"

I scramble into the kitchen, where I spoon the lasagna onto three plates and try to quiet the old memory that's still fresh in my mind. Ayla is eating dinner for once, so Judd allows me to sit at the table, too. This happens every so often now. I still attend to Judd's every demand, but I prefer this setup to eating my own portions cold after I've served and cleaned up his meal. It's more nerve-racking, but less time-consuming.

We eat in silence. Judd indicates that he's finished by

tossing his napkin onto his plate. Then he looks at Ayla and says, "Let's go out tonight, baby." It sounds more like a command than an invitation.

Ayla isn't in the mood. "You know I've got a big day tomorrow," she says through half-slit eyelids.

Judd's face hardens and I lean back on instinct. "I guess you'd better sober up, then."

Ayla shrugs and lethargically brings a forkful of lasagna to her lips. Scowling, Judd stomps into the bedroom to change clothes. A few minutes later he leaves the house, alone.

Once he's gone, I breathe easier. I clean up the kitchen and join Ayla on the couch because it's too hot to go back upstairs. Since Judd is withholding the stronger stuff, she alternates smoking and drinking from a wine bottle she had stashed under the cushion. We sit there staring at old music videos on the muted television. On screen, girls in skimpy clothes slither-dance through nightclubs, frolic in ocean waves, sloppy-kiss tough guys on motorcycles…it's all sex, drugs, and passion. I don't know anyone who actually lives like that, except maybe Ayla when she was younger. But I have a feeling it wasn't so glamorous.

Suddenly, the words explode from my mouth.

"What's his name, Ayla? The man you had sex with to conceive me?" I ask it that way on purpose. There's no father in this equation.

Ayla shoots me an amused glance. "Why? You gonna hunt him down, knock on his door? You think he's been pining all these years for the daughter he didn't know he had?" Ayla laughs sharply, but it's cut short by a strident cough, which she stops with a fierce drag on her cigarette.

When Gram used to smoke, her eyes would crinkle as she inhaled. You could tell that the nicotine and the routine of the act relaxed her. Watching Ayla now, I see how differently she approaches *her* habit. Instead of a long, deep draw, Ayla takes quick little puffs, squeezing the cigarette too tightly between her thumb and forefinger. She looks so impatient and angry that I almost feel sorry for the poor, abused thing clenched in her hand.

"I just want to know his name," I press. I'm not even sure why, but I'm burning for it all of a sudden, as if it's something tangible I can hold onto—like Gram's watch.

When Ayla ignores me, I shout, "I deserve to know the motherfucker's name! Is that too much to ask?"

"Yeah, Bones." She sighs. "It is, 'cause I don't *know* the motherfucker's name."

This comes at me from left field. Of course she knows his name. He was the boy she left home for. The one who lured Ayla into his druggie world, knocked her up, and then split. Gram told me all about it when I asked. She didn't sugarcoat anything.

"Bullshit," I retort. "Gram said you followed him around like a lovesick puppy."

"Oh. Mama's talking about Danny." Ayla says it like Gram is sitting right here with us, participating in the conversation. Then she smiles a little, like she's remembering something lovely. She opens her saggy eyelids a bit more, but her face hardens when she looks at me. "Yeah, she would think you were Danny's."

Wait, if not Danny…then who? Ayla knew Judd back then, I realize. Oh God. If I'm Judd's kid…I stare hard at the TV—like someone paused me for a minute—but my mind is not on pause. It's spitzing and fizzing and buzzing with panic. But no, it couldn't be Judd. Ayla said she didn't know the guy's name.

Ayla sits up a little. "Alright. You wanna hear a story? Danny was my first love. He was beautiful. Sweet. I'd have followed him straight to hell if he asked. Heh, pretty much did. We used to go to this house out in the woods. Kinda like this one. That's where everyone went to get loaded, have a good time.

"We didn't think anyone but our crowd knew about it, but one night an off-duty policeman showed up and flashed his badge. Everyone scattered. Except me and Danny, 'cause we were in the bedroom with the music on loud. We were the only ones still there when the cop busted through the bedroom door. By then Danny was too wasted to know which way was up, but I wasn't."

Ayla looks down at the disgusting carpet in front of the couch, scrunches her bare toes into it. "Wish I'd been as baked as he was. The cop told Danny to run home and not to come back. He didn't let me off so easy, though." She takes a drag on her cigarette and exhales a thin stream of smoke.

"Did you get arrested?" I ask when Ayla pauses.

Her face goes tight. "I got pregnant."

My eyes flash around, figuring things out at lightning speed.

"He handcuffed me first," Ayla continues in a small voice, "and I just went somewhere else. Up to the ceiling, like I was watching a movie. Didn't feel a damn thing until it was over. And when he was done? He left me there. Alone." She reaches over to the small table next to the couch and grabs the neck of a wine bottle, then takes a long sip before wiping her mouth with the back of her hand. "So there's your answer, Bones. Never had a chance to ask your *daddy* what his goddamn name was. Or if he was even a real cop."

"Don't. Call him. My daddy," I snarl through clenched teeth, surprised to find my voice so brittle. Surprised at how I can muster so little pity for Ayla even while feeling like all my bones are cracking and crumbling to dust. As if Ayla and I are connected, and she is not the addict sitting on the couch beside me, and I am not the spawn of a rapist.

After a minute, I assert desperately, "You were with Danny too. How do you know I'm not *his*?"

Ayla scoffs. "I knew the first time I saw you, crying your ugly bald little head off." Her gaze glides over my face. "You got the cop's eyes."

She turns away and sucks deeply on her cigarette until there's no tobacco left in it. I am glad Ayla doesn't look at me again, because I'm staring at her outline now, at her thin body battered by years of drug use. The curves and lines that make her up are getting blurrier and blurrier, and my pretty, pale blue eyes that everyone loves so much, are filling with seventeen years' worth of tears.

Ayla moves to get off the couch, but I stop her with one last, urgent question. "If I had been Danny's, would you have wanted me then?"

She stands up, sways a little. She turns to me and answers

with conviction, "No." Then she shuffles into Judd's bedroom, clutching the neck of the bottle, and shuts the door.

Shakily, I stand up and race outside, into the woods. I run fast, because if I stop…if I stop, the earth will swallow me up.

Soon I'm at the edge of the pond, stripping off my clothes, tumbling recklessly into the black abyss. The frigid water steals my breath, but I wade in until my toes feel the lip of the sandbar dropping off, deep. With one small gasp, I plunge below the surface.

Inside the belly of the pond my tears flow freely, indistinguishable from the pond water itself. Now I have some answers at least, to questions I never even imagined asking. This is why Ayla hates me, has always hated me. *This* is why she can lie there and not care what Judd does to me. Any indignity he imposes on me is nothing compared to what she suffered. Perhaps I'm meant to pay for my father's sins? Perhaps I deserve to…

The hoot of an owl is the first thing I hear when I break the surface. I haul myself onto the big log and stretch out there, naked in the moonlight. Bats dive overhead between the trees and I silently invite them to come, come and get me.

Chapter 33

Half an hour later, I sit on the bench in the woods outside the Mastersons' house, not quite knowing why I'm there. The back of my T-shirt is soaked where my wet hair lays coiled.

It's dark out—country dark, which is just one step shy of cave dark—and the wind rustles the tall corn stalks surrounding the farmhouse. Some of the corn has been harvested already, but several acres still stand. Chloe says they wait for it to dry out and then sell it for animal feed. Her family doesn't keep animals anymore, but they had goats when she was little. I've seen pictures of her holding the babies and feeding them with a bottle. There are pictures of her and Brick, too, sitting in the hayloft of the little barn on the far side of the property. The first time I saw those photos, I said she and Brick could have been poster children for some farmer's group, with their rosy cheeks and big smiles. Chloe still smiles a lot, but I've never seen Brick show so many teeth in real life. Now that he's told me about his parents, I guess I know why.

I sit, hidden in the trees, and watch the house. I can see the TV flickering through the windows of the great room. I'm shivering despite the warm air, and after several minutes I start feeling like the stalker I accused Chloe of being. So I shuffle out of the woods and knock on the side door.

Mr. Masterson greets me with a big smile and a little hug. "Oh, Andrea, you're sopping wet. Did I miss the rain?" He peers up at the star-studded sky as I enter.

"No." I force myself to laugh. "I went swimming in the pond."

"By yourself? At night? You crazy teenagers." He shakes his head and leads me into the great room, yelling up the stairs for Chloe.

On the big sectional couch, Brick is leaning back with his ankles crossed, knitting alongside Chloe's mom. I do a double take. *Knitting?* I mean, I know that historically men were the master knitters, but today it's a more common hobby for women. Still, he only seems slightly embarrassed as he glances up. We stare at each other curiously, him with his needles poised to do the next stitch and me plastered down in my wet tee. We both say, "Hey."

"What are you making?" I ask politely. "They look beautiful."

Mrs. Masterson smiles and says, "I'm working on a sweater and Brick's knitting a scarf."

"Cool," I say and fall silent, thinking how nice it would be to live in a home like this. Brick was lucky to have an awesome aunt and uncle ready to open their doors—and their arms—for him when things turned bad.

Worried about dripping on stuff, I stand way back behind the couch and watch the television—some legal thriller—until Chloe bounds down the stairs and flings her arms around my shoulders, almost toppling me. "No fair, you swam without me!"

"Jesus, Chlo, chill out," Brick chastises as I stumble under the weight of her attack.

She tugs on my hand. "Come upstairs. I'm trying to figure out my outfit for Saturday."

Saturday? Oh yeah, the dance I got suckered into. She leads me up to her spacious yellow bedroom. Before I can ask, she throws me a towel, which lands on my head.

"Thanks," I say and begin rubbing my hair dry.

"Are you cold? Here's a dry shirt." She tosses it, and this one lands on my shoulder.

While I turn my back and change into her yellow tee, Chloe disappears into her closet and emerges with a copper-colored dress, which she lays flat across her bedspread.

"I was thinking of wearing this, with tights and tall brown boots."

I turn around, the damp towel spread across my shoulders, and assess her ensemble. "Oh, that's gorgeous," I breathe. "You'll look so good."

"You think?" she bubbles. "Because there's this guy in homeroom…"

"Not Mr. Cavanaugh, I hope."

"I could only dream it," she says wistfully. Then she shakes her head a little, snapping back to reality. "But no, this guy's a freshman. Totally legit. His name's Ryan and I can't stop staring at him. Of course, it helps that he sits in front of me. My God, the back of his head is so fine. Anyway. He and his friends are going to the Harvest Dance in a big group, but on Friday he asked me if I was going to be there. When I told him probably, he said he hopes he'll see me!" she squeals.

I smile, relieved that Chloe is finally having some normal high school experiences.

"I need help with the jewelry, though. Can you look through my options while I try this on?" Without waiting for an answer, she scoops up her dress and skips to the bathroom down the hall.

Chloe's jewelry box is open on her dresser and I start pawing through it. I want to share in her enthusiasm, but I'm still burdened by the weight of Ayla's story. Then I wonder if it could be just that—a story. Maybe Ayla was lying about the cop, all of it. She's lied about plenty of other things. But deep down I know her story is true. Just as I knew Gram would never kick Ayla out for good. The shameful knowledge makes my stomach tighten up like a corkscrew.

Chloe's dilemma is a good distraction. I pick out some long gold earrings and a chunky bracelet to match. I'm pretty good at this girly stuff. Gram loved dolling me up for parties when I was younger, and we went all-out for *my* first high school dance two years ago. We started the tradition in junior high—every autumn Gram would take me shopping, then out to lunch. Even though I avoided the actual dance floor at the events, it was still fun dressing up and watching everyone. Last Fall, I got a cerulean blue sheath that matched my eyes. Delaney said it was *divine.* That's back when I was obsessed with Ben Stankowski…God. It seems like I've lived an entire, harrowing lifetime since then.

When I hear the bedroom door creak open, I whirl around, holding up the jewelry and saying, "I think these will be perf—" But it's not Chloe. "Oh, hey." I lower my hands.

Brick shakes his head. "I can't believe you went swimming. That water must be freezing right now."

"Well, I kind of needed to wake up," I say, but don't elaborate.

Brick didn't come up here to talk about the pond, though. He leans against the wall and slips his hands into his pockets. "Um, I didn't freak you out the other night, did I? I know I dumped a lot on you."

"No," I assure him. "I don't get freaked out easily."

"That's what I thought." A grateful smile curls up one side of his cheek.

"Thought about what?" Chloe interrupts, sweeping into the room.

"Wow!" I exclaim. "You look amazing."

My friend beams. "Really?"

Brick grumbles, "Yeah, I'm going to have my hands full keeping those freshmen boys at bay."

Chloe rolls her eyes, then commands, "Just be sure to let Ryan through."

I stifle a laugh as Brick's face becomes concerned. "Ryan? Who the hell is Ryan?"

"Ease off, cowboy. Your cousin's old enough to have a Ryan." I come to Chloe's rescue, linking arms with her in solidarity.

"We'll see," Brick mutters, leaving. Probably to go downstairs and alert the Mastersons to this new threat in Chloe's life.

"Maybe I shouldn't have mentioned Ryan." Chloe giggles after he's gone. "Good thing my parents are more laid back than he is."

"Don't worry," I tell her, holding out the gold earrings. "I'll distract Brick on Saturday while you and Ryan hang out."

Chloe arches her eyebrows, but I ignore the insinuation. There's nothing like that between Brick and me. Besides, romance is the last thing I need—or want. I'm still getting used to simply having friends again.

"You're sure about the gold?" Chloe asks, looking in the mirror. "I have this other stuff, too." She pulls out the bottom drawer of her jewelry box, and my eyes pop at all the sparkles. "Dad gave me these earrings on my eleventh birthday. They're real diamonds!" She holds them up, smiling. "And these pearls were my grandmother's."

"Well," I say, tilting my head. "Pearls are too conservative for a Harvest Dance, I think. The earrings are gorgeous, but I like the gold better with your outfit and your eyes. Ooh wait, what about this?" I pull out a glittering cut glass and diamond bracelet that catches all the light in different ways, reflecting the copper in Chloe's dress like a shimmery penny. "This would be *so*—"

"No," Chloe says abruptly. "I never wear that one."

"But—"

"No." She shakes her head. "I don't…like to wear that bracelet."

Sensing something deeper there, I say, "Okay," and put the bracelet back in the drawer. "You should wear whatever makes you feel prettiest, Chlo."

"I trust you," she tells me, looking in her full-length mirror again. "Gold it is. I hope Ryan thinks I'm pretty when he sees me."

I stand behind Chloe in the mirror like Gram used to do with me. And I use Gram's words when I assure her, "That boy will be over the moon."

Then we both double over, giggling.

Tuesday means back to school, but with the Harvest Dance a mere five days away, there is no actual learning taking place. Instead, there are ballots to cast—for the Harvest Dance King and Queen, as well as their adoring Court. There are volunteers needed for decorating and cleanup, for bringing food and punch, and for checking school IDs at the door. My mouth drops when I hear this. *Seriously?* Are dances at Belmont so spectacular that other people actually want to crash them?

I am at my wit's end by the time I slump into trig and drop my forehead on my desk, acting as dramatic as Chloe. After a moment, I feel Brick's hand massaging my neck and shoulders. "Rough morning?" he drawls.

Raising my head a bit, I nod. "If I hear one more word

about this stupid dance, I'm going to hide in the cornfields on Saturday night."

"Chloe would hunt you down," Brick says with a chuckle. "And I'd help, because you promised her."

"Don't remind me."

"You know, you might enjoy the dance, Andrea."

I shoot daggers at him with my eyes.

"Or not," he says, retracting his statement and his hand.

The class quiets down as Ms. Sampson enters the room. Then a small vibrating noise comes from Judd's phone, which is on top of my math book. I snatch it and hit mute without even looking. At the same time, my hand shoots up and I ask to be excused to the restroom.

With a curt nod from Ms. Sampson, I am out of there like lightning. Unfortunately, there are three giggling girls clustered in the nearest bathroom and the next one I try is being cleaned by the janitor. So I hit Judd's contact icon as I walk down a deserted hallway.

"The hell's *wrong* with you, makin' me wait so long?" Judd bellows.

"I was in class!" I whisper desperately.

"I don't care if you were in China. Do I need to remind you who's callin' the shots?"

I visualize the whiskey bottle sailing past my head. "I'll be faster next time."

"Good. Meet me at the market. And girl, you'd better run."

"Right now?"

"Right now." The line goes dead.

Shit. I hang up the phone and briefly wonder if Brick will get my books. That means I won't have them to study with tonight. Oh well, it's not like we're doing any real schoolwork this week. I slip out the side door, jog across the dusty baseball diamond toward the road, and don't stop running until I see Judd's black sedan parked in the back row of the market's parking lot.

Slipping into the front seat, I try to catch my breath, overdoing it on purpose—just in case Judd thinks I wasn't booking at an all-out sprint. We're already pulling onto the road when he shoves the red dress at me.

"Put it on."

"In the car?" I ask, horrified.

"Get in the back if you want. But trust me, there's nothin' I ain't seen."

I climb into the back and try to change without exposing too much of anything. My knees knock together nervously. I'm hesitant to ask Judd where we're going, since I can see how tense he is, but I have to know.

With the detested dress hugging my body and me sitting in the backseat, a whole arm's length away from Judd, I venture, "What do you want me to do?"

"Nothin'. Donovan wants to see how well you take direction."

"Why?"

"Because he does."

"Why the dress?" My voice shakes.

"He thinks all his ladies should wear dresses."

The words "his ladies" freeze me in terror. "I'm not going anywhere with him," I insist.

I half expect Judd to twist around and shut me up with the back of his hand, but he doesn't even acknowledge my words. As if I don't count. As if I'm nothing but the polluted, unwanted offspring of a rapist.

Then the horrible image of Ayla and the cop pops into my head. It's not hard to imagine Donovan doing the same thing to me.

"I'll turn you in," I say recklessly. "I know everything about your business. I'll tell the police who you are, where your drugs are hidden, the delivery routes, everything!"

I wait for my words to take effect, but Judd just laughs. "You think you know something? You know nothin'. Smoke and mirrors, girl. I've been doing this longer than you've been alive." His lip curls up over his yellow teeth. "Are you threatening me? When I finish with you tonight, you'll be lucky if you can move."

My stomach flips because I'm sure he's serious. But at least that means I won't be with Donovan tonight.

It's a time trial.

A test, like when Judd makes me call him back so fast on the phone. They're *training* me. That's the word Donovan uses when we meet him at the log cabin that's so far out of town we could be in Kentucky. I don't know where we are because Judd tied a blindfold on me several minutes before we got here. Now I'm standing next to the car, staring at Donovan and his henchman in front of a cabin deep in the woods. Donovan's hair is not slicked down today, but hangs in waves around his hooded eyes. If I didn't know better, if I saw him on the street, I'd think he looked cute. My stomach clenches. I can imagine naïve girls falling for him, dancing right into his trap.

He inspects me with that self-satisfied smirk, as if he knows I'll be his someday. Then he gets close enough to rub a lock of my hair between his fingers. I wrench away with disgust, even though Judd's eyes are boring into me, warning me to play nice.

"You're too soft on her," Donovan chastises Judd as they turn and walk away.

"She's under control," Judd assures him.

"These girls are like horses, Judd. You break 'em right away, or they'll always be ornery…"

Then they get too far away for me to hear any more of their disgusting talk. I glance at the cabin again, and something in the window catches my eye. No, not something. *Someone.* As quickly as I lock onto the set of eyes peering beneath the curtain, they are gone. I can't even be sure I didn't imagine them.

I surreptitiously search the windows, but no one appears again. As the men drift back toward the car, Donovan calmly threatens, "You're running out of time, Judd. Payment's due soon. Or she's mine."

Then Donovan's eyes slice over to me, and I realize I was meant to hear his threat. He reaches out swiftly, grabs my wrist and waits for me to react. Somehow, I know I shouldn't. I hold perfectly still until his grip relaxes. He trails a finger lightly up and down my arm.

Unlike Judd, who just wants respect and obedience, Donovan *enjoys* making me uncomfortable. To him, it's a game. When he releases me, I step back instinctively, bumping into the creepy bald guy whose job was to keep an eye on me while Judd and Donovan talked. Baldy isn't that intimidating, though, at least not in comparison to his cold, calculating boss. Until I met Donovan, I didn't think anyone could scare me more than Judd.

The two of them walk away again and Baldy looks down at his phone, bored. With the edge of my dress, I frantically rub at the spot on my arm where Donovan grabbed me, where his sweaty fingers pinched my skin. I want to get his smell, his essence, his *intention* off me.

When the men are done hashing things out, Judd pushes me back into the car and reattaches the blindfold, pulling it painfully tight. He's angry. Since I can't see, I silently count the seconds until we're on the highway. He takes off the blindfold after 1,720 seconds, but I keep counting. Someday, if I tell the police exactly how far away the cabin is from Haydon, maybe they can find it.

On the drive home, Judd seethes. I can tell by the way he yanks me from the car into the house that the meeting did not go as he'd hoped. Once we're in the cellar, he makes good on his promise by thrashing my legs with his belt. Somehow, Judd's fury seems to have more to do with Donovan's displeasure than my earlier threat, though.

I barely sleep that night. My legs throb like crazy. But that's not what keeps me up. It's Donovan's voice in my head, *Payment's due soon. Or she's mine.* And it's the memory of Donovan's eyes on me. He's always had a hungry look, but today I saw something even scarier—resolve.

I sit up and start to hyperventilate. Everything in my life seems to be accelerating erratically, like a spinning top veering toward the edge of a cliff. By Judd's count, I owe him eight hundred and fifty dollars. Maybe if I find a way to get him that money, he'll be off the hook with Donovan and I'll be off Donovan's radar as well.

I cup my right hand around the pretty silver watch and squeeze it. "I'm sorry, Gram." I whisper. But it's the only chance I've got.

Chapter 34

Since I'm not really sleeping, I get up extra early, tiptoe outside and head for the woods. The sun has barely risen, but Brick's green Explorer is parked on the street outside Judd's house. When I see it, I stop in my tracks, my eyes widening. Brick is slouched in the driver's seat. "What the…" I mumble to myself and march over.

As I approach, he sees me. He sits up and calls through the driver's window, "Hey, I brought your books—"

"Shh!" With a glance back at the house, I wonder how much of the road Judd can see from his bedroom window. I don't want him catching even a glimpse of Brick—for both our sakes. "Can I get a ride?" I ask quietly.

Brick nods. I quickly swing up into the passenger seat and we take off.

"This is really early, even for you," I say, trying to conceal my annoyance.

Brick's jaw twitches, but he stares straight ahead at the road. "I was worried about you."

I make myself laugh, though it rings false. "Because I ditched school? We weren't exactly learning anything."

He steers with his left hand while his right reaches into the back seat and emerges with a reusable grocery bag, which he drops into my lap. Inside it are all the books and papers I left in trig.

"I covered for you with Sampson," he says. "I told her you got sick and went to the nurse."

"Thanks," I say.

"Since when does Andrea Hathaway skip school?" he asks a moment later. "Since when does little miss 'I've-never-been-in-trouble-before' risk suspension by bolting in the middle of trig?"

"Um. Since yesterday, I guess." It's really hard to keep my voice light when my mind is fixated on the word he used—suspension.

I grab the oh-crap handle as Brick turns the Explorer onto a bumpy dirt road, brakes hard, and shoves the gear shift into park. He turns to me and stares, expectant.

"*What?*" I finally ask.

"Why'd you leave school yesterday? Who called you?" he demands.

I meet his glare with one of my own, but my mouth is clamped shut. This is the last thing I need. I have too much on my mind, too much to take care of with Judd, with Donovan. And I can't protect Brick and Chloe if they continue to push at me with these questions and show up at Judd's house uninvited.

When he realizes I'm not yielding, Brick slumps back in his seat, his hand over his eyes. "I'm really worried about you, Andrea. I was up all night."

I decide to play it lightly. "I'm sorry about your beauty sleep, but as you can see, I'm fine."

"You're not fine," he argues and then looks at me half angry, half concerned. "Look, I get that you want everyone to think you're this tough chick, aloof, too cool to be bothered with—"

"That sounds about right," I agree and stare out the window, aloofly.

"But I see something very different," he presses, gently. "I see a girl who thinks she's alone in the world. A girl who's guarded and...sad."

Whipping my head around, I say, "Guarded, maybe. I'll admit that I don't like people in my business. But pick another adjective because I'm definitely not *sad*."

"Okay, here's a better one..." Brick's brown eyes level me across the front seat. "Scared."

"You think I'm scared?" I scoff.

"I think you're terrified."

His accusation hangs in the air between us for a moment, then plummets.

"Screw you, Brick Mason." I fumble for the door handle, jump out of his SUV, and wade into the woods. They're dense here. Burrs cling to my jeans and tennis shoes.

Brick leaps through his own door and yells, "See? There you go, running away. I'm your friend, Andrea. Why won't you talk to me?"

I don't answer. I haven't been careful enough with my words—that's why I'm in this predicament.

"You don't have to be afraid of me," Brick calls desperately.

"Afraid of *you*?" I laugh, wrestling with a tall cluster of reeds impeding my path. I grit my teeth and yank at the reeds, scraping up my palms. "I'm not afraid of anybody."

There's a pause. And then, "Not even that guy you live with?"

I freeze. Spin around and face Brick, who is now only a few feet away. I stare hard at him. His eyes bore right back at me with the same intensity. "Why would you—?"

"It's the way you jump whenever he calls."

"You have no idea what you're talking about," I say coldly.

Brick's eyes zero in on mine. "And it's the way he dragged you into your house yesterday."

I stare, dumbfounded. A thousand emotions whip through me like wind. "You're...spying on me?"

"No. I was waiting for you to come home so I could give you your books."

While I search for my breath, I glance down at the small patch of woods between us. Brick walks closer, carefully. "But I saw the way you shrank away from him. I saw the way he held onto you." Brick's hand slowly moves to my arm, touching me softly in the exact place above my elbow where Judd pinches me, where he yanks so hard I think my arm might pop loose from my shoulder. "Please tell me what's going on," he says. "I can help, or I can just listen, and it'll be our secret. But you need someone..."

Breaking out of my trance, I snatch my arm back. "Stay the hell away from me. Stay out of my life. I mean it." But I'm not convincing anyone. I wasn't ready for this, wasn't expecting to be called out today. I hate this feeling, this loss of control, this sensation of being exposed.

Brick's eyes are glossy, his jaw set like stone. "What does he do to you? Andrea..." By the look on Brick's face, I don't have to guess what he's thinking. He saw me in that horrible dress, after all. Shame floods my neck, turning my pale skin a deep crimson.

"It's nothing like that! He just pushes me around, makes me help him with his business."

"What kind of business?"

I cross my arms, upset that I've told him this much. "Direct sales."

He stares at me for a long minute. Then his eyes widen, like he's figured something out. "You mean drugs, don't you? Holy shit..." He takes a step back.

"No, Brick! God, you have some imagination. He sells stuffed bears, clothes, small appliances...It's like a home shopping channel but through the Internet. Sometimes I have to dress up to do product demonstrations, like yesterday." I grab his arm, desperate for him to buy my story. "It's demeaning, but it's not illegal."

Brick's eyes are incredulous. "You almost believe it yourself, don't you? That it's all okay? Andrea, you're in serious trouble. Let me help you."

"I don't need your help. I'm handling it." I grit my teeth and explain, "My Gram's dead. My mom's sick. I don't have an Uncle Pete and Aunt Lil like you do. You don't know, sitting up there in your big house, how much worse it could be. How much worse *he* could be. So just get off my case because I know what I'm doing."

But he isn't listening. He's walking fast to his Explorer, opening the back door, fumbling through his backpack. And I'm trailing him to make sure he doesn't do something stupid like call his uncle, or the police. "Brick—"

He thrusts something into my hands. "Here. Take my phone. He probably monitors that other one, right? Take this. I want you to call my house if you need help. I don't care if it's three in the morning, you call and I'll come—" He is frantic, his words colliding.

I push the phone away. "No, I can't—"

"Andrea, please!"

"No." If Judd sees me with this phone, or hears it, or finds it...

As usual, Brick reads my mind. "Hide it somewhere. Turn it off until you need it. Save the battery."

His eyes are bloodshot and so worried that I'm stunned, flattered, by how much he cares. I think about Judd's whiskey bottle coming at my head, the cold night spent in the cellar, the welts currently plastered across my legs. But I can't bring myself to tell Brick that if it ever gets to the point where I need him to rescue me, it'll probably be too late.

Instead I say, "Just write down your number. That way

you'll have your phone if I need to reach you."

After thinking about it for a minute, he scribbles his number on a paper and hands it to me. "*Any* time. I mean it."

"Okay." I put the slip of paper in my pocket.

He runs both his hands through his hair. "Look, I can't just forget what I saw. So don't be surprised if my truck's parked in front of your house every night from now on."

"Brick, *no.* You can't come near the house again. Chloe either. You'll make things worse for me. Jason's irritated right now, but in a few days he'll be fine."

"Why?" he demands.

I look away, sick that I'm telling him any of this. But it's the only way to keep him from opening his own stupid mouth. "I owe him some money. I just have to pay him back."

"Jesus, Andrea! He's a grown man and you're a junior in high school. What could you possibly owe him money for?"

"I told you, he takes care of my mom. He doesn't do it for free."

Brick looks confused. "You said he paid you. That all the money you earned was in some trust. I thought you didn't have access to it."

"Yeah, but I'm getting a check soon. Inheritance from my Gram." It's sort of true, I think, since it's her watch I'm going to sell. "Then everything will be fine."

Brick shakes his head. "This is all kinds of wrong. You shouldn't have to do any of this. Can't you go to the police—"

"They'll take my mom away. Plus I don't *want* to go to a

foster home, okay? I need to be in a good school district. I need to get into a good college. Can't you understand that?"

Finally, Brick seems to comprehend my motives. Grades and college and focusing on the future are things he does understand.

He presses his lip together, deciding. "Swear to me that you're not in danger."

"I swear." I say it fast and then sigh in exasperation. "You're blowing this way out of proportion. It's really not that bad."

His eyes look deeply into mine, searching. "I really hope you're right."

Brick seems calmer now, and all I can do is smile a bit and roll my eyes and hope that I've convinced him.

We stand in silence for a minute, decompressing. Then we slowly climb back into the Explorer. I pull on my seatbelt while Brick stares at the woods. "Are you hungry?"

I'm always hungry. I shrug. "A little."

"I spent all night in my car. I'm exhausted and famished." He glances at me over his shoulder. "Wanna ditch school again?"

"Okay." I'm not sure I want to spend the entire day with Brick, though. The events of the last half hour have totally unnerved me, and part of me just wants to find a quiet place to digest everything. But I may need to do more damage control. I have this sensation of being split wide open, with all my secrets dangling dangerously in the breeze.

At the same time, being with Brick feels easier now. Even though I fed him half-truths, he is the first person who has come close to knowing anything about my real life. My secret life. And despite how worried I am about the money and Donovan and Judd, I want more than anything to hold onto this new feeling of intimacy, this lovely feeling of not being so utterly alone. My other problems can wait a day, I decide. They can wait.

We get breakfast to go. Brick suggests running into the deli at the market, but I shake my head and he doesn't question it. He drives through McDonald's, then steers down some gorgeous country lanes to a patch of woods I've never seen. With our Mickey D bags and a blanket Brick snagged from the back of his SUV, we duck under a chain and head down a service road. I follow his lead through the thicket, lost in my own head.

"This road leads to the far side of my uncle's property, behind the cornfields," he explains. "There's a nice little brook back here. It's a good place for a picnic."

I don't respond, just plod along next to him. The October sky is smoky blue, the leaves dressed in their autumn shades.

It's not until after Brick has arranged our little picnic spot and I'm sitting with my bare feet dangling in the ice cold brook that I speak again. "What'd you tell Chloe about yesterday?"

"Nothing." Brick's answer comes from behind my back and I purposely don't face him.

"Why not?"

"She's so happy right now, excited about the dance. I haven't seen her that way in a while."

"Good. Don't upset her." At least we agree on that.

For a few minutes, the only sounds are the gurgling brook

and the screams of a red-tailed hawk high up in the trees. Then I hear Brick crumpling up one of the paper bags. "You'd better come eat or there may be nothing left."

It takes me a few minutes to find the will to move. When I finally drag myself away from the brook, there is still plenty of food waiting for me, set up nice and neat on one side of the red plaid blanket. Brick lies stretched out with his hands clasped behind his head, his sweatshirt balled up for a pillow. With his eyes closed, he looks boyish—far younger than his nearly-eighteen years.

I sit on the blanket and start nibbling an Egg McMuffin. I'm glad Brick isn't looking at me, glad he's so tired that he can't keep his eyes open, because I need to be alone with my thoughts. I need to plan. Unfortunately, the answers aren't clear. I only have the one idea. If it doesn't work…I don't know. Running away isn't an option anymore. There's no Buick, no money, no way that Judd and Donovan wouldn't hunt me down. Or worse, go after Brick and Chloe in my absence. I've made a royal mess of things.

When I'm finished eating, I hug my knees and watch Brick's chest move up and down for several minutes.

I don't worry about the tears that start sliding down my cheeks, about the hurt and worry bubbling up and pressing against the surface of my throat, about how I'm letting down my defenses with Brick a mere three feet away, dozing lightly. It's strange, this in-between place. This place where Brick knows something isn't right with me, but he doesn't know exactly how wrong things are.

"Hey," he murmurs after a while, stirring from his slumber and catching me crying. I don't bother trying to hide it. He lifts his arm and, with that simple gesture, beckons me.

Crawling across the blanket, I rest my head against his bicep, curling onto my side next to him. His right arm curves around me, the warmth of his body making me feel tender and cared for and safe. Brick's touch cuts right to my core. And it's not because I'm having some romantic notion about him, either. It's because I haven't been held like this in so freaking long. Maybe not ever.

And then, like a poison-tipped arrow gliding through time and space, the pain I've been holding at bay for the past ten months comes at me fierce, poking through slits in my armor. More tears seep out from the corners of my eyes, unstoppable.

"I miss my Gram." A small sob hitches out along with my words. "I miss her so much."

Brick's arm tightens round me, but he says nothing. After a ragged breath, I add, "I didn't get to go to her funeral. I don't even know where she's buried."

Pause. "When did it happen?"

"Last December, right before Christmas. She had a heart attack. I was the one who found her." Now that I've cracked the dam, information gushes out. "I stayed with her until the paramedics came, but I knew she was…gone."

"I'm so sorry," he whispers.

I sniffle, try to get myself under control. "I don't know why I'm thinking about her right now, anyway. Do you think about your mom a lot?"

He's quiet for so long I don't think he's going to answer.

But then I feel his chest inhale and exhale against me, and he says, "I try not to. It's easier not to. But of course I do."

I nod and rub my nose. "And your dad? Do you think about him?"

"All the time," Brick responds, choking on the words.

I reach up and place my hand against his arm, the one that's draped across me.

"When does he…get out?"

"Three more years. Just before I turn twenty-one."

"Wow," I breathe. "That's a long time."

Brick lies very still as he speaks. "He got the minimum sentence for manslaughter. They might've cut a plea but he had a previous DUI. Aunt Lillian couldn't represent him, but she worked with his lawyer. She was very level-headed, unlike the rest of us."

I don't know how to respond. So I just listen.

"Uncle Pete can't stand to hear my dad's name. He'll never forgive him for killing his sister. He only wants to talk about my mom and how great she was, and I just…can't deal with it, so I walk away. I guess it's rude, but it's better than when I first got here. I used to snap at people, teachers even."

"Really?" I marvel. He seems so in control now.

"Yeah. There's a reason I know Mr. Greeley so well." He laughs a little, and I do too. It feels good, the laughter. A different type of release. When it dissipates, Brick admits, "I have to work really hard at it. I'm not as strong as you, Andrea."

We fall into silence and it takes a while before I feel it, his hand soft on my shoulder, his finger moving around in circles.

"Andrea." Over and over he repeats my name, like a prayer. A plea.

"Stop," I whisper after a while. "Please stop saying my name."

His mouth quits, but that's all. He continues to trace circles on my skin, waiting. I know it is my turn to speak. And I *want* to tell him the whole ugly truth about my life. But as always, tar or glue or cement—or fear—keeps my lips sealed.

Eventually it occurs to me that Brick is not tracing random patterns on my arm. He is writing my name in cursive, over and over again, like it is something special, something to be cherished. Something worth saving.

"What happened to you?" he finally whispers.

What can I tell him? That I've learned to gauge my safety by reading the level of lust in a man's eyes? That I've been homeless, and so hungry that I break the law in exchange for food? That he was right about the drugs? That there are grown men who want to keep me and my mother as their play-things? That I'm in more danger than I ever realized?

No. If I tell him any of those things, I will be putting him and Chloe in the exact same danger. And I won't do that, not when they've been so good to me.

The best route is denial.

"Nothing happened to me." My voice is as flat as the cornfields.

For a moment, Brick is silent. Then I feel his breath on my shoulder where his finger was just circling. "Of course it didn't," he says and kisses me there with the lightest touch, that of a feather.

Chapter 35

Turns out Gram's watch isn't worth much. The guy at the pawn shop offers me fifty bucks for it. When I balk, he shrugs and tells me to bring him some gold instead. But gauging by the price of the merchandise in the shop, I'd have to hunt down a heck of a lot of gold to match my debt.

"I need a thousand dollars," I say desperately.

The guy laughs in my face, his beer belly jiggling against the glass on his side of the counter. "The only jewels that fetch that kind of dough are diamonds, baby."

"Diamonds?"

"Yeah. And the more unique the piece, the higher the price. Happy hunting, kid."

I leave the shop with my heart in my shoes, and with Gram's watch securely attached to my wrist. I know nothing of diamonds—Gram never spent money on that kind of jewelry. All I can think of are engagement rings. But what are the chances that some woman is going to drop her engagement ring in the next few days, and that I'm going to happen to find it? Not likely.

Outside, the late afternoon wind bites at my cheeks and whips my long hair into my face. The Indian summer is history, gone as quickly as it arrived. The temperature dropped to the thirties today and I'm freezing my arms off in just a T-shirt and my long black vest, but there's no chance in hell I'm asking Judd to buy me winter clothes.

I pull on my swirly pink and black ski cap, the one that kept me warm when we were living in the Buick last winter. The one that smells like home.

With my hands balled in my jeans pockets, I look up and down the streets, the buildings as gray as the sky, as gray as my mood. It took me forever to walk here. All for nothing.

I begin the trek back to Haydon, my strides long and brisk. I feel beat down, so tired of trying to survive. For a while I think of nothing, just clear my mind like Ayla's hippie friends in their yoga poses. *Downward Facing Dog*. That's me, all right. It takes every ounce of willpower for me to continue walking in this direction, to not veer off into a completely new life. I should have left Ayla months ago when I had the chance, because now I'm stuck. Now I have people to protect. Now I have connections that I should never have made.

As I trod up Judd's driveway an hour later, I hear him and Ayla shouting inside the house. Ayla can swear worse than a sailor in a white squall, and from the sound of things, there's quite a storm brewing. I shuffle around in the dirt near Judd's car for a minute, trying to stay warm while I decide what to do. It's a crap shoot as to whether I'll be able to sneak upstairs or get caught in their crossfire. I decide it's not worth the gamble. Better to come home later and hope that Judd has calmed down, passed out, or gone to a bar to drown his sorrows.

I turn and sprint through the woods toward Brick's house, toward safety—and if I'm honest with myself—toward the soft, sweet kiss he placed on my shoulder.

Mrs. Masterson answers the side door. She purses her lips in disapproval when she sees me standing there shivering. "The kids are both out," she says regretfully. "Brick is with some friends and Chloe's at the store with her dad."

With chattering teeth, I thank her and turn to leave, but she reaches out and puts her hand on my shoulder, stopping me. "I should let you freeze out there," she says with a wry smile. "The way you teenagers run around without coats. I've wasted more breath arguing with Chloe about dressing appropriately for the weather." She shakes her head as I rub my arms.

"Yeah, my mom says the same thing." What a liar I am.

Mrs. Masterson nods toward the house. "Come on in and have some hot cocoa before you catch pneumonia. I'm not about to send you home without warming you up first."

Since my only other option is to hunker down in the woods and shiver for the next couple of hours, I accept. As I step into the cozy country kitchen, the soothing notes of instrumental music float out from a speaker on the counter. I immediately recognize

Liszt's Hungarian Rhapsody No. 2 from my Musical Masters elective. As it segues into Pachelbel's Canon in D, I smile a little. Guess I learned something in that class after all.

I spy a pile of knitting heaped on the counter and some of Chloe's schoolbooks open, like she left in the middle of a tough algebra problem. Instantly, I'm overwhelmed with a sense of longing. For this. For Chloe's life. Even for Brick's, tragedy and all.

For twenty blissful minutes, I sit at the big planked wooden table and sip cocoa and munch on cookies and chat with Chloe's mom. Mostly we talk about school and books. It's the best conversation I've had with an adult in a long time. She's impressed that I'm so well read, and I blush with pride at her compliments. I wish I didn't have to leave this place, this moment, but eventually I finish my drink, and Mrs. Masterson reaches over to pick up my mug and carry it to the sink. That's when I notice her wedding rings—three small sparkling diamonds set into a thick gold band— and beside it a marquee-shaped stone that glimmers in the light from the chandelier.

And then the terrible, perfect idea hits me.

"You can borrow one of Chloe's coats to wear home," Mrs. Masterson says. "Or I can drive you."

"A coat would be great. Even a sweatshirt's fine. Thanks."

"Okay." She walks toward the mud room. I take a breath.

"Actually..." I say. "I think I left my T-shirt here the other night when I stopped by. Would it be okay if I grab it from Chloe's room?"

"Of course." There's not even a hint of suspicion in her voice.

Upstairs, I shut the bedroom door quietly and hurry over to Chloe's jewelry box. My hand is shaking as I pull out the bottom drawer and poke my fingers into the mass of sparkles, seeking the one item I know Chloe doesn't wear, ever.

Dangling from my fingers, the diamond bracelet shimmers like a million stars. It looks unique. It looks expensive. But what if I'm wrong? I won't have another chance. I stuff the bracelet into my jeans pocket and then pluck out the glittery diamond earrings that Chloe showed me the other night. The earrings her father gave her for her eleventh birthday.

I'll bring these back. I'll only use them if I have to. I tell myself this over and over as I push them frantically down into my other pocket.

As I'm closing the little drawer, I catch sight of my reflection in the mirror. A lump forms in my throat because all I see is a pretty girl with ice blue eyes and an evil soul. A girl who takes what she wants. A girl who may be more like her father—and her mother—than she wants to admit.

My heart pounds. My eyes sting with tears that disappear almost as fast as they form.

I have to survive, my mind argues.

But that doesn't make it right.

Before the guilt overwhelms me, I turn away and do a quick sweep of the bedroom. My shirt is laying near the top of her laundry pile. I'm sure it would've been returned to me clean and folded and smelling like lilacs.

Oh Chlo, I think as I snatch it, *your worst mistake was ever wanting to be my friend.*

A few minutes later, I hurry out of the Mastersons' house tucked snugly into Chloe's brown puffy winter coat. I'm only a few car-lengths down the long paved driveway when I stop, pull the bracelet from my jeans and fold it into my fist. It felt too heavy sitting in the bottom of my pocket, like a boulder whose weight could pull me under the earth and hold me in some devil's prison, which is probably right where I deserve to be. I stare at the bracelet, feeling sick. *What have I done?*

"Hey. What brings you out on this blustery evening?"

Brick's cheerful voice, with its unmistakable southern drawl, is *right* behind me. I jump and spin around and clutch at my chest. I think I also yelp in surprise, but who could be sure with the way my heart is hammering in my ears?

"Oh my God! Don't you know not to sneak up on girls in the dark of night?" Infuriated, I push at his chest while he laughs. And then I notice the end of Chloe's bracelet dangling from my grip.

Unfortunately, Brick notices too. "What's that?" he asks, curious.

Crap. If I act weird about it, he'll get suspicious. Anyway, what are the chances a 17-year-old boy knows what kind of bling his cousin owns? Chloe never wears this bracelet, and I highly doubt Brick has gone snooping through her jewelry box.

I open my palm. "A bracelet."

Brick's face is a complete blank as he looks at it. "Pretty," he says flatly.

I breathe a quiet sigh of relief. "Yeah. It was my Gram's."

He slips his hands into his jeans pockets. "Shouldn't it be on your wrist?"

"Well. It's a little big and I was afraid it would slip off in the woods, so..." I shrug and stuff it back down into my pocket. "Anyway, where were you tonight?"

He frowns. "At Mike's, watching Ole Miss get their asses handed to them on a platter."

"Ole Miss. Is that your team?"

He nods. "That's where my parents went to college. We used to go to the games a lot, so I'm required to be a fan. But this season?" He shakes his head. "They're killin' me."

I look directly at Brick's face for the first time since he appeared. There it is again, something pensive in the way he's watching me. I remember how worried he was when I left school Tuesday, how he confronted me about Judd, how we snuggled together so tenderly by the brook. What would he think if he knew I'd stolen this bracelet from Chloe's bedroom? He'd never speak to me again. He'd retract all his concern and kindness, his loyalty and friendship. And he'd be right to do it.

"Sorry," I say hastily, turning away. "I have to go—"

"Wait. Is everything okay?" But I don't wait.

"Yes!" I call over my shoulder. "See you tomorrow."

I sprint into the woods, gaining speed. Instead of taking the familiar path back to Judd's house, I veer left, along the Mastersons' property line where I'm hidden by the trees and the uncut corn. I run until the fields disappear and the brush grows thicker and I'm sure I must be near the brook where Brick and I picnicked. From this side, though, everything looks different. Somewhere above me, an owl hoots. As I walk deeper into the woods, I lose all sense of direction.

I'm hoping to find the service road and regain my bearings because it's pitch dark and eerily quiet, and I'm more than a little spooked. These woods cover more acreage than I originally thought. I could wander around, lost for hours, before finding my way back.

The service road eludes me, but I figure the narrow path I'm on must lead somewhere familiar. After several minutes of walking, I spot movement ahead, tiny lights bobbing around. Instinctively, I crouch low, slither off the trail and tuck myself behind a large bush. Through the shrub's leaves, I spy two men coming my way, carrying flashlights. Breathing silently through my mouth, I am grateful for the dark brown color of Chloe's coat and my black-as-night hair.

Hopefully the hikers will pass by without noticing me. In case that doesn't happen, I'm poised to run. As they get closer, their voices roll across the wind.

"Don't see why we couldn't do this in daylight," grumbles one of the men.

"You scared of the dark, Jackson?" the other teases.

Jackson shoves him. "It's frickin' cold, that's all."

"Such a pussy. Maybe you should ask Judd for a blankie next time?" The guy snickers.

My eyes grow wide.

"Very funny. Let's just hurry up and grab his shit and get

back to your place. He's probably waiting."

The men can't be more than six yards away now, but they move off the trail to my left. A brighter light fills the area and I pull myself into an even tinier ball. This new light spills out from a small shed, well-hidden behind a cluster of trees. A windowless shed like the one Judd takes me to work in every Friday night.

The men duck inside and then reappear with bulging backpacks. I catch a glimpse of the first guy's face in the light and immediately notice the bright red scar above his eyebrow. When he orders his friend to hurry up, I recognize his voice as the one complaining before, the one named Jackson.

I don't move until they are long gone. When it feels safe, I start to tiptoe along the path again, looking over my shoulder every five seconds.

Smoke and mirrors, Judd told me the other day in the car. Is this what he meant? That what I know of his operation is just a tiny slice of the whole? Maybe these woods are crawling with hidden sheds. Maybe all the little rundown houses that dot the edges of the forest are inhabited by Judd's workers. Maybe his operation is a lot bigger than I thought.

It's almost midnight when I stumble into Judd's driveway with my feet half-frozen, my nose running, and my body numb. The house is dark and still. I creep up to the attic and pull the cord that illuminates the light bulb. Below it waits my empty, soft bed.

After shoving Chloe's jewelry inside my pillowcase, I strip down to my underwear and slip between the sheets. I shiver for hours, but it's not from the cold.

Chapter 36

Thank goodness the pawn shop is open twentyfour-seven because I couldn't bear to hold onto Chloe's jewelry for long. I leave Haydon when it's still dark and arrive at the strip mall before daybreak. The guy with the beer belly is working again. I walk in and set Chloe's bracelet on the counter.

"You're back!" He greets me with mock enthusiasm and a knowing smile. "And you've brought diamonds." Pleased, he picks up the sparkling bracelet and begins to examine it.

I hate seeing his stubby fingers manhandle such a precious thing, but I can't look away. I want to make sure he doesn't try anything funny, but watching forces me to feel the full weight of my actions. As he looks closely at each stone with a special magnifier, I swallow over the lump lodged in my throat. My hand itches to snatch the bracelet back. But I don't.

After a few minutes, he sets the bracelet down between us. "Five hundred and eighty."

My jaw drops. "It's worth way more than that!" Actually, I don't know this to be true. But I *need* it to be true, so that's what I say.

The guy raises his eyebrows. "You got a receipt? I don't buy stolen merchandise."

Uh oh.

"I didn't steal it," I say hotly, as if insulted. "It was a gift from my dad, and it's worth a lot more than five-eighty."

He seems to buy my story, probably because he wants to. "Well. It might've cost a thousand new, but I can't sell it for that. This is a business, kid."

I narrow my eyes at him. He knew exactly how much I wanted. He had an unfair advantage in these negotiations.

"Take it or leave it," he says and gives me a moment to decide.

Angrily, I reach into my pocket and pull out Chloe's earrings. "What about these?"

He pulls out his eyepiece again and takes a look. This time, he says, "They're good quality. I'll take the pair for three hundred."

So that's it. I got what I needed. Eight-eighty will buy my freedom.

I hesitate, but not for long. With a nod, the deal is done. Chloe's jewelry is swept off the counter and into a plastic container, and my hands are holding onto the cash like a vice.

"Want a bag for that?" the guy asks.

I don't answer—just stare at all the green—so he goes ahead and places an opaque bag on the counter for me. "We all do what we have to, kid," he says, then walks away with the jewelry.

As I turn to leave, my eye catches something in a glass case. I peer closer and see a flat-sheathed blade—short, sharp, and small enough to hide in my pocket. The tag says $35.

I call the man over and ask to see the knife. It fits my hand perfectly and makes me feel…unbreakable. "I'll buy it for twenty," I bargain.

The guy laughs as if he likes my spunk. He agrees to my price, and I leave with the knife tucked securely in the pocket of my jeans.

I jog all the way back to Haydon so I can meet my friends for the ride to school, but when I reach the Mastersons' driveway, Brick's Explorer is nowhere to be seen. He always parks it in the same spot, creature of habit that he is. But today there's nothing but an empty patch of asphalt to stare at, and it somehow makes me feel empty, too. I check my watch. I'm not late, but apparently they left for school without me. That's not like them. A twinge of worry squeezes my heart. I hope Brick didn't mention the bracelet to Chloe. But why would he?

The bag of cash is stuffed in the deepest pocket of my cargo jeans, and I feel a little uneasy carrying it around. But I'm certainly not leaving it at Judd's house. I glance toward the woods and consider hiding it inside a log or buried by the pond but ultimately decide it's safest with me.

At a steady run, I make it to school on time, but I'm a mess of sweat when I arrive. I'm also starving and exhausted, and I feel like a space cadet through my morning classes. In trig, Brick's seat is empty. I keep staring at the door, waiting for him to burst in, but he doesn't show. Halfway through class I start to panic, adrenaline shooting through me. What if he did something stupid like go and confront Judd? Oh God.

It's hard to keep myself from sprinting down the hall to the cafeteria after class. When I spy Chloe waiting in our usual spot with a pinched look on her face, my heart skips a beat.

"Chloe! What's wrong?"

She rushes over and we both turn away from the cafeteria and walk down the hall toward the North wing, which is always the least populated at lunchtime. Her hand grips my forearm so tightly that I know, I just *know*, something horrible has happened to Brick. My stomach feels like it's turning itself inside out.

"I'm freaking out!" she explodes when we're far enough away from the throngs of students. "I don't know what to do…"

"What happened? Is Brick okay?" I have to try really hard not to shout these things.

"Brick?"

"Yeah, he wasn't in trig."

Chloe looks baffled. "He said he told you. He and my dad had to sign some papers for his mom's estate this morning. He's coming later."

"Oh." I sag with relief. Then I wonder *why* he didn't tell me. It's not like Brick to be forgetful. But Chloe's face is still scrunched up and worried, so my adrenaline shoots right back up. "What's wrong then?"

"I've done something awful." She paces back and forth in the deserted hallway. Her breathing is rapid, and her words spill fast. "I've been trying on my outfit for the dance every night this week, and playing around with different jewelry and shoes, you know? Not that I don't trust your opinion on the jewelry," she adds hastily. "But just for fun."

"Yeah?"

"Well, last night I couldn't find my diamond earrings."

I take a step back. Feel the boom in my chest. The bag of cash burns in my pocket, like the telltale heart.

"I looked everywhere for them," Chloe goes on, oblivious to my reaction. "I even went through the vacuum bag, in case I'd dropped them and my mom had cleaned up. And then, when I was looking through my jewelry box again, I realized that I'd also lost that diamond bracelet. The one you said would look so perfect with my outfit. Remember?"

"Yeah," I say again. "The one you don't like?"

"It's not that I don't *like* it. I just don't wear it. I mean, that bracelet is more important than—" She stops moving and I swear she's going to burst out sobbing right there in the hallway. Her eyes fill and her little hands ball into fists. I grasp her shoulders hard.

"Chloe, don't cry. It's just jewelry."

She shakes her head miserably, the tears bubbling out. "It's not just jewelry. It was my aunt's bracelet. Mom brought it back from Mississippi for me, but I never wore it because I thought it would upset Brick. His mom loved that bracelet. And now I've lost it! And Brick...won't have it later when he wants it, for his wife or his daughter someday. I'm such an idiot!" She grasps her head with both hands.

While she berates herself, everything in my line of vision begins to mesh into a thick stream of liquid color. I back up into a row of lockers because I'm pretty sure I might faint.

If that bracelet belonged to Brick's mom, and he saw me with it last night…Listened to me lie and say it was my Gram's… The realization hits harder than one of Judd's punches. Brick knew all along. He knew as soon as he saw it in my thieving little fist.

I cover my face with my hands, feel the panicked heat blister through my fingers.

"I know!" Chloe wails, mistaking the meaning behind my gesture. She plops down cross-legged on the floor and buries her head in her lap. "What am I going to do?"

I slide down next to her and think, *You are going to hate me. When Brick tells you the truth, you are going to spit in my face and call me all sorts of horrid names. You are going to say I betrayed you, our friendship, everything.*

I should come clean right this minute.

But my survival instinct is too strong. I have a wad of cash in my pocket that could set me free from Judd. Without it, I'll be whisked away to Donovan's cabin to face who-knows-what horror.

Chloe is practically sobbing now. "Brick said he didn't want it, that he didn't need some damn bracelet to remind him of his mom. But *my* mom said he might change his mind someday, when he's not so…raw. I was just supposed to keep it—" She hiccups. "—safe!"

I absently pat Chloe's hand but my mind is stuck on what she just said about Brick and his mom's bracelet. All this time I've been clinging to Gram's watch like it means something, like it means *everything*. Meanwhile, Brick knew better.

"What am I going to do?" Chloe wails again.

I purse my lips and force myself to focus. "Put it out of your mind for a couple of days. I'll come over on Sunday and we'll turn your room upside down. I promise we'll find them. Okay?"

"But I already looked. I looked everywhere!"

"When you're upset, sometimes you miss things. Give it a few days, Chlo. That's what I always do. Just trust me."

Nodding miserably, she raises her head and lays it against my shoulder. "I do trust you."

I stroke her hair and work hard to keep from throwing up.

Brick finds me in the hallway as lunch is ending. I sense his presence before I hear the request. "So, I heard Sampson piled on the work today. Mind if I borrow your notes?" His voice is soft and slow and melty, and I realize that I love the way Brick drags out certain words. The way his Southern dialect makes me feel like he has all the time in the world, and he's saved it just for me. I'm going to miss that. I'm going to miss everything about him.

Luckily, my head is buried in my locker so I don't have to look at him. Without speaking, I hold out my math notebook in his general direction.

"Thanks." I can hear the soft whir of pages being flipped. "I'll give it back after school."

"No rush," I mumble.

Maybe he'll walk away now. *Please, Brick, walk away.* I won't be able hide my guilt from him. He'll read it on my face, no matter how composed or aloof I try to make it look. He's already proven that he can see through me.

There's a shift in the air, like he's leaving, then it stops. "What's wrong?" he asks, noticing that my head has been in my locker too long.

My heart pounds. My legs want to sink through the floor, the dirt, the layers of earth's crust, mantel, and core—until I'm on the other side of the world being reborn as a cactus or a hemlock or some other kind of toxic plant that no human will ever be tempted to touch.

"You knew." I say quietly, my shoulders low.

A heavy silence follows. Finally, he exhales. "Yes."

"When are you going to tell Chloe?"

"Sunday," he says definitively. "After we all go to the Harvest Dance."

Of course. He doesn't want to ruin the dance for her. And that means I have to show up too, as promised. Slowly, I close my locker and turn toward him. My eyes naturally fall at the level of his chest and I don't move them. He's wearing a blue and gray striped shirt. I know if I reached out to touch it, to touch him, he would recoil.

"You can return the bracelet," he suggests flatly. Even though we both know fixing things wouldn't be that easy.

"I don't have it anymore," I tell his shirt.

When he doesn't respond, my eyes finally dart to his face, and it's all there for me to see—the hurt, concern, suspicion. My throat is closing up, but I push the crazy promise through anyway, "But I'll try to get it back for you, okay?" Somehow, I think. *Somehow.*

He laughs sharply. "Not for me. For Chloe."

I nod, past words.

"Did you give it to your *boss*?" Brick's voice is tight, a spring in a mousetrap.

"What? No. It has nothing to do with Judd," I insist, knowing I still have to protect my friends.

"Who's Judd?"

Startled, I realize my mistake. "I mean, J-Jason."

Brick smiles sadly. "Hard to keep track of all the stories you tell, isn't it?"

I stare at him, shamed into silence. His eyes are so full of distrust now, so wary. I can feel his anger and hurt growing the longer we stand here. I can't leave things like this. Panicked, I recover my voice enough to blurt, "Brick, when I took that bracelet, I had no idea it was your mom's. I'm…I'm sorry."

"Andrea." He says my name coldly, so different from the way he spoke it at the brook. "You still don't get it. It was never about the bracelet."

He spins around and walks away. I stare at his stiff, retreating back until long after it disappears around the corner and the bustle of students have filled up the space between us. Then I slump against my locker.

I have survived so many things this year. And there are pieces of my soul that were shattered months ago, but it's not until Brick is out of my sight that I feel truly, utterly broken.

Chapter 37

My fingers sail over the keyboard on the library computer. I've spent the entire afternoon scouring yearbooks from the past decade, looking carefully for anyone with the first or last name of Jackson. None of the students looked like the guy I saw in the woods and the quad. So I've moved on to the Internet, using every free people-finder I come across. Unfortunately, "Jackson" is an irritatingly common name and most of the listings don't include pictures. I am close to giving up when I decide to try the social networks. I type in "Haydon, Ohio" and the name "Jackson" and wait for the search engine to do its thing. Good old Facebook comes through. I find him on the second page, his red scar peeking out from under a fuller head of hair than he has now. Keith Jackson. That's it. That's all the information I can get without "friending" him, but it's more than I had before. It'll have to be enough.

Before I leave the library, I create a new anonymous email address and write down everything I know about Judd's and Donovan's business dealings. Then I look up and type in the email addresses of four different detectives at the Columbus Police Department—just in case Donovan has one of them on his payroll. I schedule the email to be delivered at 6:00 AM Sunday morning.

I open my own email program and compose a note to Brick, this one set to be delivered three days from now. It takes a few minutes before I figure out how to say what's in my heart. Finally, I type, *Someone really smart once told me "what we do in life echoes in eternity." I know that I can never make things right with you and Chloe, but I hope you can believe that I truly, fiercely regret what I did to you both. By the time you get this, I won't be in your life anymore, or ever again. I'm going to start over in a new town, a new state, where I can be a different, better person. But I want you to know that I will be sorry for eternity. And I will forever be grateful for your friendship, which I never deserved. If all goes according to plan, you will find Chloe's jewelry in an envelope beneath the bench in your woods. —Andrea*

I quickly swipe at my eyes. Then I erase my browsing history, close down all my programs, and focus on my next task. I'm going to need all my wits about me for this.

The plan started forming as I watched Brick disappear down the hall earlier. It's crazy and dangerous and a total long-shot, but it's what I should have done to begin with. I was just too much of a coward.

KeithJacksonKeithJacksonKeithJackson. I repeat the name over and over in my mind as I head out to the quad. It gives me something to concentrate on besides the knife, the huge sum of cash in my pocket, and the knot of nervous fear in my gut.

School's been out for at least twenty minutes, so the quad is pretty much empty. That is, except for the group clustered by the trees on the northeast side. I slip into my old tough-girl swagger as I approach. The guy I'm looking for is the leader of the group Brick cautioned me and Chloe about early in the year. He is sitting under a leafless tree, laughing at something another kid is saying. He rubs the fuzz of his flattop haircut with his palm and squints up into the sun. Mr. Greeley may not have figured it out yet, but I knew this guy was the ringleader way back in August. After months of venturing into all those crack houses, I'd learned how to spot who was in charge.

I walk over and stop directly in front of him.

"'Sup?" he says, looking me up and down.

I nod my head to the side, indicating I'd like to talk privately. He rises languidly and leads me away from the group to a more secluded area. "Yeah?"

"Jackson sent me," I say quietly, my heart pinned up in my throat. I hope there's not some secret password I need to know.

The guy looks away and then back at me, nonplussed. "Jackson?" he repeats, like he knows a hundred of them.

"Yeah," I say hastily, as if annoyed. "Keith Jackson."

This seems to satisfy him. Thank you, Facebook.

"And? You want to buy something?"

"No. I want to sell something."

The kid cocks his head. Then he asks, "How long you been

at this school? A few months?" His thumbs hook into his belt loops and my heart skips a beat. He thinks it's a setup.

"Look, I'm legit," I assure him, talking fast. "I work for Judd. Jackson wants to do a side trade with you, but he doesn't want Judd to know. That's why he sent me." I'm hoping name-dropping will work in my favor.

The guy's eyebrows crease, but he says, "I'm listening."

I glance around furtively. "He got a little extra snow from an outside source," I say, using the same street name for cocaine that Judd does. "I'm supposed to bring it to you tomorrow night."

"How much are we talking?"

"Twenty Gs." My voice sounds so much smoother than I feel. All those months of acting have paid off. "And a little extra for you."

The kid, whose name I don't know, tells me where and when to meet him. I nod once, then walk briskly across the lawn and don't look back.

If I can skim enough cocaine from Judd's canisters while I'm working tonight, I can pull this off. Then I'll have plenty of money for everything. I'll pay my debt to Judd, go to the pawn shop and buy back Chloe's jewelry, then try and convince Ayla to leave town with me. We only have to make do for a couple of months on the remaining money—just until January, when Gram's next check will arrive. And this time around, *I'm* controlling the cash. And if Ayla won't come with me...I'm going alone.

I pat my pocket where the little knife lies flat against my thigh. Amazing how a two-inch piece of metal can make a girl feel so brave.

Not brave enough, though. The walk home turns into a sprint when I realize how late it is. Judd told me we had a lot to do tonight and I'm not in the mood to put up with his punishments. As I skid into the driveway, I find myself facing a familiar blue BMW. Donovan's here.

And not just him. Two other cars are parked in the driveway as well. I've never seen so many people at Judd's house. Suddenly, I am scared enough to consider taking off now, making a run for it with the cash in my pocket. But eight-fifty is not enough to make things right with my friends and then they'd still be in danger. Plus, what about Ayla? No, my original plan is better.

I sidle inside and straight into some kind of meeting. Judd, Donovan, Donovan's bald sidekick, one of the dealers from our delivery routes, and…Keith Jackson. They're all hovering over some maps spread out on the coffee table.

Ayla is nowhere in sight, so I linger in the background until Judd notices me. As soon as that happens, he pounces. "Where the fuck were *you*?"

All eyes turn to me.

I mumble, "If you wanted me, you could've texted."

Judd growls, "Girl, I'm gonna—"

But before he can get another disgusting threat out of his mouth, I shut him up. "I was getting your money."

There's a pause. Then Judd smirks. "Well, boy-howdy! You hear that, Donovan?"

"I hear a lot of squawking." Donovan's eyes crush me as he

steps forward to stand next to Judd.

"So your big plans came through, Bones?" Judd cackles. "I don't believe it."

I reach into my pocket and pull out the bag of cash. I toss it to Judd because I don't want to get within arm's reach. "Believe it."

His eyes widen as he draws out all the bills. "Well, I'll be damned..." He starts counting.

"It's all there," I assure him, trying to sound tough. "Now we're even."

As soon as the words are out of my mouth, Judd and Donovan look at each other and bust out laughing. Soon the other men in the room are snickering, too. I keep my cool, but inside I'm confused. This is what he wanted. This is what he said I had to do.

"There ain't no 'even,'" Judd gasps between guffaws. "But I will say I'm surprised." Then his eyes darken. "You didn't steal it from me, didya?"

"No!"

"Where'd you get it?" he presses, taking a step closer.

I take a step back. "I stole it from someone else."

Someone near me titters, but Judd doesn't blink. "Is this 'someone else' gonna come looking for it?"

"No."

He hands the bills to Donovan, who begins counting them again. "Your mama gave me the last of her debt today, too. When it rains, it pours, eh?" Judd says to the crowd. Everyone chuckles. I wonder how Ayla repaid her debt, but part of me doesn't want to know.

The men return to the maps on the coffee table. At a glance, I can see the woods drawn on the top map, with little paths snaking around and several square boxes marked with Xs. The sheds, I think. Judd notices me looking and points toward the cellar. "Go help Ayla. *Now.*"

My feet shuffle listlessly across the room and snag on the peeling linoleum in the kitchen. I look back and see Donovan shoving my payment into his pocket like it's a handful of change. He and Judd laugh about something and turn back to their plans.

Suddenly, everything is crystal clear. This hell won't end with an eight hundred dollar payout or a high school diploma. Not in two years or twenty. Despite Judd's plans and promises, I am certain that these men will never let me go. The deal I made so hastily with Judd back in April, when I was starving and scared, is eternal.

I walk numbly down the cellar stairs. All the lights and lanterns are on, and Ayla sits hunched in a chair, biting her fingernails to the nub. They are so red and raw it hurts to look at them. A few ripped garments lay across her lap. She jumps when she hears me. "Damnit, Bones!"

"Are you okay?" I ask because something is off about her, something more than usual.

"It's changin.' It's all about to change." She sounds worried.

"What do you mean?"

She gestures around the cellar and I see what she means. Every box is turned upside down in the middle of the room. All around us are toys, clothes, appliances—the last of Judd's merchandise. "We're getting rid of it all?"

She nods. "There's some new plan. Judd won't give me details, but after we unload this stuff…everything's gonna change. I don't like it, Bones."

"It's okay," I say, determined. "We'll be on our own soon." Grabbing a baggie off the table, I stride across the room, pry the lid off one of the canisters, and reach down to pull out the hidden container of the powdery stuff. I knew it would be here. Judd always keeps the cocaine close to him, never in the sheds. I load the baggie as full as I can, then seal it. There's no scale handy but I'm pretty sure it's enough to satisfy Jackson's dealer at the high school.

"Bones!" Ayla hisses in surprise. "You're using now?"

I want to shake some sense into her, but instead I shake my head. "Just selling. Trust me, Ayla. I'll take care of us from now on." Glancing furtively at the stairs, I stuff the baggie inside my pants. I feel the gratifying poke of my knife as I reposition everything. "What are we supposed to be doing, anyway, the usual?"

Before she can answer, Judd opens the cellar door and leads Baldy downstairs. The bag of cocaine feels as heavy in my pant-leg as Chloe's jewelry did in my pocket. I bend over and pick up some toys so Judd can't see my face. He rattles off instructions and leaves Baldy to oversee us.

We work into the wee morning hours, hiding the drugs and breaking down boxes, until I'm so tired my head keeps bobbing down to my chin. When we finally finish filling the orders, we're sent upstairs. I want to stop in the kitchen for some food, but Keith Jackson is in there so I dart past. Ayla comes with me up to the attic because the men are working through the night and using Judd's bedroom. They are still making plans, murmuring about "the new operation."

With Donovan around, Judd's not taking any chances. Shortly after Ayla and I are sent upstairs, the lock on my door turns. I'm used to it, but Ayla starts trembling and scratching at her arms, agitated. I really have no patience for her sudden fear and paranoia. How does she think *I* live?

After hiding the contraband cocaine, I pull out my stash of food and share everything that's left. Eating settles Ayla's nerves. She even says "thanks" between bites. After that, I turn off the light.

It is the strangest thing, lying in the dark beside the woman who gave birth to me, our hipbones touching. I feel like I should say something, or she should. We're so tired, though, that both of us drift off without uttering so much as "good night."

I dream of another bed, in another house, in another lifetime. I am four years old and nestled into the curve of someone's body, my hair lightly stroked. A lullaby is whispered more than sung, near my ear. Sighing contentedly, I feel whole and good and right. Even before I wake, I'm aware that this is not a dream. It's a memory. *My* memory—not one from Gram's book. And though I am certain the person lying with me was Ayla, I still find myself murmuring "Gram" as I roll over.

Fingers poke me. "I ain't your Gram, Bones. Wake up."

My eyes don't feel like cooperating, but I force them open. I'm sure they look puffy and red, like Ayla's do. Except that her irises are the color of autumn with green flecks in the middle, and mine are the color of a misty spring sky.

I look toward my hexagonal window, at the pink-tinged sunrise beyond. This is it, I think. Tonight, I will be done with this place, with this world. And maybe even with my mother. I glance around the attic room and say a silent goodbye since I might not have time to do it later. Then my gaze lands on Ayla. She is half dressed and her body is skeletal. My nickname would fit *her* better, I think.

"Why do you call me Bones?" I ask suddenly, knowing this may be my last chance to get any information from her. I wasted those chances with Gram, but I won't make that mistake twice.

Ayla looks a little surprised at the question, but she answers. "It…reminds me of when you were born."

My eyes narrow, wondering if this has something to do with my rapist father. "What about when I was born?"

Ayla's face clouds. "You were too small. Undernourished, I guess. They kept you in the hospital until you gained weight." Now her voice turns bitter. "The looks those nurses gave me…like I was scum. And just because I wanted a cigarette." She stands abruptly and turns away.

As usual, it wasn't about me or my health. It was about how *Ayla* felt. The bitterness I feel is so acidic, I can taste it. Gram was wrong about Ayla. She'll never change. Maybe I won't even ask her to come with me tonight. Maybe it isn't my job to save her. But I do have one more thing to say.

"It wasn't my fault, you know. What he did to you." My voice is strong, clear.

I wait for some response, anything, but Ayla stands perfectly still.

"It wasn't your fault, either," I add, softer.

She nods once, a movement so slight that I could've easily missed it. And that's all I get.

Downstairs, the men start thumping around preparing for the busy day ahead. So we do the same. After breakfast, the cars are loaded. Ayla is riding with Judd and Keith Jackson. Donovan orders me into his blue car with Baldy. I glance at Judd for confirmation, but he doesn't see. Reluctantly, I climb into Donovan's backseat. I don't like being separated from Judd and Ayla, crazy as that sounds.

Before we leave, Donovan turns and gives me a once-over. He presses his lips tight. "My girls wear dresses," he says.

I scramble out of the car, biting my tongue. When I see Judd still loading supplies into the other trunk, I decide to risk everything. Turning to Donovan's open window, I say loudly, "I work for Judd, actually. I'm only supposed to take orders from him."

Judd smirks at this and Donovan looks like his face is going to explode. Donovan hollers at Judd, "You hear that?"

"Told you she was loyal," Judd responds like he's pleased with me. He is almost jovial when he says, "Go put on that dress anyway, girl. Make Donovan happy."

So I do. Even though the tight red dress Judd picked out makes me feel like the lowest form of trash. And there's no place to hide my knife, which I'm inclined to bring along. Deciding it's not worth the risk, I leave it hidden with the bag of cocaine and Gram's watch.

As I come downstairs, I notice the maps from the night before laid out on the kitchen table. No one is around. The men are all out in the driveway. I look down at Judd's cell phone cupped in my hand and make the decision. Flipping the phone to camera mode, I tiptoe into the empty kitchen and snap photos of every paper on the table—codes and instructions and addresses. Maps of Louisiana and Florida, which make me wonder if Judd is planning to move me and Ayla away from here. My hands are shaking and I have to steady my elbows on the table so the photos don't come out blurry. If anyone walks into the house right now, I'm dead.

Moments later, I race outside to Donovan's blue BMW, where his eyes pierce me like a saber. Judd, however, is still grinning from my earlier show of allegiance. I'm glad that I've increased the tension between those two.

Now, I just have to hope Donovan won't hurt me for it.

Chapter 38

I pray that we'll caravan behind Judd and Ayla, but we are on completely different routes all day. In our car, Baldy is the lookout. Donovan does most of the deals himself while I stand beside him and steel myself against the men's roving eyes. Donovan is friendly with some dealers, all business with others. As for me, he plays the part of a gentleman suitor. He holds the doors open, puts his arm around my shoulder…whispers that I'm distracting everyone and then laughs. I tolerate what I can and try not to dodge away.

Sometimes Donovan leaves me in the car with Baldy and goes inside alone. I casually ask Baldy some questions about the business, like, "So what's the new plan?" and "Is this Donovan's normal route?" because the more information I can give the police later, the better. But Baldy sits there mute, like I didn't say a word.

The deliveries go on and on. I chew my lip, wondering when—wondering *if*—we're going to hook back up with Judd and

Ayla. At five o'clock the last box is empty and Donovan pulls onto the highway toward Haydon. I finally relax a little and gaze out the window. The sky was full of colors earlier today, smoky blues and grays punctuated by bulbous white clouds. Now the magenta sunset sneaks in and takes over the horizon. I think of Chloe and our Sunday sunrises, and ache at how much I'm going to miss her.

I try to pinpoint where things went wrong, but there are too many spokes on that wheel to count. All along, I thought I was being so smart. But maybe being book-smart and being life-smart are two different things. Perhaps I have more of one and not enough of the other. How else to explain it, me pushing Brick away? Stealing from Chloe. Betraying the only two people I've cared about in the last twelve months. If I'm so smart, then why… why do I feel so stupid?

Instead of heading straight back to Haydon, Donovan stops at a diner where the waitress is infuriatingly slow. He doesn't ask what I want, just orders me an iced tea and a salad with no dressing. "I know how you women like to watch your calories," he says.

I don't argue. I also don't eat, because my stomach is clenched too tight. I can't stop looking at the clock on the wall. Chloe and Brick expect me by six-thirty at the latest, and I need to change clothes and retrieve the baggie from Judd's attic first. I really hope they wait for me. This is my one chance to do something nice for Chloe before she finds out what a horrible person I am.

"You late for something?" Donovan asks, following my gaze to the wall.

"No," I say quickly and take a forkful of the dry green leaves. His dark eyes watch me choke them down.

Judd's car is already in the driveway when we pull in at six-forty. I can hear the music and smell the joints being smoked as we enter. Judd calls Donovan into the kitchen for a hit, and the way Donovan glances at me makes me worry that he's going to insist I come play, too. Luckily, his cell phone buzzes at that moment and when he answers it, I bolt for the stairs.

In the attic, I rip off the nasty red dress and throw it across the room. I pull on my long black skirt and the dressiest black top I own. Shrugging into Chloe's brown coat, I shove the cocaine-filled baggie into one of her puffy pockets and the cell phone into the other. Then I slip my knife in next to the cell phone and give it a pat.

It's going to be a long night. I still need to get to the farmhouse, let Mrs. Masterson snap some photos, and head to the dance. Then somehow I have to ditch Chloe (hopefully Ryan will be around to help with that) and sneak to the baseball dugout at ten o'clock for my "meeting." Once I hand over Judd's cocaine and collect the cash, the most dangerous parts of my plan will be over.

With a couple thousand dollars in my pocket, I'll buy back Chloe's jewelry and leave it under the bench in the woods. I'll text Brick from Judd's cell phone, warning him to be careful and protect Chloe until Judd is arrested. Then I'll snag Ayla and we will leave Haydon forever. I'm so excited, thinking about the end. I know I can do this. I know it.

But time is ticking. I need to get out of Judd's house, fast. At the top of the attic steps, I pause and listen. There is music playing and low voices emanating from the kitchen below. Luckily, this is the time of night when Judd and Ayla celebrate their hard work and cash infusion, oblivious to everything else. And since Donovan's still here, I'm sure he's partying too.

Leaving the lights off, I tiptoe down the steps toward the front door, sliding my hand along the hallway wall until I reach the knob. In the darkness, I slowly turn it, breathing silently through my mouth. The door eases open, inch by inch, and when the space is large enough for me to slip through—

A massive force slams the door closed.

I nearly jump out of Chloe's coat as my hand slips off the knob. Gasping, I look up. Donovan's palm is flat against the doorframe. His eyes are two black nails boring into me through the swirls of his hair.

"Thought you didn't have anywhere to be," he snarls.

"I forgot...it's a thing, at school," I stammer.

"You meeting someone?"

"Uh huh," I say, hunched between him and the door because there is nowhere else to go.

Donovan's eyes slice me. His head tilts, amused. "So you got the delivery my boy's waitin' on?"

As his words sink in, all the color drains from my cheeks. *No, no, no.* Ayla betrayed me. I should have known she would. Donovan laughs at my stunned expression. Then his smile disappears, his hands grip my shoulders, and my feet are six inches off the ground as he slams my back against the front door. "You made a big mistake, little girl," he says in a toxic voice.

I don't know how I manage it, but I hear myself respond in a low, defiant voice: "I'm not afraid of you."

He offers me a sinister smile. "Then that's your second mistake." And everything is a jumble as I'm dragged down the hall and through the kitchen, then shoved roughly to my knees in the middle of the living room.

Judd and Ayla both seem confused by the two of us bursting in and by Donovan's sudden aggression toward me. I inch back and huddle against the wall by the TV, my long black hair hanging in front of my eyes like a curtain. I feel like a feral animal, trapped.

"I just got an interesting call," Donovan announces, cutting off the music. "Looks like our sweet little Bones is pulling some dirty tricks on us." To me he says, "Did you think Marcus wasn't gonna run your silly story by Keith first? I thought you said this girl was smart, Judd!"

Marcus? Oh. He must be the dealer at school. I feel a deluge of relief that it wasn't Ayla who sold me out. Emboldened, I shake my hair back, sit up and holler, "You wouldn't have known a thing if—"

Donovan spins around and kicks me in the chest, cutting off my words, along with my air. I double over, spewing undigested bits of salad and saliva onto the floor. I fight for oxygen, unable to inhale properly. "Give it to me," Donovan commands. "Or I'll scrape it off your body."

Still wheezing, I reach into Chloe's pocket and pull out

the bag of cocaine because I don't want him rifling through my pockets and finding the cell phone—or the knife. Donovan seizes the powder.

When Judd sees the baggie full of his precious cocaine, his eyes widen in surprise, and then narrow. "After all I did for you. Bones, you lyin' little—" He lunges toward me but is stopped abruptly by Donovan's fist.

Judd staggers backward and sinks onto the couch, heaving and swearing. Blood gushes down his chin, his nose clearly broken.

"Incompetent fuck," Donovan scoffs. "Can't even control a little bitch like this. Lucky for you, I know how to handle 'em."

My stomach plunges as I realize that Donovan just *claimed* me.

While Judd writhes, Donovan hauls me to my feet and looks me up and down. "Tsk, tsk. Judd, you played this one all wrong," Donovan chides over his shoulder. "She's far too pretty to be a runner. I'll make a lot more off her in the stable."

From the couch, Judd gurgles, "You got your payout. I found these two—they're mine." But he's in no position to argue.

"You can have the junkie," Donovan nods his head in Ayla's direction. "I'm keepin' this pretty little thing. After a few days with me, she won't be so feisty."

I grit my teeth and think, *I'll die first.*

Donovan wets his lips. My stomach churns at the look in his eyes, the one I have known to watch for ever since Ayla brought me into her filthy underworld. Then his hand, fleshy and pink, comes slowly toward me. I back up against the wall, but there's nowhere else to go.

I cringe and then freeze as his fingers make contact with my skin. He caresses my cheek, then runs his whole hand over my face, lips and neck—as if marking me with his scent. Frantically, my eyes seek out Ayla. She's standing near the cellar door, still as a statue. Everything about her appears wasted—her body's too thin, her bones too visible. Her face is gaunt where it used to be vibrant. And her eyes look scared, scared for *me.*

Determined not to end up like her, I slap Donovan's hand away from my face, ready to fight him tooth and nail. But he simply smirks like he's already won, and somehow I know he's broken girls far *feistier* than me.

"We had a deal, you sack o'shit!" Judd springs to his feet, which causes Donovan to step away from me. While the men exchange insults, I slide my hand into Chloe's coat pocket and search for the hidden blade. The handle feels like heaven and hell in my grasp. I click it open.

Holding it straight down by my side, I make a desperate dash for the hallway. Donovan sees my move and easily blocks my path. He doesn't see the knife, though. "Now, now, our little party's not over yet, Bones." He smiles.

Blood pounds up through my ears as he steps closer, closer, close enough. Just before his fingers reach me, I squeeze my eyes shut and thrust the knife into his gut.

His hand drops. His mouth roars. Something warm and wet seeps into the crevices between my fingers. I press my lips tight to keep from retching.

I did it…*I actually did it.*

Triumph surges through me. But something's wrong.

Donovan has a strange, pained look on his face, yet he's not bending forward, not falling back. His grubby hand is suddenly around *my* wrist and he's squeezing and twisting, twisting until my fingers are forced to separate and the knife is out of my grasp. Gone.

Crazy with fear and adrenaline at the loss of my weapon, I thrash and hit Donovan in the face, all over his head. Despite my efforts, Donovan pulls me in closer, tighter, until I feel something— his belt buckle, I think—pinching sharply against my stomach.

I scream, hoping some neighbor will hear, hoping Brick is parked on the street, ready to call the police. Ayla watches anxiously, but she can't save me—she's proven that a hundred times over.

Frantically, I whip my head around to scan the room and then I reach out for Judd, of all people, beg him to help me. I beg better than I ever did for mercy or scraps of food. But he just grunts dismissively, turns and marches out the front door, mopping his nose with his elbow.

Donovan's lips twitch into a smug little smile at Judd's departure. I push against Donovan's huge chest with all my might, but I can't get away. He's too strong. We are mashed together like partners in some monstrous dance, and my stomach feels damp with his blood and the knife is somewhere in his possession, and I am sweating, crying, panting with the exertion of the struggle. Desperate, I try to find a way to raise my knee to his groin—the best defensive move I know—and then a blur of flesh streaks through the kitchen.

It's Ayla. She's holding something large in her hand—a lamp—and I squeal as it crashes over Donovan's head, large pieces showering us both. It doesn't take Donovan down, doesn't even cut him, but he loosens his grip on me enough to turn and deliver a backhand so powerful that it lays Ayla out cold. As he does this, my knife falls to the ground with a thud, dripping red with Donovan's blood. Only his right hand is squeezing my arm now, so I raise my leg and point the heel of my black boot straight down. With furious strength, I pierce the top of his foot so hard I feel the crunch, and know I must have broken some toes.

Donovan howls and releases me instantly. I dart across the room and am almost to the hall when he recovers enough to snag the fur hood of Chloe's coat, yanking me backward. I flail. And then I see Judd standing in the doorway.

There's a gun in his hand.

For a moment, there is nothing but Judd and the gun and the pale blue door half open behind him. My brain is screaming, and all I want, all I've ever wanted, is to *get beyond that door.*

Donovan cusses behind me, injured but still tugging on Chloe's hood. I am directly between him and Judd now, trapped. Still, this time I won't stop fighting. I make my arms go slack and allow Chloe's coat to slip off my shoulders. Donovan stumbles backward, left with nothing but the shiny brown material in his meaty hands. I dash for the door.

Judd raises his gun, but I just keep running toward him, waiting for the pain, the bullet, the end.

The shot is so loud and so close to my ear that it mutes all sound. A blast of heat envelopes the side of my face and my chest quivers with the vibration of the discharge. I fall forward in a slow-motion sort of leap, watching the floor rise up to meet me. I am overwhelmed with shock and fear and even an odd sense of peace at the certainty of my impending death. I wonder if Gram will be there to meet my soul.

My knees smack the floor, but I push myself back up. Somehow, I'm still moving forward. The bite of a harvest wind slaps my cheek as I stumble out of the house, into the woods. I stagger toward the clearing and across the soggy leaves, past the shed and the pond, all the way to the Mastersons' in a sort of misty midnight dream.

Maybe it is a dream. Maybe I'm already dead. But until I know for sure, I keep moving, shuffling, tripping, and getting up again. There is a deafening silence around me. I shake my head to clear away the sensation of my ears being stuffed with cotton. It doesn't work.

Finally, I see the big country house, lit up and welcoming.

The garage door is open so I just keep going. Inside the house, through the mudroom, across the kitchen tile. I hug my torso, wet with Donovan's blood, and try to walk straight. Smooth steps now, one after another.

In the foyer, my eyes land on Brick first. He's dressed in a gray suit, clean-shaven, a dress coat hanging over his arm. I hear the jingle of his car keys, see his head turn when I enter. His eyes scorch me, furious, and his voice sounds far away, down a tunnel, when he accuses, "You were supposed to be here an hour ago..."

Then I see Chloe, red-faced from crying, still beautiful in her copper-colored dress and her hair all done up. Her mother stands beside her, a protective arm across Chloe's shoulders. I'm too late. Brick must have told them.

I turn away, not knowing exactly who or what I'm looking for, until I spot the group gathered around the table in a corner of the great room. Four men playing poker. I recognize two of them—Chloe's dad and Mr. Greeley, the assistant principal.

I mean to walk over and tell Mr. Greeley everything, everything I know about Judd and Keith Jackson and Marcus and Donovan, but the table is floating farther away the more I try to move toward it. I turn in a circle, disoriented, see pieces of Brick, Chloe, Mrs. Masterson, all of their lips moving but no sounds coming out. I try to say "I'm sorry," but I can't hear my voice either. And I can't hold all this inside anymore.

Breathing raggedly, I hug myself tighter, drop my head and start to sob. The movement tires me and my arms fall to my sides. Mr. Masterson's voice breaks through the barrier first, "My God, you're bleeding!"

I glance down at my abdomen, red and slick. "No, it's not mine…" I say faintly. He catches me as my body goes slack.

Now I'm lying flat under shallow water and all the commotion is occurring above the surface—panicked voices, someone hollering to call an ambulance, something pressing hard against my side. Pain sears through me, subsides.

When I force my eyes open, there are many faces swimming in the sky, distorted by the waves. Chloe is gaping at me, shrieking.

Her father pulls her away. Someone talks rapidly into a cell phone, pacing near my feet. Chloe's mom kneels beside me, cutting the bottom of my shirt and sucking in air through her teeth. She presses a towel against my stomach, tells me not to move, that everything will be okay.

"Okay," I agree weakly, but she shushes me and I feel pressure again. I wince and catch sight of red liquid seeping through the towel in her hands. By the looks on everyone's faces, you'd think I was dying. Maybe I *am* dying. Frantic, I search the room with my eyes. "Brick?"

"Right here." His voice is the most soothing of all, near my ear. He moves to where I can see him and I realize he's been cradling my head in his hands. His eyes are wide and he is trembling.

"I lied to you...so many times," I gasp.

He nods, tries to smile gently. "No shit."

"Ayla, my mom. She's at the house, with them...she's hurt."

"The police are on their way," he assures me. "Just hold still."

I breathe for a minute, noticing that the air rattling in my chest doesn't feel right. I think of Gram. I whisper, "I'm scared."

"Shh, you're gonna be fine." Brick touches my hair, runs his hand along my temple. "You're unbreakable, remember?" But his voice catches.

I reach for his hand, latch on. We stare at each other, though my eyelids keep closing.

He dips his head down and comes up crying. "*Damn* you, Andrea. Don't you go anywhere."

I'm too tired to promise anything. Brick stays with me,

squeezing my hand until I hear sirens wailing in the distance, and their lullaby puts me to sleep.

Chapter 39

I am adrift between reality and hallucination. Trapped in a void that looks and feels like a series of narrow tunnels, shadows pulsing from the corners. I am running barefoot on hard-packed dirt. Slowly, the tunnels fill with a light like liquid smoke. I'm blinded, but unafraid. As the darkness melts away, she stands waiting with her gray-streaked hair, eyes the color of ripened walnuts, and the too-soft skin that age bestows.

"Gram!"

The word cracks in my throat like a brittle leaf. She smiles softly and opens her arms. I rush into them with fervor. I fall against her, and she cradles me, and I smell her and breathe her and feel her softness. We are together again, wrapped in love. For a brief, beautiful moment, I am filled with happiness.

It doesn't last long—not nearly long enough. As Gram slips away, I squeeze tighter, wanting frantically to hold her in this place, this moment. But I press my cheek so hard against her chest that she breaks apart and, with a poof, the substance of her fades. I am left hugging nothing but air. My heart plummets.

"Her BP just dropped. Andrea…I need you to open your eyes. Can you hear me? Try to answer," a voice coaxes from another world. But I am busy falling into a bed of soft light.

"Andrea, come on. Open your eyes. *Open* them." The urgency in the lady's voice makes me think this request is important, so I try to comply. It's like climbing through layers of mud.

When my eyelids open, shiny hospital lights reach down into my irises and pull me back, out of the tunnel, away from Gram.

"Heart rate's heading back to normal, BP stable. Keep your eyes on her monitor," someone above me directs.

Then the first voice, "Andrea, stay with us. We need you to wake up."

I try, but it's so hard. The bright tunnel pulls at me. Back and forth, back and forth…until everything goes dark.

I awaken with a grunt to find a nurse poking my arm with a needle. "The doctor's coming soon," she slurs, and her face fades away.

They wake me again when the doctor arrives. He's tall, with hair that reminds me of ripe summer apples. He starts talking, but I miss some of the words.

"…given a blood transfusion, no surgery. The knife didn't puncture…vital organs."

The doctor's white lab coat flaps against his leg.

"…stab wound was quite deep. You're very lucky."

Stab wound? Me? I blink rapidly as the puzzle pieces come

together. As soon as I understand, the pain hits me hard, like a fist sinking into my ribcage—except it's hot and sharp. My fingers tenderly explore the bandages across my abdomen.

"I didn't feel anything," I tell the doctor, confused.

He nods. "That's the numbing effect. Your adrenaline, the shock, it can mask the pain at first."

"It hurts now," I whine, which is an understatement.

"We'll try to help with that," he says and a nurse begins bustling around. "How's…hearing, Andrea?"

"Intermittent."

The doctor raises his eyebrows in surprise.

"SAT prep," I offer, and he smiles.

"Do you have any ringing or buzzing in your ears…now?"

I shake my head.

"Good. You'll have some impairment for a few days, but let's hope…"

He continues talking, but there's another poke in my arm and the pain starts to fade. I am so exhausted. I can't keep my eyes open.

Chloe's mom is the first person I see outside of the hospital staff. When I open my eyes many hours later, she is sitting in a chair near my bed, writing furiously on a clipboard. My surroundings come sharply into focus.

"Mrs. Masterson?" I say groggily.

She rises, offers me a calm smile and a drink of water with a straw. I slurp for what seems like forever. She refills the cup, and

I drink some more.

"How are you feeling today?" she asks, smoothing back my hair and propping a pillow gently behind my head. I glance out the window at the bright autumn sky. It's a new day.

"I'm alive, I think."

She smiles again, but then her face grows serious. "You're very lucky to be alive."

"Maybe," I say softly. I'm thinking a little more clearly now and I realize that because I'm alive, there will be questions—and consequences. I have no idea what comes next, but I know that I lied, I stole, I sold drugs, and I stabbed someone.

"Call me Lillian from now on," she states, all business. "I am not your friend's mom right now. I'm your court-appointed advocate and your lawyer, if you'd like."

"Lawyer? You don't have to—I don't need—"

"They'll appoint someone else if you'd prefer. It won't hurt my feelings. But yes, Andrea, you do need a lawyer."

I let her words settle in my brain. Of course I do. For the past year, there's been a whole pot of trouble brewing around me, and we're all finally boiling in it. I nod. "Okay."

"My job is to help you. But in order to do that you need to be completely honest with me. And we both know that honesty hasn't been your strong suit."

Feeling like a deer in headlights, all I can do is stare. My lawyer stares right back.

This is not the same soft-spoken Lillian who sat discussing literature with me over hot chocolate. She doesn't beat around the bush. But that's okay. I want someone tough on my side for once.

"I don't want you talking to the police unless I'm with you," she says. "Not a word. They're going to come in here asking questions. All you need to say is that you want your lawyer present before you answer anything."

"Okay."

"No reporters, either. No matter how much they tell you they're trying to help, they won't have your best interests at heart. This isn't going to be easy," she warns.

I have a sudden urge to laugh, because nothing is ever easy for me. But it would probably pull at my stitches and hurt like hell.

"Okay," I say again. I am so relieved to have someone else, some responsible adult, in charge of things. For once. Finally.

"Good. I have a lot to tell you." She hesitates and her voice softens. "Are you up for it right now?"

I meet her eyes. "Ayla?"

For some reason, I'm certain that she's dead.

"She's not hurt. She's been taken into police custody."

Letting out the breath I was unconsciously holding, I don't ask anything else about her. That's enough, for now.

"And Judd?" I ask, suddenly panicked.

"He was apprehended in Kentucky. Authorities caught up to him within a few hours. His trunk was full of cocaine and firearms."

My eyes flutter shut in relief. Judd's been caught. My friends are safe.

After a pause, Lillian continues slowly, "Police found one

man dead at the house. You might know him as Donovan, though that's not his real name."

The whole room wobbles, and for one terrifying second, there's no air. Then it all comes whooshing back. "Oh, God, I did it. I stabbed him. I'm a murderer," I whisper, my hand covering my mouth.

Lillian steps closer to the bed and gently touches my shoulder. "No. You were acting in self defense. And in any case, his stab wound was superficial. The cause of death was a gunshot to the chest."

Slowly, I remove my hand from my mouth and try to make sense of her words, try to remember that night…I stabbed Donovan. Then Judd showed up with a gun. I ran toward him. He fired.

But not at me.

"Judd shot him?" I ask, shocked. Even I can hear how young and frightened my voice sounds.

Lillian nods.

I turn my head, overwhelmed. Tears begin to stream down my face, but I don't really notice until Lillian hands me a tissue.

"You've been through a lot of trauma. I'm going to help you in every way I can, but you also need to concentrate on getting well. How about you rest now and I'll come back in a little bit?"

She pats my shoulder and walks toward the door. Before she leaves, I croak, "Mrs. Master—I mean, Lillian? I'd rather get it over with."

That's one truth. The other is that I don't want to be alone.

Lillian comes back, picks up her clipboard and nods. "Okay. We'll go slow, but I've got lots of questions."

I glance down at the dressings taped to my stomach. If I shift even an inch, my whole body throbs. Leaning back against the pillows, I set my jaw and say, "I've got time."

I tell Lillian everything, starting with Gram's death. Once I start talking, it all gushes out. I even include my experience with Charlie at the foster home. It's impossible to prove what he did, but at least it's on record now. At least someone else knows. I do what Lillian asks—I am completely honest, even when it's shameful to describe what Judd did to me, what Donovan wanted to do, and what I put up with from Ayla. I tell Lillian about the photos I took of the maps, about Donovan's cabin in the woods, and the face I think I saw in the window there. She doesn't seem appalled by any of it, but that's her job. The telling takes hours, and I don't stop until I've let it all go. When I finish, my nose is clogged and my eyes are swollen from crying. My whole body feels heavy with exhaustion, but my heart...my heart is a million times lighter.

Chloe sits on the side of my hospital bed, one leg bent beneath her, the other hanging over the edge. Her free foot swings back and forth and I watch her brown Mary Jane, mesmerized. This is her third time visiting me in the four days I've been here. She has brought me chocolate, colas, magazines, and makeup. On top of that, she calls my hospital room every night at nine o'clock to say goodnight. She is amazing. This is what I keep telling her.

Hopefully she'll believe me someday.

At the moment, she's chatting about how Ryan talks to her every day now in homeroom, how they're sort of kind of almost an item. I try to listen attentively and ask all the right questions because she so deserves it, but my mind is elsewhere.

When she falls silent, I casually bring up what I really want to know, what I've wanted to know all week but was afraid to ask. "What's Brick up to?"

Her eyes shift. "He's been pretty busy."

I struggle to keep my voice light. "Doing what?"

"Oh you know…studying. Knitting."

"Knitting?" I repeat. I get stabbed and he's too busy *knitting* to stop by or call? I know I betrayed him and Chloe both, but I thought after the way he looked at me when I was injured… maybe it was just pity. I stole from his dead mother, after all. Why *would* he forgive me?

"Um…yeah." She nods vigorously. "He's been doing a lot of knitting."

Frustrated, I toss the school books Chloe brought me onto the table by my hospital bed. For once, I don't even care about homework.

Chloe looks at me and twists her lips. "I wish you could come home with us."

I don't respond right away, because it hurts to admit that once again, I am officially homeless. Then I think of how badly I wanted Delaney to say those words to me after Gram's death and how she never did. Chloe is the best, most wonderful friend, despite all the crappy things I've done. Now, seeing the worry lines stretched across her forehead, I feel a mama bear urge to protect her.

"No one's giving you a hard time, are they? At school?" I ask suddenly.

"No, but people ask about you. They didn't mention your name on the news, but everyone knows. They think it's exciting—they're like the paparazzi."

A flash of anger heats my skin. "Well, you don't have to say anything. And you can't let people push you around. I know Brick's there, but—"

"Don't worry about me, Andre. I can handle them." She pats my head. "It's you who has to be strong."

After a moment, I snort. Once again, she's got it all figured out and I still don't. For the first time, though, I'm grateful *not* to be going back to school—to the stares and assumptions. I'm glad I won't have to face the condemnation of the other kids—*white trash, drug pusher, crack head.* I could take it, but that doesn't mean it wouldn't hurt. They'd just better not revile Chloe, better not lump her in with me. She doesn't deserve it.

Chloe tucks a strand of hair behind her ear and a familiar glint strikes my eye, forcing me to blink. How did I not notice this? I grab her hand and gape at the diamond bracelet on her wrist. "Wha—you got it back!"

Chloe smiles, a sight as dazzling as the diamonds themselves. "Yeah. Brick figured you went to the closest pawn shop. But he said he'd only buy it back if I actually wore it once in a while."

"And your earrings?"

She shakes her head. "They were sold."

Our eyes meet again.

"I'm so sorry, Chlo," I whimper. I had so many other things in my mind, things I was going to say when I got up the courage, but that's all that comes out.

Chloe's eyes are wide and dry. She shrugs. "Like you said, it's just jewelry."

"No. It's about friendship and trust. And I'm terrible at both." I sigh heavily. "I don't know why you want anything to do with me."

Chloe is quiet for a minute, playing with her bracelet. "I just think," she begins slowly, "that you were desperate. It's not like you stole from me to buy an iPad or something. You were scared of him. Weren't you?" Her voice is sweet and tentative, because she doesn't know all the details of what happened to me. Lillian left it to me to divulge whatever I wanted.

I feel myself tearing up at Chloe's blind faith in me. "I was terrified," I admit, using Brick's word from that day in his truck. "But that doesn't make it right."

"No, but it makes it forgivable. No one's mad at you, Andrea. Just be honest from now on and let us help you. That's all we want."

"I'm not very good at letting people help me," I admit, sniffling. "Even when I lived with my Gram, we kind of did things on our own."

"Well, now's your chance to try something new." She grins impishly.

As I consider that, the nurse walks in to announce the end of visiting hours. Chloe slides off my bed and ruffles my hair in farewell. "See you tomorrow," she calls over her shoulder. My eyes are full of gratitude as I watch her go.

I really don't deserve a friend like Chloe. But maybe she's right. Maybe I should try something new, and be the kind of friend *she* deserves. I have to try. Because I owe her, and I love her so very much—smiley faces and all.

Chapter 40

My hearing is tomorrow morning. Lillian paces around my hospital room, in full attorney mode, prepping me for the harsh questions the judge may ask. "You're a juvenile with no priors, you were clearly in danger, and you did alert the authorities with those emails, so I doubt charges will be filed," she says, "but you need to be ready for anything." She explains that even though Judd and Ayla both pled guilty to their charges in hopes of getting lighter sentences, that doesn't mean I'm off the hook.

"What are you going to say when the judge asks where you want to live? Have you thought about it?"

"Yes. I want to be emancipated," I tell her excitedly. "I can go to school and take care of myself. I've been doing it all year anyway."

Lillian stops pacing and looks at me. Her eyes are kind when she says, "Honey, no judge will emancipate a minor with a history of dealing drugs—even though you were coerced. I'm sorry, but people aren't going to give you the benefit of the doubt on that one."

And no one is going to want to foster a 17-year-old with a history of drug dealing, either. Oh, and when you factor in the tiny detail that I *stabbed* someone, it's clear that I'm doomed. I'll end up at Wheaton, the local institution where castoff girls stay until they age out. I looked it up one night when Chloe left her laptop at the hospital for me to use. Worst of all, Wheaton feeds into a "Needs Improvement" school district that barely has enough funds to keep the electricity on. The school has no honors program, no extra curriculars, nothing.

I cross my arms sullenly, not caring if I look like a pouting child. Lillian gently asks if there's anyone—a relative, an old family friend—who might take me in. She has asked me this before and I told her I'd think about it, but the truth is, I'm alone. I can't even imagine going back to Indianapolis now. I might as well resign myself to "the system."

"Andrea—"

"I'm tired." I abruptly turn over in bed, even though it makes my stitches throb.

She pauses, then tucks her papers inside her briefcase. "Okay, get some rest. I'll see you tomorrow."

Tomorrow. The word sits like a rock in the pit of my stomach. Tomorrow I'm getting discharged from the hospital. Tomorrow I'm going to face the judge. Tomorrow my life will change, again.

Lillian hesitates, then leans over and kisses the top of my

head. I stare straight ahead and listen to her heels click-clack down the tiled hall, diminishing into silence. My eyes fill, and I just let them.

Courtrooms in real life aren't nearly as quiet as in the movies. My hearing begins with a bunch of legal jargon flying back and forth between Lillian and the judge and the prosecutor. I hear the man on the other side of the room say the word "incarcerate," and I break out into a cold sweat. It's hard to breathe in here, where everything looks so massive—the presidential portraits on the walls, the dark-paneled judge's bench, the pillars. If I wasn't in the hot seat, I might think it was cool. As it is, I'm struggling to keep mine.

Lillian is a superstar, though. She doesn't let the other lawyer ask me anything directly. I hear her argue for leniency because I was "coerced," "abused," and "in fear of my life." The man at the other desk hesitantly agrees, but wants to be sure we have the facts straight. I try to sit tall and look poised, but I feel vulnerable and…so *angry*. Of all the days for me to feel angry, this is the worst possible one. Finally, the judge calls a recess and I'm escorted into chambers to speak with her privately. She enters from another door, glasses perched on her nose, black robes flowing. She hands me a cup of ice water and we sink down into two leather chairs. This is better, quiet.

"It'll be easier to talk in here, don't you think?" she asks, and I nod. Then the questions begin. The judge is nice, professional, and seems to believe everything I tell her. I cry a little, even though I told myself ten times this morning not to do that.

Some of her questions are easy—factual, logistical. But some of them are tough. Mostly because they make me think hard about what I did, and why—and what I didn't do, and why not.

"Andrea." The judge shuffles through some papers and then looks at me squarely. "Your drug screenings were clean, you're an honors student, and most of your upbringing was in a stable environment with your grandmother." After a pause, she continues, "You knew that carrying drugs, selling them, was illegal. You did it anyway, and you didn't tell anyone. Why?"

"Because..." I falter, feeling the sting of how unfair this question is. How unfair it is that I have to relive this nightmare, when it's all there in my written statement. How everyone wants to know the same thing—*why*—and how I don't have a good enough answer.

"Did Judd pay you?" the judge inquires.

"No."

"Did he buy you jewelry, electronics, clothes?"

"No!" I repeat hotly, then clarify, "Well, clothes once, but he wasn't happy about it. And he gave me a cell phone, but it was just so he could reach me."

She waits to see if I'm going to add anything else, so I do, after swallowing hard. "I didn't have a choice. I was...scared. He hurt me, and threatened me all the time. He even threatened to hurt my friends if I told! I couldn't—I mean, he said he had connections with the police, with everyone—" I stop myself because I'm getting worked up and Lillian told me not to let that happen, no matter what.

"Okay," the judge says calmly. "I'm just trying to understand why someone like you didn't realize that you had chances to ask for help."

What she's really asking is, how could someone so smart— an honors student, no less—do something so stupid? I bite back my anger. This woman has no idea what it's like to wake up every morning with one goal—surviving the day. She has no idea what it's like to live in constant fear of men like Judd and Donovan. I want to stomp out of this room, turn my back on the judge, tell her off. But I can't. So I stare at my hands, balled in my lap. She doesn't push me. As the silence grows, her words reverberate in my head.

You had chances to ask for help.

I think of Delaney, Essex, the church lady, Belmont and Mr. Greeley, Brick and Chloe, her parents. And then, sitting there in the plush chambers of the judge's office, I suddenly realize the truth in those eight syllables. As impossible as my situation felt, there were people I could have turned to. Why *didn't* I? Was it really my fear of Judd, and my reluctance to face the unknown in the foster system? Locked in the deepest part of my heart, I know another answer.

As a kid, I never understood why Gram let Ayla in every time she came crawling home. Why she cared lovingly for her daughter knowing Ayla might rob her blind on her way out. I know exactly why I didn't turn on Ayla now. It's as clear as if Gram were whispering the words in my ear—*she's family, love, and she's sick. You don't give up on family.*

I hadn't given up on Ayla, hadn't deserted her, because deep down I knew Gram wouldn't have. And despite the distance of death, I wanted to make Gram proud of me, wanted to be like her. Like *her*—and not like Ayla or my father.

Slowly, I meet the judge's eyes. "I needed to stay with my mother. I needed to protect her." Mostly from herself, I add silently.

"I figured that was part of it," the judge says gently.

I inhale a deep, shuddery breath and ask a question of my own, "What will happen to her?"

The judge steeples her fingers, purses her lips, and considers. "Well, I'm not directly involved in that case, but she'll most likely end up with a combination of incarceration and rehab."

"She won't go to rehab," I say with certainty.

"She won't have a choice."

Oh. I allow myself a flicker of hope that rehab will help Ayla. Maybe…maybe.

Before we return to the courtroom, the judge looks me in the eye and says she's very sorry this happened to me.

I appreciate her words, but the facts don't change—I knowingly sold drugs. For that, I get nine months of probation, mandatory counseling, and 100 hours of community service. When I turn eighteen, my record will be wiped clean, but for now, I am a ward of the state. As predicted, there's a bed waiting for me at Wheaton.

When it's all over, I give Lillian a tight hug in the glass-windowed foyer of the fancy courthouse. "Thank you for everything. Will you tell Chloe goodbye?" I nearly choke on the words.

"I will, honey. But we'll see you soon. After you get settled in a bit."

Lillian has good intentions, but I won't hold her to that promise. I know how these things work. Once you are out of someone's direct line of sight, they forget all about you.

I nod, blink quickly, pull myself together. Then I walk across the shiny floor to where a social worker waits with my belongings. A few clothes, my watch, and Gram's photo album. Someone retrieved them from the crime scene, and they all fit nicely into one brown paper bag.

This is what my life has been reduced to, I think bitterly, as the social worker hands it to me. All I can do is take it.

Chapter 41

The Wheaton Home for Girls is located in an old downtown neighborhood. It's not a particularly nice area, but not a dangerous one, either. The building is large and ancient, four stories high with peeling white paint and lots of character: a pitched roof, casement windows, and a wide front porch. A grim-faced counselor woman meets us at the front door and tells me the first rule before I even step inside—Girls on probation aren't allowed off property without permission.

Then I get the tour. Wheaton is one of those places that could use a serious makeover, but I don't mind. It's better than being stuck in some sterile institution with fluorescent lights and squeaky floors. The downstairs has been gutted and is comprised of a huge kitchen and dining area, with a rec room tucked in the back. Upstairs, it's a mouse maze with little plaster-walled rooms, hidden staircases, nooks and crannies. At least if the other girls hate me, it will be easy to hide.

There are all sorts of girls living here. A few make my former tough-girl act seem like a joke. Some are sullen and withdrawn. Others appear outgoing and fairly well adjusted. But I won't judge too fast. Fights break out on occasion, but I stay far away from that scene. I don't really associate with anyone except my two roommates, Tiana and Reese. And even them not more than necessary.

Having roommates isn't something I'd imagined, and at first I resent sharing space with strangers. But each night as I toss and turn from nightmares involving shiny knives and the gristle of gunfire, I find myself relieved not to be alone when I wake up sweating, my sheets tied in knots. Sometimes they whisper, "Are you okay, Andrea?" and I can tell their concern is genuine. I think everyone here has nightmares of some kind.

I'm still officially "healing," so for now I have no chores, no school. There's a backyard, a big screen TV, and a phone in one of the sitting rooms. I've received several calls from Chloe, and our conversations always cheer me up. I never dial her number because I'm afraid of who else might answer. I wouldn't know what to say to Brick. Sometimes I think it might be better for Chloe if she forgets about me like Brick did, and moves on. But that's her call. I certainly won't be the one to do the abandoning. Besides, I need her now more than ever.

Lillian phones a few days after I arrive at Wheaton and delivers an update. The police found huge amounts of marijuana, cocaine, and other substances in those sheds. They got a ton of information off the pictures I took with Judd's cell phone, recovered from the pocket of Chloe's brown coat. Keith Jackson and Marcus were both arrested, and the cops are still watching the dealers Judd supplied. As I suspected, Donovan was involved in more than drugs. He had his hand in human trafficking as well. They located his cabin and found Baldy living there with two teenage girls—both runaways from Tennessee. The girls were returned home last night.

There's more—Ayla had her sentencing, and it is pretty much what my judge predicted. One year in a secured rehab facility followed by two years probation. Lillian says I can do my community service at Ayla's rehab clinic if I want.

I don't know what I want.

After a short silence, Lillian asks how I'm holding up. I'm about to lie and say, "good," when I remember Chloe's words. *Be honest. Let us help you. Now's your chance to try something new.*

I take a breath and give it a whirl. "I'm really worried about school. I'm getting behind and they won't let me do anything but rest." I relay what my therapist said the other day—that I have a different kind of work to do now. But it's not enough. "I'm going to the doctor next week to get my stitches out," I explain. "And I'm hoping he'll clear me for school. I don't want to lose this semester." I hesitate, then lower my voice and add that I've looked at the other girls' books and the work is really basic, stuff I learned years ago.

"I've got some ideas about that, Andrea. There are other options, like online schooling, that might work for you. I'll let you know what I find out."

"Really? That'd be great," I say, just as relieved to have someone looking out for me as I am about the idea of having options.

"How's Wheaton?" Lillian probes.

"It's not as bad as I thought. I mean, it's not great, but it's better than Charlie's or Judd's." I could stop there, but I go on. "There are a lot of adults here, counselors and therapists, who seem, you know, interested in my life. I'm not used to that," I say with a sad little laugh.

"And how are the other girls treating you?"

"Fine," I answer. Even though there are fifteen of us living here, I'm still kind of lonely. I tell her that, too. "I don't know, Lillian. I'm just trying to make the best of things."

After another pause, Lillian says, "That's all really good to hear, Andrea." And I know she isn't talking about my situation. She's talking about the way I opened up to her, about my honesty.

Before we hang up, Lillian once again says she'll see me soon. But soon isn't right now. It isn't tomorrow. And even though I'm starting to believe that she *will* keep this promise, each day waiting feels like eternity.

On my seventh day at Wheaton, a local cosmetology student arrives to give us all free haircuts. I go downstairs more from boredom than anything else. The woman is young, with bright red lipstick and platinum hair streaked blue. She hums to herself as she sets up a chair and a cart of tools near the sink in the kitchen. While I wait with the cluster of girls, Tiana tells me the cosmetologist aged out of Wheaton herself a few years ago.

When it's my turn, the young woman smiles gently, as if sensing my wariness. She begins combing out my tangles and notes that she hasn't seen me before.

"I've only been here a week," I say.

"Sometimes new girls want a change," she says as her cool fingers separate my dark locks into smooth sections. "Sometimes, they want something drastically different. A clean break from the past."

I consider this. It might feel liberating to ask for a pixie cut, or a short bob, or a bunch of layers to reinvent myself once again. Maybe I could do something so outrageous that I wouldn't look pretty or innocent anymore. And even though I do feel fairly safe now, I won't be sorry to lose the long strands that Donovan took such interest in, that Judd liked to yank.

I am about to tell the woman to chop it all off when something powerful stops me, like a brick pressing on my chest. A moment of clarity. Cutting off my hair might feel good at first, but it might also feel like hiding. And I am so sick of hiding. The fact is, I *like* my hair long. And I don't need a new identity. What I need is to reclaim myself. To be brave and strong, and unbreakable. To be me.

"Just a trim," I say firmly.

She nods, then goes to work gently massaging my scalp. I don't think this is part of her job, but I'm grateful for her touch. It's funny how you miss sensations like that. I picture Gram standing behind me, smiling and stroking my hair, reflected in our antique mirror, and for the first time in months, I feel certain and unwaveringly proud of a decision I made.

When I return to our room, Reese is lying on the top bunk paging through a fashion magazine. She stares as I enter and flop gently onto my bed. "Wow, Andrea. You look so pretty," she says.

Pretty. My instinct is to bite her head off, but I don't.

Instead, I consider the blue eyes I inherited from my father, the yellow bruises courtesy of Judd, the pink scar Donovan seared on my stomach. They are all a certain kind of pretty—the kind that is earned by overcoming some hardship and emerging stronger on the other side, with more durable traits. Like Brick's resilience and Chloe's compassion. I understand now that our *choices* make us who we are, not our genes. And from this moment forward, my choices are going to be great.

I look up at Reese, fourteen years old and in need of so much. I smile at her and say, "Thank you."

That night, a counselor finds me in the hallway and tells me I have a phone call. I assume it's Chloe, so I'm not prepared when the counselor adds, "Her name's Ayla. Says she's your mother."

My whole body tenses.

Ayla is calling me? Why? To yell at me for ruining everything she had going with Judd? Or to apologize? Isn't that something they have to do in rehab—make amends?

Part of me is curious about what Ayla has to say. Part of me hopes that she's calling to tell me she's beginning to turn her life around, that someday in the future she wants to have a relationship with me. And that the next time she looks at me, she will try really hard to see something other than her rapist's eyes. But I don't trust her, and it's too soon. It's too soon for her to have made any real kind of progress. It's too soon for me to forget what she put me through.

The counselor looks at me kindly. She knows what I've decided. "What do you want me to tell her, sweetie?"

"Tell her...not yet," I say and walk away.

Someday. Someday I will be strong enough to face Ayla. Someday, if she is really clean and really trying to fix her life, I will help her. Someday I'll be as forgiving as Gram. But not now. Right now, I'm taking care of me.

Chapter 42

November in the Midwest is a dreary affair. The sky transforms from a grayish blue to a drab silvery color reminiscent of soot. The chill seeps through the cracks and the window moldings and the door jambs of Wheaton. I take to wearing my ski cap twenty-three hours a day. It would be twenty-four, but there's a "no headgear" policy at dinner.

One blustery afternoon the week before Thanksgiving, a counselor named Sherri finds me staring at a bookshelf in the downstairs library. I was looking for something to read, then sort of zoned out. This happens a lot lately. It's a symptom of post traumatic stress, so I'm told.

"You have a visitor, Andrea!" Sherri trills in her typical bubbly voice. I swear, if the Angel of Death showed up at our door, she'd greet him with a smile. "I'll send him in, okay?" she chirps.

"Okay." I sigh. It's probably my probation officer, here to go over my community service options. I am so not ready for this.

But as she leaves, Sherri adds over her shoulder, "He's got some serious accent."

I freeze. When my brain thaws a moment later, my head snaps up. Brick is standing in the doorway three feet from me. I'm so excited to see him that I sort of catapult myself into his arms without thinking, and he has no choice but to catch me in a lopsided embrace. The instant this happens, I pull back, flames of embarrassment heating my neck and cheeks. *What am I thinking?* He hasn't called and he didn't come visit me in the hospital, and he's probably only here to tell me to stop talking to Chloe and to leave his family alone once and for all. I'm sure he doesn't trust me not to hurt her again. Things are not the way they used to be.

"I'm sorry," I say, flustered.

"S'okay," he says a little uncomfortably, but oh man, the sound of his easy drawl nearly snaps my heart in two.

I stare at him, wide-eyed, and he does the same. We're like two statues in a garden, and it's killing me not to jump back into his arms. I wasn't kidding when I told Lillian I was lonely.

Finally, Brick glances toward the couch and asks, "Can we sit down?"

I lead the way, and we both sit and face each other. I press my hands together and slide them between my knees. He fiddles with the loop on his backpack.

Neither of us knows where to begin, and I'm suddenly irritated that he didn't plan something out before showing up. At least *he* had some advance notice. While I'm just sitting here stewing in red-faced humiliation over that stupid, impulsive hello.

"How've you been?" he finally asks.

I shrug, at a loss. I'm not going to lie but I don't want to dump my troubles on him either.

He peers intently at me, and his gaze suddenly feels intrusive. I have no right to be annoyed with Brick, but his unexpected appearance has stirred up a flood of emotions, half of which I don't understand. As good as it is to see him, a part of me wishes he hadn't come. Part of me is downright mad about it.

"Did you want something from me?" I prompt.

He frowns. "Just to see you, is all. Make sure you're all right."

"I see," I say, even though I don't. "Well, I'm fine. In fact, I've been fine for two weeks, so you didn't really need to take time out from your needle crafts to come all the way down here." I even sort of huff at the end.

Brick shifts forward a little on the couch, his eyebrows drawn together. "Um. What are you talking about?"

I drop my eyes and curse myself for this bitterness, this anger that's clawing up my throat. But it's better than the ache of longing I feel at the sound of his voice. It's better than the shame that is knotting me up inside, good and tight. "Nothing," I say. "Chloe just isn't a very good liar. So the next time you're avoiding someone, you probably shouldn't ask her to cover for you."

"I wasn't avoiding you. I was busy," he says defensively.

"Yeah, I heard. *Knitting.*" I make air quotes with my fingers around the word.

Brick looks stunned. He blows out a breath. One puff, like

he's purging himself of me. "Wow."

"What?" I ask, harsher than I intend.

"Look, I just came here to…" He struggles for each word and it's driving me crazy that I can't read him at all.

And then it hits me and I feel like such an idiot. *Of course.* "Oh! Chloe's bracelet," I say. "Um, I don't have the money now, but as soon as they let me get a job I'll repay you. Your uncle, too. How much did you have to spend to get it back?"

Brick squints at me, his mouth hanging open, like I'm some alien he can't figure out.

"What?" I ask again, totally unnerved.

He shakes his head and suppresses either a grin or a grimace, I can't tell. "It's just that…I've never heard someone so smart say such stupid things."

Now I *really* don't know how to feel. I glare at him through eyes that are threatening tears. "Did…did you just call me stupid?"

"I called you smart, too," he points out and I briefly catch his smile before he dives into his backpack. The smile has already disarmed me, even before he pops up holding a wrapped package. "This was supposed to be for Christmas, but since I missed your birthday in September—thanks for mentioning it, by the way—I had to hurry and finish. Happy birthday, Andrea."

I stare at the bulky package he has set in my lap. The gift is wrapped in brown paper with silver angels on it. I slowly peel the wrapping away, trying to reclaim control of my senses. Soon I'm holding a fuzzy black scarf with pink cursive letters woven through it. It looks hand-knitted. It *is* hand-knitted.

"You…made this. For *me*?" My voice is thick with emotion.

"Not bad, eh?" Brick says proudly, then admits, "Aunt Lil helped with the script." He reaches over and stretches out the scarf so I can see the word the pink letters spell: *Unbreakable*.

I am speechless.

"I figured this might suffice until you get that tattoo," Brick says. "And it matches your ski cap. Right?"

Biting my lip, I run my fingers over the soft black fabric. "I love it," I murmur, overwhelmed. "Thank you."

"There's more," he says as I loop the scarf around my neck and snuggle down into its softness. He reaches down again, pulls an envelope from his bag of tricks, and taps it nervously with his thumb. "I hope you'll like this too."

But he doesn't give it to me, so all I can do is wait.

He takes a deep breath. "I kept thinking about what you said that day at the creek," he finally explains in a rush. "About how you never saw where your Gram was buried. I can't imagine how that would feel, to not know. Sometimes I think about my mom's plot, try to visualize it, even though I know it's just her body there. It's…important, for some reason."

"Yeah," I say, understanding.

"So I made some calls and found her. Your grandmother." He hands me the envelope.

I blink. "You found her? But I looked on the Internet last spring and I couldn't…"

"It took a while. The cemetery is in the country, way outside of Indianapolis, not even listed online." He nods at the envelope that is now in my hand. "Take a look."

Not sure what to expect, I slide out a thick piece of paper. On the top is a logo—a pen and ink drawing of an iron archway inscribed with the words "Washington Grove Cemetery." Beneath the logo is a letter from the cemetery's director confirming that Gram was indeed buried there, with the date of her burial and the exact location of her plot. All the information is correct—her full name and last known address and the dates spanning her fifty-eight years on earth. As her last will and testament directed, she was buried in the plot adjacent to her husband, who died thirty years earlier. The letter ends with an assurance that a bouquet of flowers will be set on her headstone, as requested.

I finish reading and swipe at my eyes. In spite of the tears, I don't feel sad. I feel…settled.

"Are you upset? That I did this without your permission?" Brick sounds anxious.

"No," I assure him. "It's a perfect gift."

"When you're better, I'll take you there," he offers, and this kindness confuses me. Everything about his visit confuses me.

"I thought you were writing me off." The words just come out, uncensored. But I'm glad. Why beat around the bush with him if I'm vowing to be more honest with everyone else?

Flustered, Brick says, "No. Okay, I *was* sort of avoiding you, Andrea. But finding your Gram and making your scarf…they were just excuses. I had other reasons."

I knew it. I brace myself to hear what he really thinks. How angry he still is about the jewelry, my lies, dragging his family into my messed-up life.

"I couldn't see you like that, in the hospital," he says quietly. "It was bad enough when you collapsed in our living room, bleeding—" His hands tremble against his thighs. To hide the shaking, he clenches them into fists. "I shouldn't have believed you that day when you said you weren't in danger. I *didn't* believe you, really, but I let you go, back into that man's house. And when you took Chloe's stuff, I turned on you. And then you got really hurt… and I could have prevented it all." He squeezes his eyes shut and I can see that he has been beating himself up about this. "I'm such a coward."

"Brick, no. You saved me. You and Chloe. Your whole family…"

But he's not listening. He's just shaking his head hard like he wants to punch something—maybe himself. So I change tactics and quip, "Don't blame yourself, Brick Mason. I'm a very good liar."

The scoff leaps from his throat so fast I feel offended. "You're a *prolific* liar, Andrea. Not a good one. No, I let myself believe you because it was easier."

"Easier than what?"

"Than trying to figure out what to do with a girl who was in trouble but didn't want help. A girl that I—" he breaks off. Then finishes "—that I didn't want to lose."

There is a long stretch of silence. I'm looking at Brick and Brick is staring at his clenched hands. I notice his pale skin, the few dark freckles around his nose, and the long, caramel lashes framing his eyes. I think about how he held me while I lay bleeding on the floor. I think about the awful, raw look on his face when he told me about his parents. I remember that he's been through hell, too. I place my hand over his fist.

"Didn't you think you could trust me?" he finally asks in a hoarse voice.

"Trust had nothing to do with it," I say gently. "I was trying to protect you. And Chloe."

Brick looks up at the bookshelves, shaking his head in dismay this time. Then he turns back suddenly and his eyes slay me, the way they look determined and devastated and tender all at once. "I'm sorry I didn't protect *you*, Andrea." He leans in, holding my gaze. "It won't happen again."

I should protest. I should tell him it was never his job to protect me—and still isn't. But it's too much of a relief to share this burden, and I can't refuse it.

Behind Brick's head, the book spines start oozing into a colorful, drippy mess. I blink hard, but the dam doesn't hold anymore—not with Brick next to me. Looking at me. Really *seeing* me, surrounded by all my messy truths.

For the first time, I invite someone else to witness the full misery I've been living. It's all there, streaming silently down my face. When our eyes lock again, he holds out one arm to me, just like he did at the creek.

I fall against his chest and allow him to hold me together as I let everything go.

Later, I stand at the bottom of the porch steps and watch Brick drive off with a casual see-ya-soon wave. The wind blows so cold it puts tears in my eyes. But the real crying is done.

I reach up and pull off my ski cap, and the wind immediately lifts my hair high off my shoulders. I can feel it all fanning out behind me, tangled and free.

I'll bet it looks so damn pretty.

THE END

Discussion Guide

1. Andrea starts her story by talking about how pretty her mother is. Beauty and its perils is a theme throughout the book. How is being pretty a good thing? How is it a bad thing? How does Andrea view it? Does her view of being pretty change over the book? How does it differ at the beginning and at the end?

2. Another theme is being smart or stupid. Andrea prides herself on being a good student. Why is getting good grades so important to her? Is Andrea book smart or street smart? Or both? Give examples that show how she is or isn't smart about her choices.

3. Choices and decisions, whether they're good or bad, safe or dangerous, is also a theme. Make a list of the different choices Andrea makes throughout the book. Do you agree with her decisions? Why or why not?

4. How do you know who to trust? Can you even trust yourself, your own instincts, and choices? Andrea thinks of herself as smart, but she discovers that intelligence only gets you so far. She needs to ask other people for help, but doesn't reach out to any of the adults around her, to any of her friends. Why do you think Andrea does this? What holds her back?

5. Family values—especially the roles of grandmothers, mothers, and daughters—run throughout the story. Andrea tries to take care of Ayla, her mother, though her mother doesn't take care of her. How does Andrea care for Ayla? Does Ayla ever care for Andrea? How does Gram care for both of them?

6. How do the adults in the book help Andrea? How do they hurt her? What roles do adults play in this story? What roles do kids play?

7. Why is the book called "All Out of Pretty"? What does that refer to? Do you think it's a fitting title? The book could have been called "Unbreakable." Would that be a better title? Why or why not?

8. Andrea thinks of herself as pretty, smart, and unbreakable. Is she all of those things? What incidents in the book prove her right in her opinion? Which prove her wrong? Which of these three characteristics is most important to her? Give evidence for your stand.

9. Andrea also considers herself to be a moral, good person, but she does immoral, unethical things, like sell drugs and steal. How does she justify these actions to herself? Is she a good person despite doing these things? Why or why not?

10. Is Andrea a strong or weak person? In some instances, she stands up for herself and her friends without hesitation. But other times, she cowers and backs down. List some scenes from the book when Andrea acts strong, and some when she acts weak. What do you think you would do in similar situations? Does it take a stronger person to endure a bad situation, or to run away from it?

11. What is the bond between a mother and a daughter, despite challenges like addiction and neglect? Why do people stay in toxic relationships? Why does Andrea stay with Ayla?

What would you do if there was only one person left in the world that you were tied to—and that person was pulling you into dangerous situations?

12. When Brick learns Andrea is in trouble, he wants to help her but doesn't know how. How do his decisions affect Andrea? What different choices could he have made and what do you think the outcomes would have been? How would you save someone who didn't want your help?

13. When Andrea learns the truth about her father, she feels anger, guilt, and confusion. How does having a parent that is a criminal affect a person's identity and self-worth? How do Andrea's feelings about her father—and her mother—change throughout the book?

14. Brick's feelings for his father are also confused. How do you forgive someone who has done something so unforgivable? Should Brick talk to his father or shut him out? What would you do? Do Brick's feelings toward his father change throughout the book? Do we get a sense of what his father means to him?

15. There's a parallel between Brick's parents and Andrea's, though it's never spelled out. Ayla is a drug addict and Brick's father drinks too much. How do these parental behaviors affect their kids? What does it cost them?

16. What does keeping secrets do to a person over time? Why does Andrea choose to keep her secrets? Do you agree with her reasoning? Is it possible to have authentic relationships and grow close to others if you are never truly honest with them?

Photo by Ellen Loeffler-Kalinoski

Originally from Ohio, Ingrid Palmer writes young adult fiction in the Colorado mountain town where she lives with her husband and two sons. When not writing books or enjoying the great outdoors, Ingrid works as a freelance editor. She has a master's degree in journalism from Northwestern University and is a graduate of the Denver Publishing Institute. *All Out of Pretty* is Ingrid's debut novel. To learn more about her, visit www.ingridpalmer.com.